wicked

sexy Tales of Legendary Lovers

wicked

sexy Tales of Legendary Lovers

EDITED BY MITZI SZERETO

Published in the United States by Cleis Press Inc.,
P.O. Box 14697, San Francisco, California 94114.
Printed in the United States.
Cover design: Scott Idleman
Text design: Frank Wiedemann
Cleis logo art: Juana Alicia
First Edition.
10 9 8 7 6 5 4 3 2 1

"The Ballad of Scott and Zelda," by Maxim Jakubowski, first appeared in *The Mammoth Book of Historical Erotica,* Carroll & Graf, 1999. "Seduction," by Anonymous, first appeared in a different version in the fall 1997 issue of *The Cream City Review*. "Letter to Valentino," by Mitzi Szereto, first appeared in *The Erotic Review*, Sept. 2004. "Elvis, Axl, and Me," by Janice Eidus, originally appeared in the story collection *The Celibacy Club,* by Janice Eidus, City Lights, 1997. "Time, Movement, and Desire," by Tom Bacchus, was previously published in *Rahm*, Badboy, 1994, and in the 1996 Spanish edition, *Sueños de Hombre*.

CONTENTS

Introduction

HISTORY IS DULL, DRY, A REAL YAWN. Or is it?

That's how my writers' call for submissions began. And that's how most of us feel about the subject (unless you're a hard-core enthusiast!). But what about the people who inhabit history? Amazing lives have been led, some of which we know a lot about, some we don't. We've all wondered what went on behind the cinematic facades, the pages of type, the layers of paint as we've watched a film, read a book, viewed a work of art. Individuals commit acts of greatness and madness, lead populations to their salvation or their doom. We have this need to pick them apart, learn what makes them tick. How closely linked is their sexuality to their public personas? Let's face it, that's the question most of us *really* want to have answered! Human beings have always been curious about the sex lives of others, especially when those others have achieved reverence or notoriety. More often than not, it's the notoriety we're most interested in.

Wicked: Sexy Tales of Legendary Lovers is a collection of speculative erotic fiction—the *hows*, the *what ifs*. Combining fact with fiction, it gives us a peek into the "bedrooms" of the famous and infamous, allowing us to imagine what might have gone on had we actually been there. None of the writers in this anthology can claim to have intimate knowledge of these individuals (at least I don't think so!), but what they've succeeded in doing is to let their erotic imaginations flow, filling in some of the blanks. Characters run the gamut from figures of biblical proportions to cinema icons, music legends, celebrated authors, renowned painters and composers, Hollywood celebrities, American presidents, foreign dictators, men of science and medicine, and even the odd political assassin.

Although *Wicked* makes no claim to provide a 100 percent accurate depiction of the persons featured in its pages, what it can do is flesh out their lives with a generous dose of erotic conjecture. This collection of stories will not only thrill you, it will get you to think twice about people you've seen on the movie screen or read about in history books. Because there's a lot more to them than meets the eye.

One word of caution: As you're reading, remember to keep in mind that it's fantasy.

Or *is* it?

Mitzi Szereto
Leicestershire, England

Elvis, Axl, and Me

Janice Eidus

I MET ELVIS FOR THE FIRST TIME IN THE DELI across the street from the elevated line on White Plains Road and Pelham Parkway in the Bronx. Elvis was the only customer besides me. He was sitting at the next table. I could tell it was him right away, even though he was dressed up as a Hasidic Jew. He was wearing a *yarmulke* on top of his head, and a lopsided, shiny black wig with long *peyes* on the sides that drooped past his chin, a fake-looking beard to his collarbone, and a shapeless black coat, which didn't hide his paunch, even sitting down. His skin was as white as flour, and his eyes looked glazed, as though he spent far too much time indoors.

"I'll have that soup there, with the round balls floatin' in it," he said to the elderly waiter. He pointed at a large vat of matzo ball soup. Elvis's Yiddish accent was so bad he might as well have held up a sign saying, "Hey, it's me, Elvis Presley, the Hillbilly Hassid, and I ain't dead at all!" But the waiter, who was wearing a huge hearing aid, just nodded, not appearing to notice anything unusual about his customer.

Sipping my coffee, I stared surreptitiously at Elvis, amazed that he was alive and pretending to be a Hasidic Jew on Pelham Parkway. Unlike all those Elvis-obsessed women who made annual pilgrimages to Graceland and who'd voted on the Elvis Postage Stamp, I'd never particularly had a thing for Elvis. Elvis just wasn't my type. He was too goody-goody for me. Even back when I was a little girl and I'd watched him swiveling his hips on *The Ed Sullivan Show*, I could tell that, underneath, he was just an All-American Kid.

My type is Axl Rose, the tattooed bad boy lead singer of the heavy metal band Guns n' Roses, whom I'd recently had a *very* minor nervous breakdown over. Although I've never met Axl Rose in the flesh, and although he's *very* immature and *very* politically incorrect, I know that, somehow, somewhere, I *will* meet him one day, because I know that he's destined to be the great love of my life.

Still, even though Elvis is a lot older, tamer, and fatter than Axl, he *is* the King of Rock and Roll, and that's nothing to scoff at. Even Axl himself would have to be impressed by Elvis.

I waited until Elvis's soup had arrived before going over to him. Boldly, I sat right down at his table. "Hey, Elvis," I said, "it's nice to see you."

He looked at me with surprise, nervously twirling one of his fake *peyes*. And then he blushed, a long, slow blush, and I could tell two things: one, he liked my looks, and two, he wasn't at all sorry that I'd recognized him.

"Why, hon," he said, in his charming, sleepy-sounding voice, "you're the prettiest darn thing I've seen here on Pelham Parkway in a hound dog's age. You're also the first person who's ever really spotted me. All those other Elvis sightings, at Disneyland and shopping malls in New Jersey, you know, they're all bogus as three-dollar bills. I've been right here on Pelham Parkway the whole darned time."

"Tell me *all* about it, Elvis." I leaned forward on my elbows, feeling very flirtatious, the way I used to when I was still living downtown in the East Village. That was before I'd moved back here to Pelham Parkway, where I grew up. The reason I moved back was because, the year before, I inherited my parents' two-bedroom apartment on Holland Avenue, after their tragic death when the chartered bus taking them to Atlantic City had crashed into a Mack truck. During my East Village days, though, I'd had lots of flirtations, as well as lots and lots of dramatic and tortured affairs with angry-looking, spike-haired poets and painters.

But all that was before I discovered Axl Rose, of course, and before I had my *very* minor nervous breakdown over him. I mean, my breakdown was so minor I didn't do anything crazy at all. I didn't stand in the middle of the street directing traffic, or jump off the Brooklyn Bridge, or anything like that. Mostly I just had a wonderful time fantasizing about what it would be like to make love to him, what it would be like to bite his sexy pierced nipple, to run my fingers through his long, sleek red hair and all over his many tattoos, and to stick my hand inside his skintight, nearly see-through, white Lycra biking shorts. In the meantime, though, since I had happily bid good riddance to the spike-haired poets and painters, and since Axl Rose wasn't anywhere around, I figured I might as well do some heavy flirting with Elvis.

"OK," Elvis smiled, almost shyly, "I'll tell you the truth." His teeth were glistening white and perfectly capped, definitely not the teeth of a Hasidic Jew. "And the truth, little girl, is that I'd gotten mighty burned out."

I liked hearing him call me that—*little girl*. Mindy, the social worker assigned to my case at the hospital after my breakdown, used to say, "Nancy, you're not a little girl any longer, and rock stars like their women really young. Do you truly believe—I'll be brutal and honest here, it's for your own good—that if, somehow, you actually were to run into Axl Rose on the street, he would even look your way?" Mindy was a big believer in a branch of therapy called "Reality Therapy," which I'd overheard some of the other social workers calling "Pseudo-Reality Therapy" behind her back. Mindy was only twenty-three, and she'd actually had the nerve to laugh in my face when I tried to explain to her that ultimately it would be my womanly, sophisticated, and knowing mind that would make Axl go wild with uncontrollable lust, the kind of lust no vacuous twenty-three-year-old bimbo could ever evoke in a man. Axl and I were destined for each other precisely *because* we were so different, and together we would create a kind of magic sensuality unequaled in the history of the world, and, in addition,

I would educate him, change him, and help him to grow into a sensitive, mature, and socially concerned male. But Mindy had stopped listening to me. So after that, I changed my strategy. I kept agreeing with her, instead. "You're right, Mindy," I would declare emphatically, "Axl Rose is a spoiled rock-and-roll superstar and a sexist pig who probably likes jailbait, and there's no way our paths are ever going to cross. I'm not obsessed with him any more. You can sign my release papers now."

"Little girl," Elvis repeated that first day in the deli, maybe sensing how much I liked hearing him say those words, "I ain't gonna go into all the grizzly details about myself. You've read the newspapers and seen those soppy TV movies, right?"

I nodded.

"I figured you had," he sighed, stirring his soup. "Everyone has. There ain't been no stone left unturned—even the way I had to wear diapers after a while," he blushed again, "and the way I used my gun to shoot out the TV set, and all that other stuff I did, and how the pressures of being The King, the greatest rock-and-roll singer in the world, led me to booze, drugs, compulsive overeatin', and impotence...."

I nodded again, charmed by the way he pronounced it im*po*tence with the accent in the middle. My heart went out to him, because he looked so sad and yet so proud of himself at the same time. And I really, really liked that he'd called me *little girl* twice.

"Want some of this here soup?" he offered. "I ain't never had none better."

I shook my head. "Go on, Elvis," I said. "Tell me more." I was really enjoying myself. True, he wasn't Axl, but he *was* The King.

"Well," he said, taking a big bite out of the larger of the two matzo balls left in his bowl, "what I decided to do, see, was to fake my own death and then spend the rest of my life hiding out, somewhere where nobody would ever think to look, somewhere where I could lead a clean, sober, and pious life." He flirtatiously wiggled his fake *peyes* at me. "And little girl, that's when I remembered an article I'd read, about how the Bronx is called 'The Forgotten Borough,' because nobody, but *nobody*, with any power or money, ever comes up here."

"I can vouch for that," I agreed, sadly. "I grew up here."

"And, hon, I did it. I cleaned myself up. I ain't a drug and booze addict no more. As for the overeatin', well, even the Good Lord must have one or two vices, is the way I see it." He smiled.

I smiled back, reminding myself that, after all, not everyone can be as wiry and trim as a tattooed rock-and-roll singer at the height of his career.

"And I ain't im*po*tent no more," Elvis added, leering suggestively at me.

Of course, he had completely won me over. I invited him home with me after he'd finished his soup and the two slices of honey cake he'd ordered for dessert. When we got back to my parents' apartment, he grew hungry again. I went into the kitchen and cooked some *kreplach* for him. My obese *Bubba* Sadie had taught me how to make *kreplach* when I was ten years old, although, before meeting Elvis, I hadn't ever made it on my own.

"Little girl, I just love Jewish food," Elvis told me sincerely, spearing a *kreplach* with his fork. "I'm so honored that you whipped this up on my humble account."

Elvis ate three servings of my *kreplach*. He smacked his lips. "Better than my own momma's fried chicken," he said, which I knew was a heapful of praise coming from him, since, according to the newspapers and TV movies, Elvis had an unresolved thing for his mother. It was my turn to blush. And then he stood up and, looking deeply and romantically into my eyes, sang "Love Me Tender." And although his voice showed the signs of age, and the wear and tear of booze and drugs, it was still a beautiful voice, and tears came to my eyes.

After that, we cleared the table, and we went to bed. He wasn't a bad lover, despite his girth. "One thing I do know," he said, again sounding simultaneously humble and proud, "is how to pleasure a woman."

I didn't tell him that night about my obsessive love for Axl Rose, and I'm very glad that I didn't. Because since then I've learned that Elvis has no respect at all for contemporary rock-and-roll singers. "Pretty boy wussies with hair," he describes them. He always grabs the TV remote away from me and changes the channel when I'm going around the stations and happen to land on MTV. Once, before he was able to change the channel, we caught a quick glimpse together of Axl, strutting in front of the mike in his sexy black leather kilt and singing his pretty heart out about some cruel woman who'd hurt him and who he intended to hurt back. I held my breath, hoping that Elvis, sitting next to me on my mother's pink brocade sofa, wouldn't hear how rapidly my heart was beating, wouldn't see that my skin was turning almost as pink as the sofa.

"What a momma's boy and wussy *that* skinny li'l wannabe rock-and-roller is," Elvis merely sneered, exaggerating his own drawl and grabbing the remote out of my hand. He switched to HBO, which was showing an old Burt Reynolds movie. "Hot dawg," Elvis said, settling back on the sofa, "a Burt flick!"

Still, sometimes when we're in bed, I make a mistake and call him Axl. And he blinks and looks at me and says, "Huh? What'd you say, little girl?" "Oh, Elvis, darling," I always answer without missing a beat, "I just said *Ask*. *Ask* me to do anything for you, anything at all, and I'll do it. Just *ask*." And really, I've grown so fond of him, and we have such fun together, that I mean it. I *would* do anything for Elvis. It isn't his fault that Axl Rose, who captured my heart first, is my destiny.

Elvis and I lead a simple, sweet life together. He comes over three or four times every week in his disguise—the *yarmulke*, the fake beard and *peyes*, the shapeless black coat—and we take little strolls together through Bronx Park. Then, when he grows tired, we head back to my parents' apartment, and I cook dinner for him. In addition to my *kreplach*, he's crazy about my blintzes and noodle *kugel*.

After dinner, we go to bed, where he pleasures me, and I fantasize about Axl. Later, we put our clothes back on, and we sit side by side on my mother's sofa and watch Burt Reynolds movies. Sometimes we watch Elvis's old movies, too. His favorites are *Jailhouse Rock* and *Viva Las Vegas*. But they always make him weepy and sad, which breaks my heart, so I prefer to watch Burt Reynolds.

And Elvis is content just to keep on dating. He never pressures me to move in with him, or to get married, which—as much as I care for him—is fine with me. "Little girl," Elvis always says, "I love you with all my country boy's heart and soul, more than I ever loved Priscilla, I swear I do, and there ain't a selfish bone in my body, but my rent-controlled apartment on a tree-lined block, well, it's a once-in-a-lifetime deal, so I just can't give it up and move into your parents' apartment with you."

"Hey, Elvis, no sweat," I reply, sweetly. And I tell him that, much as I love him, I can't move in with him, either, because *his* apartment—a studio with kitchenette—is just too small for both of us. "I understand, little girl," he says, hugging me. "I really do. You've got some of that feisty women's libber inside of you, and you need your own space."

But the truth is, it's not my space I care about so much. The truth is that I've got long-range plans, which don't include Elvis. Here's how I figure it: down the road, when Axl, like Elvis before him, burns out—and it's inevitable that he will, given the way that boy is going—when he's finally driven, like Elvis, to fake his own death in order to escape the pressures of rock-and-roll superstardom, and when he goes into hiding under an assumed identity, well, then, I think the odds are pretty good he'll end up living right here on Pelham Parkway. After all, Axl and I are *bound* to meet up some day—destiny is destiny, and there's no way around it.

I'm not saying it *will* happen just that way, mind you. All I'm saying is that, if Elvis Presley is alive and well and masquerading as a Hasidic Jew in the Bronx, well, then, anything is possible, and I do mean *anything*. And anything includes me and Axl, right here on Pelham Parkway, pleasuring each other night and day. It's not that I want to hurt Elvis, believe me. But I figure he probably won't last long enough to see it happen, anyway, considering how out of shape he is, and all.

The way I picture it is this: Axl holding me in his tattooed, wiry arms and telling me that all his life he's been waiting to find me, even though he hardly dared dream that I existed in the flesh, the perfect woman, an experienced woman who can make *kreplach* and blintzes and noodle *kugel*, a woman who was the last—and best—lover of Elvis Presley, the King of Rock and Roll himself. It *could* happen. That's all I'm saying.

The Ballad of Scott and Zelda

Maxim Jakubowski

THIS IS HOW IT COULD HAVE HAPPENED (anachronisms and all).

Scott—December 1940

Yes, the past is a different country, he thought. Damn right. And these last few months, every single night, he had tossed and turned in the narrow bed, even when Sheilah had visited, as it all came back. Visiting his own lost life again, armed with no more than his mental passport.

To avoid the pain, he had moved into Sheilah's apartment. Hers was on the first floor. His had been on the third. He could feel it all ebb away. One slow day at a time. There was no longer much work at the studio, and he knew the book was at a dead end. Something told him he would never finish it. Or at any rate, not to his satisfaction.

She was so kind. But it just felt like charity for the poor, the under-emotional, the under-hemorrhoided, the under-cocked. He grinned broadly and filled the glass again. She had set him up with a writing board, and he kept up the pretense that the novel was making good progress. There was pain climbing the stairs, there was pain all the time, but the worst was not the physical deterioration, it was the past flowing back, reluctantly, as he couldn't just close his mind to its cruel assault.

He sipped the whiskey. The glass was soon empty. He filled it again. Not much left in the bottle. No worry, he could always phone out for another delivery.

All this booze made him want to pee. He snickered. It just came in and seemed to flow through his body like water and come out the other end so quickly. He avoided his drawn, gaunt face in the bathroom mirror. He now spent most days in his faded blue dressing gown, with a pocket full of pencils and one always balanced over his ear. The great writer at work. And play.

Another glass, then. Yes. At least the whiskey kept him warm inside.

Sheilah had arranged a doctor's appointment for December 20, but he had managed to get it canceled on the pretext of some problem with his writing. He had no need to be told what was wrong with him. He knew all too well. The slow usage of time. He also knew that it wasn't illness or his body giving up on him that would kill him in the end. Because he just wouldn't allow that. The drink would do it so much faster and more efficiently. And painlessly. Just as it kept him alive right now. And erased all the memories of the past. The so-called golden days. St. Paul. New York. The Côte d'Azur. Paris. Hollywood.

He hoped the alcohol wouldn't kill him at least until Scottie graduated from Vassar. He would write her again tomorrow with advice. And maybe, with a bit more work and attention, he might actually finish the novel by February. It was just that he had lost much time following the heart scare, when he had fainted outside the Schwab drugstore in November. The medics had said it was his heart, but Scott knew. It was the booze clawing away at his insides. But he needed it so much. Couldn't get through the day without it. Ironically, it kept him alive as it killed him.

He looked, and suddenly the whiskey bottle was empty. No matter. Tonight they had agreed to attend a movie preview of *This*

Thing Called Love at the Pantages Theater. And he would wear his Brooks jacket, the pink shirt, and a bow tie. Made him look like a dandy. He smiled.

Stock up on more booze afterward. Yep.

F. Scott Fitzgerald, American author, died the next day. He had written the letter to his daughter, Scottie, in the morning, and was lounging in an armchair after lunch, making notes for an article, eating a chocolate bar, when he suddenly stood up, reached for the mantel and collapsed to the floor. A moment later he was dead.

His wife, Zelda, was unable to attend his funeral in Rockville, Maryland, on December 27, a raw, wintry day, and asked her brother-in-law Newman Smith to attend in her stead. She had not seen Scott for over a year at the time and was living in Montgomery, Alabama, with her mother. She had recently been released, with a letter that paroled her to her mother, from Highland Hospital—where she was being treated, unsuccessfully, for her precarious mental condition.

It's Always Forever—St. Paul, Minnesota, and Princeton, 1920

The novel has sold. She has agreed for them to become engaged. The family wasn't too happy about it, but then Scott knows they never approved of him that much before, even. Irish and from the other side of the tracks and all that.

They are blissfully happy.

He loves the way Zelda kisses him, how her tongue invites his in, twists moistly around his tongue and plays mischievously with it, streams of saliva blending as the kiss lingers on and on and on, and he soon runs out of breath and she releases him and giggles in her customary lovely way.

The feel of her lips against his, the way she sometimes nibbles the lobe of his right ear (which gives him an instant hard-on, which causes him to clumsily shift around on the spot, attempting to conceal from her eyes the unseemly bump in his pants as they linger in each other's arms in the back of his shiny new automobile).

The distinctive smell of her breath, which lingers all around him for hours, nay, days, even after she is back with her family, like a cloud that evokes her flesh, her eyes, her body.

Is this the magic of love? Scott wonders.

He has longed for this for ages, it seems, and still can't believe it is all coming true after he had given up in despair so many times.

"What are you doing?" he asks. Zelda is fumbling with his belt.

"Close your eyes, silly," she answers.

He does. Obedient.

Jesus Almighty, she is unbuttoning him, and her fingers are delving in his undergarments!

"I'm reliably informed it's called a blow job," she says under her breath, lowering her head toward his penis as her nimble fingers roll his foreskin down and the head emerges. To be engulfed by the volcanic crater of her mouth.

Scott keeps his eyes closed.

Zelda! Zelda! He would never have expected this from her. The girl is just fantastic....

She licks, she sucks, he grows to what he feels might be monstrous proportions, but she is not fazed and continues her tactile inventory of his cock, as that familiar tingle in the pit of his stomach begins, moving fast toward the sac of his balls, and he shudders as his future wife, his dearest Zelda, relentlessly continues her task. Her auburn hair bobs up and down on his lap.

He knows he can't tell her, but this is not the first time a woman has done this to him. No. There was the Belgian whore, the one with the scar on her cheek and the empty breasts hanging too low, back in that brothel in the north of France, during a furlough while he and his battalion mates waited to be assigned to the front. He can't even remember her name now. All he can recall is the way she spat his seed out onto the stone floor after he had come to orgasm, and departed with not even a word to service another American trooper in an adjoining room. They were all too scared of possible diseases in those foreign climes to go the whole hog and actually purchase a full-blown fuck.

Scott grins at the memory. A few days later, the end of the war was declared. He had never been to the front. No glory.

And now Zelda is doing this wonderful thing to him.

Her mouth full, she quietly keeps on sucking him as he feels that unstoppable wave of depraved pleasure course through him. He tries feebly to warn her, to tell her she should pull back, but Zelda will have none of it, and attacks his member with even more relish.

He explodes, feeling the warm surge of his seed burst through and flood Zelda's mouth. The ejaculation seems to go on forever. And still she will not release him, lapping up the come; he can actually feel her, hear her, swallowing it, and his heart just melts on the spot, waves of mighty emotion swirling inside his head and chest. God, I love this woman, he thinks. I will never love another the way I love Zelda now. And forever. My intended. My wife. My extraordinary St. Paul flapper.

Soon, it will be time to drive her home to her parents' house.

Scott shivers.

"I love you so much, Zelda. Words just won't suffice. They can't express even a small part of what I feel for you."

She looks up at him and smiles quizzically, as if trying to interpret the precise meaning of his words.

She smiles again, as he clumsily stuffs his cock back into his woolen undergarments, slightly ashamed at being openly exposed to her gaze like this, even after what has just happened.

"It's OK, Scott, darling," she says. "Next week I shall come to Princeton, and stay the night...."

"You mean?"

"I will become your lover. You will undress me and make love to me. Properly."

Once more his heart just lurches.

Screaming in the Cathedral—New York, 1923

The world is at their feet. The King and Queen of literary New York. Prophets of the Jazz Age. Life has become an endless party. The money goes around. The liquor flows.

There can't be more to life.

Or can there?

They get back to the apartment after a somewhat wild party at the Waldorf for a visiting French soprano. The nanny has already gone to bed. Scottie, whom Zelda insists on calling Pat—they had first named their daughter Patricia, before changing the name to Frances—is sleeping soundly in her nursery overflowing with toys.

"Darling, I know I've had too many already, but it would be

nice if you could make me one final cocktail. Would you?" Scott asks, as they both kick off their shoes in the carpeted lounge of the Park Avenue townhouse they are renting. (The price is exorbitant, but so what?)

"Make your own."

She is frowning. Her cheeks are slightly flushed.

"What's up with you tonight?" he asks, puzzled by her sudden change of mood. Earlier she had been as happy as hell.

She avoids his eyes, looks away.

"I saw you with her," she spits out.

Scott is nonplussed.

"Who? I don't know what you mean, Zelda."

"That blonde actress. I saw the way you were talking to her, you know..."

Scott bursts out with laughter.

"Jesus, Zelda. I was being sociable. She's the daughter of one of Scribner's biggest shareholders, for heaven's sake!"

"Her breasts were spilling out of her cleavage, for Christ's sake, she was like an ambulant peep show and you sure enjoyed the landscape of flesh on display, didn't you?"

Breasts are a delicate subject. Since Scottie, hers have somehow shrunk, whereas most women's would have grown a bit after a first child, she had been told.

Scott ignores her comment and walks over to kiss her.

Her breath reeks of gin, but then probably so does his. Wordlessly, he unbuttons her front and ceremoniously unveils her chest. Her nipples harden, lengthen, as he uncovers them. He kisses her there with tenderness, allowing his tongue to linger warmly as he circles the sharp tips of her small breasts. He moves back half a foot and takes them into his hands, cupping them, then looks her in the eye.

"But yours are the ones I like," he whispers gently.

And he is not lying. He loves the fact that they are small, that he can hold them both in the hollow of his outstretched hands as if he were weighing them like fruit; he adores the way the nipples lengthen under the warmth of his fingers, or the moistness of his tongue, and their color reacts by shifting between indescribable shades of pink and light brown.

He enjoys undressing her so, as he does now. One garment

at a time until she stands there quite nude in front of him, legs slightly apart for support in her current slightly inebriated state. Her reddish hair, cut short in a mischievous-looking bob according to the day's fashion, the long expanse of white skin, the plains of her flesh and the modest valleys of darker hue between her breasts and in the shadow of her belly button. The sturdy Irish legs. The luxuriant growth of hair around her cunt. He closes his eyes awhile and smells her, and soon the distinctive odor of her aroused sex reaches him and he feels himself harden.

She lets her hand move down to her cunt and spreads her vagina lips open to his hypnotized gaze. She is wet already.

"Fuck me, then. Now. Me. Not her," Zelda demands.

He quickly sheds his evening wear, his movements a tad unsteady.

"Shall we move to the bedroom?" he asks, as he pulls the shirt above his head and the cuff links from his left sleeve fall to the wooden floor.

"No," she answers, "I want to do it here." She points to the large room and an Afghan carpet spread across the floor between the liquor cabinet and the plush, quilted armchairs.

Scott feels the warmth spread inside him. Ah, my Zelda, always one for the daring and the unexpected….

He struggles with his belt. When he looks again in her direction, she is kneeling on the russet carpet on all fours, her backside raised in his direction. An obscene position in which he cannot help but see both her apertures almost gaping in readiness.

"I'll switch the electricity off," he suggests, as his trousers slide to the floor.

"No," Zelda says quickly. "I want the light on."

She is so daring. His cock, quite hard already, gets tangled in the elastic of his underpants as he rushes his movements.

"Come," she calls impatiently. "I want you to do me this way, like a dog."

Finally, he is naked, and moving behind her raised rump, falls to his knees. The wooden floor under the carpet feels hard. He can feel her sweating. It's a warm summer evening and the nanny has forgotten to leave any of the apartment windows open before retiring for the night. He realizes there's something animal about Zelda's odor tonight.

He looks ahead. Her puckered asshole and its darker concentric rim of flesh looks almost as if it is breathing. He has never before seen her, seen this, so close. He is fascinated by the depravity of the situation.

His eyes move an inch or so down, and as they do so, Zelda's hands thrust backward and spread her cunt lips wide open for him, and Scott sees how wet she is.

He thrusts forward into her. There is no resistance. She is totally lubricated and gaping for him like seldom before. He sees all the way into her mysterious pinkness. He slides in.

Surely, he wonders as he fucks her, *not all married couples love each other this blissfully? Surely all the people in the streets outside, dressed all proper, coated with the veneer of civilization, do not become wonderful savages like us in the privacy of their sex lives? No, we must be unique.*

My Narrow Mind—Villa Paquita, Juan-les-Pins, France, 1926

The summer had been absolutely gorgeous and their skin had tanned grandly. Evenly. Golden brown. Of course, Zelda had to wear a floppy straw hat to protect her face from burning, but she had nonetheless come out all over in sumptuous freckles, evenly scattered across her nose, dotted across her pink cheeks and staining the invisible part of her chest like paint stains in an Impressionist painting.

They had made friends so easily with the American contingent of the Riviera set. Also with a lot of French aristocrats. Lazy days spent lounging on deck chairs and dipping an occasional toe in the warm water of the Mediterranean, while the children, little Scottie always busy with the Murphy kids, were kept happy at a short distance under the careful eye of their minders. The conversation was witty, the rhythm of summer languorous, the parties at night in a variety of glamorous villas easily reached by automobile, by the sea or in the hills, flowing with good wine and gaiety.

Wit and repartee and laughs and fun; this was another side of paradise.

Scott and Zelda found it delirious. They rented a succession of villas after a stay at the Hotel d'Hyeres. Zelda in particular loved Provence. She would later evoke it meaningfully in the only book she would ever write. At first, Scott managed to write most days, while Zelda busied herself shopping with Sara Murphy and others and organizing picnics on the beach later in the day.

America felt so far away.

Ernest Hemingway had come down to the coast for one week, but left after only three days, mumbling under his breath of their parasitic status and accusing Scott of prostituting his talent with all the layabouts down here. But nobody really took Ernest that seriously then. Just another spoilsport, and a bit too earnest anyway. Zelda wondered sometimes why Scott and Ernest managed to stay friends. There was an undercurrent of envy, she sensed. And Ernest looked at her strangely when he was around, almost undressing her with his eyes. Not her sort of guy.

Unlike some of those handsome French military types, who came and went with the set throughout the summer. Dashing, exotic, supremely elegant, whether in or out of uniform.

She was still in love with Scott. A good man, he loved her back dearly. And he attracted the sort of glamour that enchanted her. Her husband, the famous novelist. But he was also a bit predictable. Boring? Zelda wanted to write her own books, regretted the loss of her planned dancing career; she didn't just want to be "the wife."

Yesterday. A whole group of them had gone up to that famous restaurant in the hills behind Nice. Expensive and overrated, she reckoned. You were mostly paying for the view. They had all divided up into several cars afterward.

"A last drink, a coffee, Madame Fitzgerald?" the French army officer had asked.

"Why not?" she had said, without thinking. Scott had gone ahead with Gerald and Sara Murphy, already quite sloshed. By now he was probably passed out on the bed with his clothes still on.

Another man's body. Another man's touch. His kisses tasted different, the movements of his hands over her skin held new, changing rhythms. He undressed her slowly, as if performing a ritual. Stood back at regular intervals to admire her, allowing her each time the opportunity to say "No, no further," but Zelda had wanted to see where this would go. It was like an adventure. Another crazy one, like the drinking, the false gaiety, the jumping into swimming pools with her dress still on, the day she had swum so far out to sea until none of the others were nearby and she had slipped out of the cumbersome costume and paddled about until tiredness set in, stark naked in the blue Mediterranean water.

The officer had kissed her everywhere, worshipped at her altar like no man ever before, inserted his tongue in all her nooks and crannies, opened her up and delved and tasted her between the puffy lips of her cunt, which Scott had never even thought of doing. She had come twice even before he got around to fucking her.

Finally, he'd undressed. Jeez, he was big. She had stared.

"*Qu'est-ce que c'est, ma chère Zelda?*" he had asked.

"It's—it's...different," she had said.

"*Ah, oui*. I see. I am circumcised; it's for hygienic reasons. You like?"

"Yes." She nodded. "It looks...nice."

He moved closer to her. Presented himself to Zelda.

"Would you, *ma chère?*"

She would.

It was morning by the time she got home.

Scott was awake.

He was already (still?) drinking.

"Who?" he quietly asked her.

There was no point pretending, she thought.

"The officer," Zelda answered. Knowing all too well that things would never be the same again.

He set his glass down, looked slowly at her—was she still flushed?—and, slurring his words slightly, said, "I'm sure it wasn't your fault, my darling. It was his. I shall challenge the bounder to a duel."

"You wouldn't." Zelda had to smile.

"Yes," Scott replied, "and after I have avenged my honor, you and I shall then pack up and return to Paris."

Carrying Sin in My Sack—Paris, Autumn 1929

Ernest and Scott were having a pee in the toilets of the Coupole in Montparnasse. They had earlier been moaning about the state of New York publishing and Max Perkins's editorial edicts, the sizes of print runs, and likely future level of advances against royalties.

Scott broke the silence.

"Hey, Ernie, can I ask you something?"

"Sure," Hemingway said. "Shoot, buddy." He directed his

stream of urine toward the metal wall of the convenience so as to avoid splashing his shoes. Next to him, Scott also concentrated on his aim, pensively looking down at his member.

"Well," he said, "it's a bit delicate…"

"Oh, come on…"

"Do you think my cock is of a normal size?"

Ernest grinned broadly and turned to look down at Scott's still-dribbling penis, reflected one moment, then said, "Seems more or less the same size as mine, man." He pulled back from his standing position and held his own cock for Scott to see.

Scott sheepishly turned and looked.

"Yeah, I suppose so…"

Hemingway suddenly roared with laughter.

"What is it?" Scott inquired.

"I was just imagining my wife, the bitch, seeing us here with our damn cocks out on display. As it is, she said the other week that she thought we were both two queers anyway!"

"Really?"

"What does she know, eh?"

Scott slipped his penis back into his trousers. Hemingway shook the last few drops off his.

"It's just that I think Zelda finds me inadequate, you know?" he confided.

"All women want you to feel that way, you know, Scottie boy. I wouldn't let it worry you."

They found their way back to their table and ordered another round of pastis.

Scott had told Ernest some years back of the affair with the French officer, and made a whole song and dance of the duel he had threatened, and how it had scared the guy right away from the Riviera, never to be seen in their circle of friends again. What he hadn't revealed was that the French officer had just laughed and declined to participate in such a farce.

"I've never had the courage to ask her if his was bigger than mine, you know?"

"Listen, Scottie boy, you fucked that gal, that English singer, the other month, didn't you? Did she complain about the size of your equipment, eh?"

"Well…"

"It's not the size; it's how you use it," Hemingway insisted.

Scott had not told him that he had come too quickly with the British woman, and that one hour later he had been impotent and incapable of performing again. Maybe it had been the drink inside him. He hoped.

They downed their drinks.

"But," Ernest said, unwilling to change the subject of the conversation, "talking of size, I saw the Tijuana movie loop the other week at Gerald and Sara's last party. The one you couldn't attend. There was a guy in it with a monster of a cock, must have been at least ten inches. Darn breathtaking. But this girl he was with managed to accommodate it without too much strain, I must say. But when he turned around and disposed her on all fours, you could see her ass stretching to criminal proportions as he impaled her there. Memorable, Scottie, you should have been there to watch it. Now, that cock would have made you feel inadequate.... And the actress—well, if you can call it acting—actually looked a bit like Zelda, I must say. Picture was a bit grainy, and you couldn't see her face, but small boobs and a nice white ass. Could have been her sister, eh?"

He roared with boisterous laughter. Other customers looked at the two men. "You sure she hasn't been taking some side trips to the Mexican border while she is visiting her parents?"

"Come on, Ernest, that ain't funny anymore," Scott said.

"I know," the other man said. "It's just I so like to see you squirm, you Irish prick!"

"I know," Scott acquiesced. Then: "Have you ever measured yours?"

"Sure," Ernest said. "Six inches, just above average. And all in perfect working order, I hasten to say...."

"I didn't know that was the average," Scott remarked.

"Well," Hemingway added, "your average red-blooded all-American male.... Don't know about French guys..."

He laughed out loud again.

As One with the Spirit, Yes, She Goes Where It Goes—New York, 1932

Scott is in California, talking to some producers. Zelda is restless. She wants to start more dancing lessons but has been told she is too old now. A friend has told her about this discreet club, this speakeasy in the East Village where money can buy you anything. Well, money is no problem these days. Scott's books aren't selling as well as before, but a short story for the *Saturday Evening Post* or *Harper's* or *Esquire* every now and then takes care of the bills and more.

"It would be advisable if you wore this," the plain-looking woman shepherding her in says, handing her a domino mask. "Discretion is most necessary."

Zelda slips the mask on, ruffling her auburn hair in the process.

Still holding her complimentary cup of champagne in one hand, and her tasseled Italian-made handbag in the other, Zelda is escorted into a small, empty, dark room and shown to a chair at its center, facing a velvet-curtained wall.

"Do make yourself comfortable," the woman says. "I shall return in a few minutes, when you have made up your mind."

She leaves the room, and the curtain Zelda is facing opens slowly.

Behind the glass, there are half a dozen men. All quite nude. Standing against a white wall. It makes her think of an identity parade, as in the gangster movies. Each holds a square of cardboard with a number. Her first thought is that the numbers are not consecutive. 3. 6. 2. 9. 7. 12. She wonders briefly about the missing numbers, the men who are not available to her today. Then lowers her gaze and sees their cocks. Long. Thick. Straight. Bulbous. Crooked. Heavy. Some just dangle there against a thigh, others are being gently stroked by their owners as she watches.

One man is bald, but his body hair is absolutely everywhere else from chest to feet, thick and curly, his cock like an explosion of dark purple in his forest. Another has pale blond hair, his white chest quite hairless and his pubic thatch like golden down.

Another, number 6, is a black man. Tall, standing proudly, legs apart, his regal chocolate cock already at half-mast, impossibly elongated and sharp. She gulps.

Time freezes momentarily.

The men are all looking in her direction, but she knows they cannot see her behind the one-way glass partition.

The door opens and the woman returns.

"Have you chosen, madam?" she asks.

"It's difficult," Zelda says. "They are all so different. Age. Appearance. Coloring. ...Size," she adds.

"I understand," the woman sympathizes.

Zelda looks over the parade of naked men again, thoughts swirling in her head. And some guilt already.

"Some of them are really quite appealing," she blurts out. Blushing ever so slightly in the penumbra of the small room.

She fixates on the mole staring at her from just above number 12's crotch.

Sensing her indecision, the plain-looking woman intervenes.

"Could I make a suggestion to madam?"

"Certainly," Zelda answers.

"Well, has madam ever thought of two?"

"Two?"

"Double the pleasure. Even more staying power at your disposal. They can take turns, or you could have them in tandem."

"You mean...?"

"Servicing both front and rear, madam. An experience to cherish, I am told. They are all well-trained in these variations, I assure you."

Zelda finally selects 7 and 9.

She is taken to the bedroom and told to make herself at ease. The four-poster bed is the largest she has seen, sitting there like a throne, dominating the whole room. Crisp white sheets. A silken dark bedspread. A thick scarlet rug. Erotic etchings on the walls. She knows at least one of them conceals some peephole and that she is going to be watched. That is also part of the price and adds to the spice of this new experience.

There is a gentle knock on the bedroom door.

"Enter," Zelda says.

The two men walk in. In the flesh, so to speak, they appear so much larger, and number 9 looks very young. But she likes the gentle curls of hair on his chest. It was difficult to arrive at a choice. So she has settled for one with dark hair and a foreskin that wrinkles down and, even when half-erect, obscures the bulbous, mushroomlike cap of his glans. The other is cut, his cock all pink and shiny.

They approach her and the dark-haired man politely asks in a European accent, "Would madam like us to undress her?"

"Yes, that would be nice, very nice. Yes," Zelda answers, setting her handbag down. Next time, she thinks as their hands begin searching for her buttons, she will go with the black man. Something she often guiltily dreamed of in Minnesota days of old, when she was still Miss Sayre.

Seen that Tight-Lipped Grin—New York, 1934

Whole days now went by without them even speaking to each other, beyond the bare formalities of "Good Morning," "Please," or "Good-night." Sex, which he knew she had once enjoyed so much, was now perfunctory on the rare occasions that he managed to stay hard long enough without recourse to her mouth.

Scott had often wondered how it must feel for a woman, for Zelda, to take a man's cock in her mouth and pleasure it without choking. How this most intimate of violations could provide her with even a modicum of pleasure. The thought had troubled him for years. The fact that she was already familiar with this particular sexual perversion when he had met her brought a sliver of bile into his throat. He was disgusted by the idea of the other men she might have practiced on, done it with, before or since him.

The young man sitting at the bar was still looking at him.

Scott had to admit he was quite pretty, a tad feminine despite his short hair and the floppy fringe that fell across his pale forehead.

He smiled back at the stranger.

Who soon joined him at his table.

"You know I'm not that way inclined," Scott said furtively, looking around the bar to check there was no one around whom he knew. "Just interested in knowing what it would be like. Curiosity, call it. An experiment. Not that I wish to go all the way, just, you know…"

"Sure," the young man said.

"And I don't want it to be something sordid. In some public convenience, with trousers down to my ankles. Have to do it properly, in a civilized way. Be comfortable with each other…" Scott added.

"I understand," the young man said. "Do you have a place where we might go, then?"

They had undressed, with their backs to each other. Scott

was conscious his body was no longer as athletic as it had been. As he failed to turn around, he felt the young man's hand on his shoulder.

"Do you want me to suck you first?" his pickup asked. "It will put you at ease. You can do me afterward. No rush."

He lowered himself to his knees and took Scott's flaccid cock in his hand and rolled the foreskin down before enveloping it with his lips.

Scott closed his eyes. The tongue moved slowly around his stem. He imagined it was Zelda and St. Paul, Minnesota, again, and paradise and youthful days. Felt a bit the same. Pleasant. The shivers began as usual in the deep pit of his stomach before traveling down toward his now-aroused genitals.

Later, he adopted the same kneeling position and closed his own mouth on the thick cock of the young man. At first, the feel was quite unexpected. The penis felt strangely greasy under his tongue, pulsing with the beat of a distant heart. He licked it methodically, his lips gripping its surprising warmth while his tongue circled its expanding circumference. With his free hand he cupped the young man's balls and felt them yield. He pushed his lips further forward, curious to see how far he could take the cock in without choking. Surprisingly far. The young man, towering now above him, began to moan gently and rustled Scott's hair as he sucked away. Scott had lost all notion of time, his whole mind concentrating on his task.

Finally, the young man shuddered and said, "You'd better take it out—I'm going to come."

Scott pulled away just as the cock began spurting its white ejaculate.

As the come spiraled down toward the wooden floor of the borrowed apartment, he was already thinking back on the experience. It had been interesting. He couldn't really say he had taken much pleasure sucking another man's cock, but on the other hand there had been nothing unpleasant either. Yes, *interesting* was truly the right word in the circumstances. So this is what Zelda would feel as she did it. Maybe now he would understand her better?

The young man was dressing quickly.

"I'll make my own way out," he said. "It would be better if we didn't exchange names."

"Yes," Scott said.

She's Waltzin' Out the Door—Princeton, 1936

The team had lost the Varsity Challenge, and the overall mood was despondent. The woman was waiting for them to arrive back at the locker room, holding a bottle of champagne and a couple of glasses in her hand. She was visibly drunk already.

"There's nothing to celebrate, lady," McKenna said.

"I know," she said. "So I thought I'd bring you Princeton boys some consolation. So you'll be luckier next time."

Tim, who had been kept on the sidelines for most of the game and was still bitter at the coach's decision, walked up to the woman, took the bottle and one glass and poured.

"And why not?" he said. "There's nothing else to lose. And most of us won't be here next year anyway."

He passed the bottle on to the other players. The woman took a small metal flask out of her bag and took a deep swig from it.

"Atta boy, that's the way to go!"

The players had soon emptied the bottle of champagne and began trooping past her.

"Why are you off so fast? We can still celebrate," the woman said, brandishing the small flask. "It's good bourbon!"

"We're all filthy and sweaty. We have to take a bath, lady."

She hiccupped and followed the last one of them into the building as they made their way toward the giant communal bathing tub.

"I'll join you!" she said.

"You must be joking," McKenna replied.

"Not at all," the woman said, and raised her cotton skirt to reveal that shockingly she had no underwear on. "See, I'm already dressed for the occasion, boys."

The young men looked at each other. Some blushed, others shrugged their shoulders. One of them began to strip openly in front of this strange woman. "Why not?" he said.

She stripped with them.

"So which one is the captain of the team?" she asked, as she jumped into the hot water and joined the burly, muddy young men.

"I am, and today was the last time," Chris Callaghan said.

"In that case," she said, wading toward him through the steaming water, her small breasts bobbing along, "you get the first blow job."

The whole team fell silent.

She serviced almost half of them, but the water was growing cold and she suggested they adjourn to the locker room. They carried her out of the tub triumphantly over their broad shoulders, like a trophy.

By now, most of the young players, even those who had already come in the woman's mouth, were hard and excited, and any veneer of civilization had long worn away.

They all had her in a variety of positions, using every available orifice offered. She sometimes laughed, often moaned, occasionally cried, and eventually passed out. Which didn't stop some of the guys from continuing to fuck her until they ran dry.

Later, once the young men had all hurriedly dressed again in their perfect Princeton gentlemen's suits, and, shamefaced, trooped away from the scene of their lustful crimes, Tim and McKenna revived the woman with some smelling salts from the first-aid cabinet and helped her dress in silence.

They watched her move away unsteadily across the now-darkening playing fields, feeling damn guilty about what had happened, but after all, hadn't she been the one who had suggested the orgy and all its excesses?

Finally, she faded into the darkness, her soiled skirt just a minute, starlike point of white on the horizon where night and earth blended.

"Damn it," Tim said. "That was crazy. She was crazy. Who was she?"

"I don't know," McKenna said. "Earlier, on the floor, while Stewart was arsing her and she was sucking on me and White in turn, between mouthfuls she kept saying 'I'm Zelda Fitzgerald, the wife of the famous writer,' over and over again." He sighed. "Forget it, man, she was just some madwoman with a bad itch in her pants. What we all did was mad too. Better forget all about it."

"Fitzgerald? Never even heard of the name," Tim said.

"Probably some delusion of hers, anyway," the other one said, straightening his tie, thinking already of tomorrow's ball, with all the Vassar belles in attendance.

Zelda, Highland, 1948

Scott has now been dead for over seven years, and Zelda

lingers in the mental institution where she is being kept for her own good.

Most of the time she is quite lucid, and has much too much time to reflect on the golden past and its mistakes. How lives can be wasted so damn easily on the altar of lust, ambition, petty jealousy, and money worries. How time eats away at the wall of love. How nothing lasts even with the best intentions in the world. How we allow things, people, to go because we are too proud, shy, or helpless to do otherwise. How all those things gnaw at the mind during the unending hours of the night when all you can do is wonder "what if this" and "what if that" and "what if she" and "what if he," until the sheer torture is too much and you retreat into that deep well where the ghosts can no longer reach you and there are no longer any feelings.

She is being given insulin treatments and has been moved to the top floor of the main Highland building.

In early March, she writes to her mother that the jasmine is in full bloom and crocuses are dotted across the lawn.

On March 9, she writes to her daughter, Scottie, that she thinks winter is now over. She is already four months into this new stay in Highland, and Scottie's second child, a daughter, has been born.

She writes of the promise of spring in the air and the fact she sees an aura of sunshine over the nearby mountains and longs to see the new baby and its growing brother.

The following night, at midnight, a fire breaks out in the establishment's kitchen. The flames shoot up a small dumbwaiter shaft to the roof and leap out onto each of the floors.

The building has neither a fire-alarm system nor a sprinkler system.

Very quickly the fire grows completely out of control, and smoke races through the rooms of the old stone-and-frame building. The fire escapes are made of wood and soon catch fire.

Zelda sleeps. After hours of tossing and turning, peace has returned at last, and she is again on the backseat of that brand-new automobile that Scott had purchased with his first novel's advance, and she is unbuttoning his trousers and giggling madly at the bemused look on his face as she extricates his small cock from the heavy garments. She's nervous also; she's never done this before, just heard about it from the other girls at the finishing school, who tell her it's the best way to a man's heart. And, yes, she loves Scott so. After all the courting, the tantrums, and the breakups, yes, she has decided, hesitantly moving her lips toward the warm penis, feeling its awkwardly spongy texture between her moist lips. Yes, I will be Mrs. Francis Scott Fitzgerald.

She smiles in her sleep.

The fire keeps on gaining ground.

Nine women are killed that night, six of them on the top floor.

Her body is only later identified by a charred slipper lying beneath it.

She is taken to Maryland and, on a warm and sunny day, buried next to Scott. They are together again. Forever.

seduction

ANONYMOUS

JOAN COLLINS

He could go many times a day. He was insatiable. He could take phone calls at the same time, too.

Warren Beatty and me

I was standing in Nathan's at the corner of Sixth Avenue in the Village, wiping mustard off my low riders, when I saw Warren Beatty. "A hot dog," he said softly to the guy behind the counter. Well, maybe it isn't Warren Beatty. What would he be doing here? I looked more closely. Maybe I stared, though I tried to hide it. His papaya lips curled up in a smile. "It's me, it's me," he said, holding up both hands, as if surrendering. My two boys were screaming. One wanted ketchup mixed a certain way with the mustard, creating a marbleized effect on the terrazzo-tile-colored hot dog; the other had just let his brand-new hot dog slip out of the roll and onto the filthy floor. He was crying because he desperately wanted to pick it up and eat it, and I wouldn't let him.

"Do you want TB?" I asked, stamping on the frank in order to obliterate any of its desirable qualities.

Warren seemed surprised at the lack of attention to him. "Let me buy the kid another dog," he said. I just nodded, slightly embarrassed. I am very thin, and tall, especially in my platform sandals, and combine, so people (men) have told me, awkwardness and attractiveness in a way that is extremely sexy. I am also very shy. I find it hard to look directly at very handsome men, as if I have a fear of being dazzled by outer beauty—something that shouldn't count for much, but can.

Warren seemed fixated on my youngest, who was gripping my prewashed jeans with one greasy hand, tiny, filthy legs balancing in huge sneakers, taking large bites from his replacement hot dog, ketchup streaks all over his face like blood. A homeless person with a bad sunburn was trying to wrest my other boy's carefully garnished food from him. "Hey, you don't have to do that," said Warren, handing the unfortunate man a five-dollar bill. The man looked at it scornfully, pulling up his shorts with his elbows. Warren gave him five more. That sparked my interest. I am very attracted to rich men who are also liberal. They are rare finds. "Hey," he said, "how about ditching the kids and calling me at the Carlyle later?" He handed me a printed card. Both boys were crying for another hot dog each, French fries, and tropical drinks. I took the card, to be polite. "What's your number?" he asked. He didn't write it down.

Jean Rhys

Why Warren Beatty would want to go out with me is beyond me. He told me my work had intrigued him, and he needed to get to know me on some other, deeper level. I know that sex isn't just sex with him, yet I went into it knowing there would be nothing more than sex. But, as usual, I was left feeling deeply disappointed, empty. At that time I was living in an SRO in New York, a sleazy room, and he gave me a key to his suite in the Algonquin. Was it that or the restlessness, the hunger, the longing to be filled up through every hole?

Ann Landers

He came in the door and we made love. He didn't have an orgasm. He was very careful. He washed his hands a lot. Is that going to keep him from getting some sexually transmitted disease? I guess that made me wonder why I'd go to bed with someone who's known to have slept with almost everyone.

Warren and me

When I got home the phone was ringing. I rushed for it, nearly falling over the baby. The bags of food I was carrying dropped, oranges spewing across the floor, when I tripped over the baby's food-encrusted, chrome highchair leg. The kids were foraging in the spilled food for cookies while I answered the phone. "I'm busy right now," I said, as soon as I found out who it was.

"I'm lying on my triple king bed, with nothing but a towel wrapped around my privates," he whispered, in his wonderful husky voice.

"So?" I said. "I'm still busy." At one time this might have interested me, but no longer.

"I'll wait," he said. "No matter when you're ready, I'll be here. Nobody refuses me. It intrigues me. I'd come there, but I have to admit, kids bring me down."

"Go to hell," I said. I felt sorry for him because he wasn't living real life. Later, very much later, after all the bedtime rituals, and after I'd run through the apartment organizing and cleaning somewhat so we could begin trashing it tomorrow, I realized that the kids bring me down too. I lay across my mattress, barely able to move. But my mind, annexed all day with trivia, was spinning.

Martha Stewart

I had my hair done exactly right the day before. This left exactly the right amount of time so that my hair would be styled the way I like it, but not stiff, as it often looks when I come out of the beauty salon. Warren likes to be spontaneous, so I had to hold him off so I could get things (dishes, candles, bedding, a meal) just perfect. Things looked so great, I must admit; I was tempted to call the television studio to come video the entire experience.

Ruth Westheimer

Everything in Warren's world has to do with sex, living out sexual fantasies. His way of relating is through seduction. He's into all aspects of sex. Nothing is bad to him. This I like. He's even into lesbianism. The first thing he said to me was, "If you misbehave, I'm going to spank you." I felt a little self-conscious at first—like, why would he like me? But he has the ability to make you feel comfortable immediately. It's not looks, or desire to be in love, that rules Warren. He goes at it for the same reason a writer writes, or a painter paints—to discover something. Unfortunately what he really wants to discover in this way may remain elusive. He's full of contradiction and paradox.

Natalie Wood

After a few times with Warren, I felt unleashed. He'd opened up all sorts of possibilities. I recall writing in my diary, "I've been Warrenized."

Warren and me

Warren Beatty is a sexual and artistic icon. An institution, like Elvis Presley. The difference is, Elvis seduced with his art; his charisma was part of that. If he was unfaithful, he kept it a secret. His unobtainability, while he seduced with his performances, was exciting. What's compelling about someone who will screw anyone and everyone? But I know what's exciting; I'm already excited. Maybe it's the Don Juan thing—the seeker in search of some elusive knowledge, imparting a noble goal to evil, sleazy behavior. Or even the Don Quixote thing—the search for nonexistent romance and nobility by someone innocent, whose wrongheaded approach causes him to make errors that, by chance, bring him success in his search. Finally, I had to admit that the way his thick brown hair wouldn't stay back, and something sad but urgent about his blue eyes, made my nipples hard.

Jack Nicholson

I invited Warren to come to some sex-addict support group with me, but he insists he's not one. "With me it's not addiction. It's how I swim through life." Warren has a point, as well as a way with words.

Erica Jong

He was seated next to me on a Boeing 747 to Los Angeles. At first I didn't even notice it was him. "I can't believe this is all we're getting," I said, holding up a minuscule bag of mixed pretzels. He was wearing a peach cotton shirt with an open collar, and olive chinos. I liked the color combination, which looked great with his tan. That's when I realized it was Warren. He removed a crushed half-sandwich wrapped in Saran from the pocket of his tight pants, and offered it to me. It turned out to be peanut butter on white bread. "Annette made it for me," he said.

"That's so generous," I said, sipping my third glass of airline Merlot.

"I like your Teutonic nose," he said.

"Teutonic?" I was surprised. "You know I'm Jewish," I said, laughing. "I'm Erica Jong."

"Jong isn't a Jewish name," he giggled.

Does he know who I am? I wondered. His smooth arms were beige. His hair was thick and wavy. "I'm still hungry," I said.

I was thinking about food, but he looked at me provocatively from under his lowered lids. He had eyelashes to die for—long and dark, with blond tips. Which made me wonder—could Warren be the perfect zipless fuck? It was the first time I'd thought about a zipless fuck in ages. After a good, long search, I was disillusioned. And that reviewer of my novel who called me a "mammoth pudenda"...I was trying to put all that behind me. I indicated that I had to go the restroom. He had to stand to let me out (he was on the aisle, I was in the center seat) and I pressed my entire body against him as I passed, which wasn't hard in the two inches of legroom, and could have seemed accidental.

In the tiny toilet I broke out into a cold sweat. I hadn't locked the door, hoping Warren would follow me. But anyone could try the door. I was running my fingers through my highlighted curls when I heard the door click open, and before I could even turn, someone was pressed against my back.

"Quiet," he said, placing his hot hand over my hungry lips. He began kissing my neck under my hair, my shoulders. He lifted my shirt and I obediently raised my arms, like a baby, so he could remove it. I didn't care where he threw it—it was a speck of turquoise flying through the air. Warren continued pressing his warm lips, then his hot, moist tongue, along every area of my back, while I succumbed to voluptuous waves from my tingling scalp to my weakening legs. Finally I opened my bra, pulled it off, and threw it up in the air. Warren's hands immediately cupped both breasts from the back.

I tried to turn around to face him, but suddenly felt something hot between my upper thighs. I pulled up my miniskirt to help him—I no longer knew what I was doing. I felt hot lightning in my nipples as he was kneading my breasts, and as I felt the long, hot prick between my thighs. Warren took his hands off my breasts for a second, speedily pulling my red underpants down. I lifted one leg so he could pull them off, and they just remained around the other ankle.

By this time I was so wet Warren was able to rub his penis between my thighs, which at first I tightened. I could feel his breath hot and fast on my neck as his prick pushed slowly back and forth, rubbing along my moist labia. Soon the rhythm was driving me crazy, and I spread my legs so I could feel his rigid dick along my wet, swollen cunt, its mushroom head hitting my clit each time he pumped his hips toward me. Now his entire body felt like a hot, hard prick, one flexed muscle pressing against my back and buttocks.

Suddenly he slipped inside me. I pressed against him in order to push him deeper, and my hands, which were behind me holding his butt cheeks, I moved between my legs, rubbing the root of his shaft as he shoved his prick back and forth. The waves of sensation, which I felt all over, and so deeply in my thighs that I felt I could collapse, swept over me until they were too much to bear. I began to moan. Warren, who seemed about to burst, instead began another rhythm, faster and shorter strokes, but by then I was gone.

"Uuuugghh, noo, nooooooo," I screamed, as I felt my entire body contract endlessly, supported only by Warren.

"Hurry up in there," I heard from outside, "there's a long line here." I could hear Warren pulling together his clothing. He handed me my bra, my shirt, while I pulled up my red panties and pulled my miniskirt down. A quick glance in the mirror showed a sweaty, red-eyed, tousle-haired stranger. Warren pulled open the metal door, and I followed him to our seats, my eyes on his brown, tasseled Rockports.

Once more in our seats, I couldn't concentrate on anything except his body, so close, emanating tsunamis of sexual energy. "Did you come?" I whispered.

He didn't answer. "I'll have a Coke," he said to the blonde flight attendant. He looked cool and dry, as if nothing had occurred, while I felt messy and as moist as if I'd been incontinent. I too ordered a Coke. As I sipped, slowly pulling myself together, I realized that for Warren there probably exists a zipless fuck. For me there's only the search.

George Sand

What attracts me is devotion—someone falling deeply in love with me. Of course I have to be in love with that person, but I often fall in love after I see someone madly in love with me. Warren is not into falling in love deeply, or for a long time. He's pretty, he's sexy, and he's fun.

Helen Gurley Brown, editor of *Cosmopolitan*

Of course I was seduced by Warren. Aside from the fact that he's absolutely delicious, there aren't many men I haven't had. I wanted to do an article when he began seeing Annette Bening, because it might be the last chance, because it seemed that their relationship might last. But so did his relationship with Diane Keaton…or Madonna. I even thought of renting a huge ballroom, and getting all Warren's lovers, past and present, together. We decided *Cosmo* couldn't afford it. Our writer wasn't supposed to sleep with Warren, but she became curious. Ultimately, she fell in love with him before the deadline and quit writing the article altogether. She was devastated.

Hope Hancock, journalist and filmmaker

It may seem as if Warren will screw anyone, but he didn't want to sleep with me. A mutual friend said, "I bet Warren would just love you." So I was sitting there at work at the Associated Press in New York one day, and the phone rang.

"This is Warren Beatty," he said. My heart flipped. He was simply the most desirable man in the world. "Come out to L.A. to see me," he said. I had to go to Denver for a news story the next day. "Come to L.A. and go to Denver the day after," he suggested.

A huge limousine met me at the airport and took me to his magnificent house on Mulholland Drive. His Asian servant met me at the door. The table was set for two, with candles and flowers everywhere. It was so perfect I thought I was at Martha Stewart's place. Suddenly the bedroom door opened, and there he was. He looked adorable. His hair was still wet from the shower, and his shirt wasn't buttoned. He had that disheveled look I love. Then he took a long look at me, and his face fell. Our friend had thought he'd like a six-foot-four, large-breasted Amazon with a doctorate. It was a painful moment.

We sat and ate anyway, and talked about many things, including how the Tao and the Dow (you know, Dow Jones?) sound alike. I think he found me interesting, but not sexually desirable. I found him both. At least, I think I did. Maybe he was interesting to me because he was sexually desirable. He seemed to be such a pagan spirit. It's so hard to tell. He kept getting up to answer the phone. I think it was Diane Keaton—she must have called every ten minutes. I bet she could tell he had someone with him whom he may not have desired, but whom he'd been prepared to desire. I thought of what it must feel like to be his girlfriend—to be Diane Keaton, for instance, at that moment. It wouldn't feel good. But when you're the new flame, it's easy to think that you'll be THE one.

The dinner was very good, though it's hard to recall what we ate. Before his car took me to my hotel, he gave me a kiss on the cheek and said, "Jack Nicholson would just adore you."

Jack Nicholson

Warren's obsessed. I'm not. Or at least I admit I have a problem, but he won't. He says he simply loves all women. To me that's not loving women.

Warren and me

This story is not about me. But who is it about?

Liz Smith, gossip columnist

I recall a wonderful story about Beatty. It had something to do with clams—or was it persimmons? Really wild. You should call Mitch Jackson, in Hollywood.

Mitch Jackson, former gossip columnist

Persimmons? No. I don't remember any wild story about persimmons. No, nothing about clams.

What about me?

I have to admit, I was getting curious.

Joyce Carol Oates

I thought to myself, you have to try this. You have to see what this is all about. It's part of history, culture, anthropology. I thought I could write a book about the institution of making love with Warren the way I wrote about boxing. So I got up my nerve and called him at the Carlyle. We had a tryst in his hotel room. He never got out of bed all day, or out of his maroon silk bathrobe. He conducts all his business from bed. He's very much a pretty boy. There's a feminine aspect to him, which may be part of his appeal. He's practically hairless. He's also obsessed with cleanliness and disease. He asked me about my former partners, and I said, "What about you?" That made him smile. He used two condoms, one inside the other. I thought, *Is this worth possibly ruining my marriage for?* He said he didn't want to have an orgasm because he was afraid Diane Keaton would find out. I wondered, for a moment, what it would feel like to be Diane Keaton.

Being in bed with Warren is like being with a technician. He's the most fantastic lover in the world, but he was not there. It was like holding onto a raft in a story, excuse me, stormy sea. "Do I scare you?" he asked.

"No," I said. "Why?"

"Fear is good," he said.

Later I realized I should have asked him whether I scared him.

Warren and me

I felt very funny about doing this, but I took a shower, washed my hair, put on my best silk pants, and called the Carlyle. I thought it would be impossible to get to talk to him, but when I told the person who answered who I was, Warren got right on the line. He was friendly, and my fingertips and toes stopped buzzing. He sent his Mexican maid over to babysit.

"Where are jure weendows?" she asked.

"Well," I explained, "lots of apartments in Manhattan don't have windows. There are other compensations."

We were near the entranceway to his suite. My platform boots kept turning over in the thick carpet. "What about Annette?" I asked.

"Well, to be honest, I love Annette very much. And I may be ready for a real relationship soon. But I feel that marriage isn't a happy, productive way of living. I prefer shallow, meaningless relationships. They're healthier."

I found myself getting angry, and was about to leave. He took my hand in his moist, warm one, placing his other hand over it, so my hand felt like the filling in a sandwich.

"I prefer shallow, meaningless relationships, too," I said.

He made me a drink from those tiny bottles of liquor one finds in good hotels. He looked directly into my eyes. His are a deep green. I felt almost hypnotized. I certainly didn't have the power to look away while his green-eyed gaze (or were his eyes blue? They kept changing) held me. My peripheral vision disappeared in a dark glow. I was almost *in* his eyes. I took a swig of my drink.

"Don't be nervous," he said. In order to entertain me, he allowed a string of saliva to pass his lips, then to drop nearly to his chin. When it looked as if he were going to drool all over his Armani shirt, he sucked it back into his mouth with a loud slurping sound. We both laughed.

His lips…his teeth, I don't know, I felt my heart race, my cheeks burned, and my fingertips prickled as if they were asleep. My lower half liquefied and dribbled onto the bed.

Maybe he thought I was frightened, because he said, "In spite of what you may have heard about me, I'm not a vampire."

Madonna

We're twins. We're the same, but we're not. Being with Warren…well, it's like you're screwing the whole world *through* Warren.

Ayn Rand

I thought he was my twin—an overman. I was mistaken. He's a small man.

Deepak Chopra

Warren's seeking, seeking, seeking something that he should be searching for within himself.

Warren and me

"I don't care if I don't come," I told Warren. "I often don't come the first time with someone."

But Warren doesn't give up. He needs to feel you become vulnerable to him. But it's also as if he's searching for something—some knowledge—or some peace. That's what makes him so lovable. Instead of thinking of Warren as some power-hungry predator, one wants to protect him, to help him find what he's missing. He seemed to be able to hold out forever. But so could I.

"Please, baby, please," he pleaded, our bodies slippery with sweat.

The telephone rang. Wiping his face with the towel, he picked it up. I thumbed through some magazines, all with Isabelle Adjani on the covers, while he whispered in a placating, whiny tone. I felt sorry for whoever was on the phone, but I felt superior, too. Who would be stupid enough to let themselves in for that kind of vulnerability with someone like Warren? I never asked, but he told me it was Madonna. She called back at least every half hour, and Warren picked up the phone every time.

There's something about going at it for hours. It's like being pleaded with, then pounded to a pulp. One becomes very large and desirable, as well as very tiny. Your skin opens up, or melts; your relationship with real life dissolves. As he pumped, he began humming in rhythm, like Glenn Gould playing Bach, never getting louder, never reaching any crescendo.

"Oh, *God*, come," he said.

"You come first," I said.

"I'm a love god. I'm the president of Hollywood," he panted. The phone rang. "Annette," he said.

Mamie Van Doren

He used to oversalivate. It was always too wet in his mouth. Almost a drooling thing. He was just one walking gland. I was newly divorced at the time, and he was young, he must have been in his early twenties. He was very persistent.

Camille Paglia, author of *Sexual Personae*

The Greek beautiful boy is one of the West's great sexual personae…an androgyne, luminously masculine and feminine, possessing a male structure, but a dewy girlishness. The Greek penis was edited from an exclamation point to a dash. The beautiful boy hovers between a female past and a male future.

Michelle Pfeiffer

Warren and I were at this opulent party given by Luchino Visconti at his mansion. It seemed that everyone there had been Warren's lover at one time or another except Luchino, who seemed charmed by Warren, and ignored his own young male guests. I was feeling completely left out. While everyone concentrated on a champagne toast, Warren grabbed me.

"I'm going to the bathroom. In a few minutes, follow me."

I started walking down the hall. I didn't know where the bathroom or bathrooms were. Suddenly I heard him whisper, "In here." He pulled me inside and locked the door.

"What are we doing in here, Warren?" I asked.

"Let me show you," he said, pulling off his peach polo shirt and his gray slacks. He was breathing hard. He lifted me up on the sink. Someone knocked at the door. He flushed the toilet, pulled my panties aside, and kissed my crotch. I felt his hot breath as he pressed his lips to me. I felt myself expanding.

"Uh," I breathed over the sound of the flushing, as he touched my clit with just the tip of his tongue.

"Warren, are you in there?" someone called. "Madonna's on the phone."

Then he moved into me, light and quick. I held onto his hair so I could balance on the edge of the cold, blue enamel sink. I felt as if I were about to come the minute he entered me, but I didn't want to. I tasted his hair in my open mouth. Suddenly he grabbed my breasts and began playing with my nipples, holding me up with his head. For a second that distracted me, but then waves traveled from my nipples to my clit, and I was losing control. He was fucking me, and I was fucking back, rocking on his cock, and he was pinching my nipples. I was coming, and it was the hardest I'd ever come—he's the best fuck, and he knows what I like best, and he gives it to me.

"Don't stop," I said. "Fuck me hard, keep fucking me, don't

stop." I knew it felt good to him too—I knew, and that excited me even more. He slowed down a little. "*Come*," I said, "don't be afraid."

I could tell he was close. I was falling into the sink, he was thrusting so hard. I felt as if I were going to faint. He thrust, and when he thrust again he moaned a little, then hesitated, and then I could feel him pulsing inside me. But he pulled out immediately and I could see he was still hard.

"Didn't you come?" I asked.

"I loved it more than anything," he said. With difficulty he shoved himself into his tight black chinos and opened the bathroom door. I slid off the edge of the sink. My thighs were dripping wet and I wasn't sure my skirt would hide their glowing moistness. When I pulled down my short, tight black skirt and opened the door, I noticed a long line waiting for the bathroom, puzzled expressions on their faces. Warren was gone.

Diane Keaton

He's the kind of guy who will end up dying in his own arms.

Warren and me

The next day, though I had no idea what day it was, Warren begged me to stay while he went to an appointment. I hung around and took a bath. The bathroom was the size of my apartment, and the sink was shaped like a seashell. The phone kept ringing. Once, I picked it up absently, and it was Warren, calling from his car.

"Are you dressed?"

"Um-humm."

"I'm a half mile away, take off your boots."

Next time the phone rang, he said, "I'm a few blocks away, take off your slacks and shirt."

The third time I picked up the phone, a woman screamed at me.

The next time I dared pick up the receiver again, it was Warren. "I'm parking. I want you to unlock the door, lie down naked, and wait for me."

Of course, I didn't. "I have to go, " I said.

A minute later I heard Warren unock the door.

"You naughty girl. I'm going to undress you." He quickly undressed, then looked in the mirror. I was looking at him too. He's really very well-proportioned. He's got almost no body hair, and very smooth skin. Very thick hair. A little like a woman. Or maybe more like a child. I felt fat and crude.

The phone rang. Warren turned away from me, and wrapped his arms around his chest as if to protect himself. I tried to listen, but couldn't hear much. He kept nodding, and finally hung up.

"I'm going," I said. I felt all cooped up, and I was worried about the kids waking up to see a strange woman instead of me.

Just then Warren got down on all fours on the gold carpet. "Woof, woof," he said. "I'm going to bite off all your clothes." I couldn't help laughing as I tried to escape. Warren took off all my clothing, including my tight pants, with his teeth. I was charmed. He seemed to want me to love him.

"I'm hungry. Aren't you?" He ordered steak for himself and grilled salmon for me. "You seduced me," he said, smiling happily, a bit of grease at the sharp corner of his lips. I could look at his smile forever.

"You seduced *me*," I said. "I was the one who wouldn't give in."

"Camille Paglia says seduction means literally 'leading astray.'" Why was he quoting Paglia? Has he slept with her too?

"I really have to go," I said, putting on my platform boots, brushing my hair. Warren was getting some fresh clothes out. He kissed me good-bye. Whom was he getting ready to see?

Me

When I got home, the youngest boy said, "Go out." The boys loved Maria so much they wanted her to stay forever. She liked them too, and left reluctantly. Both children cried for at least three hours, and only stopped when I promised I'd make tacos like Maria's.

Mostly I was too busy to think about Warren much, but I half expected him to call. Each night I was surprised that he hadn't. Then I read about his engagement to Annette Bening in the headlines of the *Enquirer,* while on line at the supermarket, the boys fighting about who was going to wheel the cart. Could that be true? Part of his seductive charm was that I felt sorry for him not being able to make a commitment, or have a real relationship.

That night, exhausted as I was, I couldn't sleep. I went over every moment Warren and I had spent together. I pictured my tongue touring his body, touching his full, luscious lips and moving down to lick his smooth, salty neck, thin compared with his large head. Then along his hairless chest, tickling his tiny taut nipples and then his lean yet soft belly. I licked his pink, hairless balls. I pictured Warren lying there patiently, so still that only his rasping breathing and his huge, hard, beige cock, pointing toward his navel and pulsing, indicated that he was alive. I couldn't resist kissing the very round tip, with its tiny open mouth. I wrapped my tongue around the mushroom head and his hips moved slightly. I wanted to make him move, to make him moan. His eyes closed. I placed my lips around his swollen prick, and began gently sucking. I wanted to make him grind his hips and push into me. I wanted to drive him wild. I put my hands around his neat ass and held his cheeks as I moved up and down on his swollen shaft. I heard moans, and then I realized they were mine. The next thing I knew, he was up from under me, on the phone. I wanted to call him, just to speak to him for a moment, to hear his voice. Nothing more. I tried to resist, recalling Diane, Madonna, Michelle, and God knows who else, but I couldn't think of anything I ever wanted to do again. My apartment seemed airless, and everything around me dismal and dingy.

At three-thirty A.M., humiliated, I picked up the phone and dialed his number. Before it rang, I hung up. Fifteen minutes later, I tried again; I couldn't help myself. I forced myself to stay on the line if only to hear his voice just once more. My heart was drumming, the blood pounding in my head so hard I couldn't hear. Then I realized I was getting the hoarse beep of a busy signal. I pictured Madonna, Diane, and hundreds of other women. We were all trying to get through to Warren.

A Date with the Chairman

Mark Kaplan

MEI LI COULD BARELY BREATHE, she was so excited. She sat, her hands folded neatly on her lap. The plush velvet chair had more bounce to it than she thought, and it was nearly impossible to control her urge to bounce up and down as she waited for the Great Man to call her in. Her fingernails were dirty, but that was good, she reminded herself, proof that she was a Worker, one of the People. Her rough cotton shirt and pants, blue, like nearly everyone else's, were another testament to how like everyone else she was. She brushed off her clothes with her tiny hands. She wanted to be neat when she met Him. She wanted to make the perfect impression.

Again she cursed the fate that gave her such big, full breasts. Chinese girls shouldn't have such melons, she thought. They made people think she was proud, so she'd taken to lowering her chin and hunching her shoulders. She tried anything to hide her breasts from view, but she couldn't. They were too big. They were embarrassing. Now she was waiting to meet the Great Man and he would see her breasts and he would send her away. She pulled her jacket lower, but the pockets on the chest only emphasized the feature she was trying to hide. She was skinny everywhere else. Her legs were thin as canes, and her small bones were evident in her tiny wrists and slim fingers. She was pretty, she knew, but that wasn't a good thing anymore. It caused jealousy, and jealous people made up stories, and some stories could ruin your life. So she kept her head bowed and worked hard, watching blisters tear up her dainty hands. She was stronger than she looked, a good worker, and she knew that must be how the Great Man had heard of her.

He had stopped at her village while passing through the north. It was as if the emperor himself had come...only better, because Chairman Mao wasn't an emperor, he was one of them, a common man. She cheered for him as he passed, and she thought that he paused as his eyes passed her in the crowd, but she didn't dare dream that he noticed her. Then her party leader called her in and told her of the great honor the Chairman had bestowed on her by asking about her. He had put in a good word for her, told the Chairman what a hard worker she was, how, even though she didn't come from the best family, she had proven herself free from the arrogance of her grandparents. The Chairman, he said, was impressed.

Now she was here, waiting to be called in. She glanced around the room, noted how beautiful it was. It belonged to the People, to her. She was as much the owner of this room as anyone in China, but she didn't feel like the owner. She was uncomfortable, and growing more and more nervous. She felt a drop of sweat race between her breasts, leaving a cool trail along her flesh. These jackets weren't tight on anyone, except her, and she hated them for crowding her breasts together and making them sweat. Sweat was good, she told herself. Workers sweat.

When the door opened, she nearly jumped out of her skin. She stood, quickly, eagerly faced the tall thin man who appeared. He was someone famous, she knew, but didn't know who he was. His skin was dark, and he dressed sloppy. Only someone close to the Chairman could dress so sloppy in his presence. The man eyed her coldly. She felt his eyes run along her body, down her hair and her throat and stop on her breasts. She instinctively drew a hand across them, modestly shielding herself. Her cheeks grew hot and she knew she was blushing. Why was she blushing? The man smiled at her, allowed his eyes to rove to her tiny waist and thin legs. His eyes shined with lust. No, she corrected herself, not lust. It couldn't be lust. Then the man smiled again and waved her after him. She followed as he led her down the hall to a door guarded by two soldiers. The soldiers kept their eyes straight ahead of them. They were young, eager boys, and they served the country proudly. The tall man walked past them, opened the door and showed her into the room.

She suddenly felt very vulnerable and isolated. She stood in what used to be a library. The shelves still held some books, but she had the distinct feeling that these books hadn't been opened in a long time. Her grandfather had had a library like this. He loved his books. But that was a long time ago. The thin man walked her to a door in the back of the room and opened it, indicating that she should go in. He closed the door behind her, closing himself out. More sweat ran between her breasts and as she grew nervous she felt her waist become weak. This room was much more private. There were a couple of plush chairs and a couch, and a window overlooking the river. She found that her hands were shaking. There was a distinct sense of power in the room. She moved to the window, more to escape the overwhelming sense of dread than to see the view. Her chest grew tight, and she leaned against the glass, willing herself under control.

Then the door opened behind her and she felt someone come into the room. She knew who it was. His aura was so strong it practically knocked her to his knees. Her heart beat quickly, and she could hear the tremble in her breath.

"I am glad you came," he said. That voice. It *was* Him. "Your party leader told me how busy you keep yourself."

She swallowed hard. Her knees were weak and she felt that at any moment she would collapse unconscious to the floor.

"Turn around," he said. "Let me see my little sister."

Little sister. He had called *her* his little sister. It was more than she could have dreamed possible. No one would believe her. She felt the smile pulling at the corners of her mouth and raised a hand up to cover it.

"Come, come," he said. "We don't have much time."

Of course, she thought. Who was she to waste the Great Man's time? He wanted to see her and here she was, too frightened to look him in the eye. No. She shouldn't be afraid. They were comrades. He was not a god, he was a man. She could face him. She took a long unsteady breath and turned around.

Chairman Mao stood there, in the flesh! Seeing him was even more overwhelming than just hearing his voice. He was so *close* to her! Here she was, alone in a room with Chairman Mao! She could die happy now, she thought. Mao smiled as he looked her over. He had eyes like a wolf, and he approached her, took her by the arm and led her toward the couch. His touch was firm; its command, unstoppable. He guided her to the couch and sat next to her. That's when the wolf vanished. For a moment he seemed tired, so tired. It was such a *human* thing. She didn't know Mao could be tired. But he was. And she saw it. Suddenly she realized how terribly tired he must be. Leading a revolution, freeing an entire people from the shackles of the wealthy, sweeping China free of prostitutes and landowners and making sure the People shared equally in everything; it must be exhausting. When he looked at her now she didn't see the Great Man. She saw a man, and his vulnerability sent her fears packing. She touched him on the shoulder. She, Mei Li, touched Mao Tse Tung, and she asked him what was wrong.

He told her how difficult his life was, how lonely. When he saw her, he said, he knew that she was the type of person who could understand him. No one understood him.

She did. She did understand him. She nodded, and told him so. She would do anything for him. Anything he needed that she could give, she would.

His hand on her breasts was a surprise, and she instinctively pulled away. No one had ever touched her like that. Then she saw how hurt he was, and she took his hand and put it back. He had a large, beefy hand, and she felt it through the rough cloth of her shirt as he traced the shape of her breast. His other hand squeezed her thigh. It was terrifying. His grip was so strong. But there was something else. As he ran his hand along her thigh she felt herself respond to him. She grew moist between her legs, a warm pulsing heat that throbbed with every squeeze of her leg. His other hand wrapped around her, as he pulled her close. She knew what was coming, what he wanted, and she knew she would give it to him. She was a virgin and she hoped to give herself only to the man she married, but here she was with Chairman Mao, and his hand ran under her jacket and she heard herself moan as he pulled her tight. She ran her hand up through his hair. It was dirty, greasy, as if he hadn't cleaned it in weeks, but when did he ever have time for something as simple as a shower? He lifted her in his arms and she let herself go limp. She couldn't give him much, but she could give him her body, if he wanted it.

He kissed her as he carried her. His breath was noisome, and she could feel the dirt on his neck when she caressed him, but it didn't matter. He needed her and she would give him what he wanted. He carried her to a large desk and set her down on it. She was very wet now and her legs pulsed with a wanting she had never known. He unbuttoned her jacket, and her breasts, free of their confinement, exploded into the open air. They were big, but they were high on her chest. She was still young and she arched her back, letting her breasts soar into the air as Mao buried his face in them. He ran his hands along their sides, pushed them together and dug his face into the firm pillow they made. He licked them, ran his tongue along and under them, tickling her beneath her arm. Then he cupped the back of her neck and took a nipple into his mouth.

Pleasure shot through her unlike anything she had ever known. Her thigh tingled as he sucked and when his hand worked its way into her pants she was ready for him. He tore her pants loose, sending the button sailing across the floor and ripping the zipper open. She felt one of his heavy hands press her onto her back while the other tore her pants off. In a moment she was naked, and she felt his hands grab her thighs and pull her toward him. She moaned, put out her hands as if to stop him, but when his fingers violated her wet virginity she could only catch her breath in anticipation.

He thrust into her like a man possessed, stopped for a moment by the thin skin that let him know she was a virgin. He looked at her then, but she couldn't speak. She felt him inside her and she knew that Mao himself was taking her. She felt open, vulnerable and invaded, and she welcomed the invasion. Her breath came in great gasps, and when the wolf came back into Mao's eyes she couldn't look at him. He thrust himself through her last little defense and she felt the sharp tear of skin. It burned hotly for a moment, but was overwhelmed by the fullness of having him inside her. Her breath locked in her throat and her fingers grabbed his jacket. That's when she noticed that he was still dressed. But it didn't matter. He was breathing heavily now and the rank hot stench of his breath on her face made her feel dirty. He was dirty, and he gripped her hips in his hands and he thrust into her over and over. His hands were dirty and his clothes were dirty and she couldn't stop him. She didn't want to stop him. He reached under her waist and pulled her up, close to him. He grunted as he lifted her onto his throbbing member and drove himself deeper inside her than she thought possible.

She felt his hands on her hips, thick, farmer's hands that had seen so much bloodshed. His fingers dug into her soft flesh, fingers that had fired guns, killed people. Fingers that had written the Book were now bruising her vulnerable young skin. He plied into her and she felt the meat of his thighs as they pushed her legs apart. He was more than a man, he was a giant, and she was his to use as he would. She was China, and she opened herself to him just as her country had. He was hurting her, but she embraced him with her thighs and moaned for more. Then, as the power of the man and the moment rushed over her, Mei Li shuddered from her very soul.

He hitched her up once with a mighty thrust of his hips, then fell forward against the desk. His grip slackened and he let her back down so her butt felt the hard wood beneath her. Then he pulled himself out of her. He was flaccid now. He turned his back to her and buttoned his pants.

"You can stay here as long as you like," he said. Then he walked out the door.

She looked around the room now, her virgin blood dripping onto the desk. She was naked, and alone. Her thighs shook, and the trembling ran up to her shoulders. She pushed herself off the desk. She was in more pain than she thought. She limped over to her clothes and pulled them on, slowly. She was careful not to bleed too much on the floor. When she was dressed, she lowered her head and walked out of the room. The library was empty as well, and when she stepped into the hall, the guards were gone. No one was there to watch her as she hunched her shoulders and tiptoed out of the building. Still, she smiled. No one would ever believe her.

Love, Zora

Fiona Zedde

HARLEM, NEW YORK CITY, 1927

She looks like a liar in that cocked hat. A lit cigarette perches between her fingers like a dangerous butterfly with smoky wings and a glowing head. My *tante* says that she is a writer, a prevaricator by trade. Three fey-looking men, dapper in double-breasted suits and the gleam of entitlement and intelligence in their eyes, gather around her at one of La Maison Haïtienne's best tables. Their conversation is loud, punctuated equally by laughter and voices raised in dissent. Her laugh is the loudest.

I come out to take their order and I feel her eyes on me, like hands, warm and over-familiar. The men watch her and laugh, teasing her about a large appetite.

"But isn't she a sweet-looking morsel, Langston?" I hear her ask. Her friend chuckles and says something about me not being quite to his taste.

As I walk back to the kitchen, dark eyes trace the movement of my hips under the thick wool skirt. It is cool in the restaurant, but her gaze burns me. In the kitchen the other waitresses ask about them, what they like, if they are as gracious as they are intelligent. I shrug before walking back out to the tables.

When I lean over to serve her grilled salmon with béchamel sauce, her hand brushes my breast. I jump and the sauce trembles in the bowl, then, as if telling on the source of my surprise, leaks over the opaque black rim of the bowl to dribble on the table in a slow white line toward her. She apologizes and smiles, innocence itself under that wide-brimmed hat. If this were a man doing these things to me, the food would be scorching a path down to his lap by now. But her smile is beautiful. My legs can't take me fast enough back to the kitchen.

She and her friends keep up a lively conversation as I serve dinner; she talks about going to Africa and doing research on the cultures of different tribes.

I cannot resist commenting. "I don't understand why people are always looking elsewhere to find themselves. What about home? What's so terrible about the places where we were born that we rarely seem to want to go back there?" I speak for myself as well as these Negro aristocrats eating at my *tante*'s expensive restaurant. "How can we expect whites to respect us and our ways if *we* don't?"

They look at me as if I were a talking monkey, an exotic prize. Her eyes are still on me, but now there is something more than the hunger.

"You can't be from New York City," she says, mouth smiling, eyes finally on my face. "Where did you come here from?"

"Why? Do you want to visit my home?"

"Maybe." Her smile becomes full and radiant. "So are you going to tell me?"

"Maybe." I walk off to the kitchen to the laughter of her companions.

It is Friday and she is back, beautiful in another feathered hat and silk gloves. She introduces herself properly this time, then coaxes my name out of me with a teasing smile. "Do you want to go out for a drink?" she asks.

I tell her that I'm working, that I can't get away, but she offers to talk to my boss for me and convince her to give me time off to play. The writer obviously doesn't know my Tante Marie. I put her off and agree to meet her after work instead.

For the rest of the day I am nervous, my sweaty palms constantly about to drop dishes. To calm myself, I focus on the memory of her skin, with its rich complexity of shades—dark ochre and ebony and cinnamon mixed together on a deep gold palette. One day, if I get the chance, I will ask her to pose for me. My nerves vibrate at the possibility and I cannot wait for evening to come.

My *tante* knows that I like women the way she likes men, but she doesn't say anything bad, doesn't complain. She says that as long as I do the work and manage to be happy then she won't interfere. We came from Haiti for the freedom to be ourselves, and that meant the freedom to love whomever and however we choose.

She comes at one A.M., dressed in different clothes. I act nonchalant with her, as if I had not spent all day waiting.

"I'm taking you to a party," she says, touching my arm. "And what you're wearing is just fine."

What is she going to do, parade me around like a 1920s Saarje Baartman, the waitress with a brain? In the car—a loaner along with its driver from her friend A'Lelia, she confides later—she looks me over, sits close, and tells me how pretty I am. Her hands play in my hair, loosen pins until it lies on my shoulders in dark waves. I let her. She takes off her gloves and hat and puts them on the leather seat opposite us. Her hands are cool on my face.

"Do you like me?" she asks, but does not wait for my answer. Her taste is sweet, like a mango in the heat of summer, her arms and throat brushed with the fine fur of peaches. She slides her hand under my skirt and lifts it, chuckles when she finds me wet and ready. Her fingers slide into me and I watch her greedily pushing under my skirt, looking for a place to call home in the wet folds of my quim. She doesn't mind that I don't move, that my eyes only flutter half closed as she pleasures me. My breasts feed her thirst, pebble and tremble beneath her tongue and teeth as they jut past the gaping blouse and jacket.

"You taste like caramel cream," she murmurs into my skin. I forgive her the cliché as her mouth suckles and milks and I shudder quietly in passion. Her fingers plumb deep inside with a noise of decadence and of want spilling into the quiet space. My heart races. My neck bows. The air inside the car is hot. I come with the sound of a thousand sighs.

She's timed it perfectly. As the car slows down in front of the building she pins up my hair, resituates my hat. She is sliding her own gloves on when the driver opens the door. I know the smell of pussy floats out before us, announcing our pleasure like a red banner in the chill night breeze.

The party is a blur of faces and mink and gin under sparkling chandeliers. In the front parlor, they tease each other with artfully arranged breasts, scented throats, and pants that cling to firm buttocks and heavy crotches. They deliver on these teasing promises in the back room, laying each other down in groups, and couples, and threesomes, to feed and lick and fuck and laugh. She takes me through these rooms, pointing out her friends, those she's had before, recommending this one or that for whatever sexual act. The room is thick with sex. The trembling of dark buttocks, a wet exchange of passion, soft moans, high-pitched screams, low growls. All eroticize the air. Her voice is a caress at my ear, but she does not touch me.

We leave the loving rooms behind for one of A'Lelia's many conversation parlors. The black intelligentsia gathers there, sharing gossip, ideas, and glasses of champagne. We settle into a low couch that is already crowded, but people make room for us. She invites me to share my opinions, to show my worth and seduce our sudden audience with my tongue. Her warm hand on my knee lets them know whom I will go home with tonight.

"Zora Neale, you were always a selfish bitch," a woman pressed close to my thigh murmurs through her marijuana haze.

For the rest of the evening, she does not touch me, only watches and smiles. When she says good-bye to her friends, they laugh and tell her to call them next month when she comes back up for air. During the taxi ride back to her apartment, we are quiet and separate on the thick plastic seats. Conversation floats out of her, one-sided. She tells me that she is in school, is working on a play with her friends. Her brother will be at the apartment, but that will be no problem. It is all the things that she does not say that make the ride tense. Her gloves are on again. The coat fits her body well. Her eyes hum over me like music, touching in gentleness where they had not before.

"I want to make you lose control," she murmurs as I step past her to get out of the cab. When it pulls off into the fog-shrouded night, her eyes focus completely on me. "May I?"

"If you can."

The apartment is warm. She says that it is her one true luxury, this voluptuous heat. For a moment the sight of her taking off her coat and gloves entrances me. I do not notice the other person there. Her brother. He is curled up on the couch watching us. A book lies waiting under his wide-stretched fingers. He is thin and brown, like her. Perhaps one day he will be as handsome. She introduces us, asks if I would like something to drink, and then, when I decline, pulls me away from her brother's knowing smile into her bedroom.

She turns on the gramophone, lifting the heavy needle to place it on the record. Ethel Waters's voice settles into the room. Her hands warm as they undress me, exploring the terrain of my skin like an unfamiliar country, as an archeologist coming in for some foreign dig, an anthropologist unearthing a lost tongue. Her mouth is greedy and hot. She is gentle, unbelievably so, as if she herself cannot comprehend the tenderness of her hands, the loving rhythm of her movements.

"I want to know you," she says, then touches every part of me, each dip and rise of flesh, as if memorizing me. "Tell me how I make you feel." Her fingers slip into my navel, circling the sweat-slick indentation. Fingertips trace the light fur on my belly, marking me. I can only sigh and moan and shiver.

"Tell me."

Her mouth settles on my cunt, bringing out the language of my people as she strokes my lips, parts the weeping delta that is my exile on her shores. I tell her in Creole of the mad rush of feelings, like dancing to the pounding rhythm of Vodun drums, when she touches me. How her tongue inside me calls up the tides of the Caribbean and the hot flush of a Haitian sunrise; how in the glory of my highest ecstasy, I hear the chanting voices of my countrywomen and the slapping of feet, the crescendo of all my senses working together until for a moment I am deaf, blind, dumb, my palate without taste, my fingers numb. Until she, in her low voice whispering "baby" and "sweetheart," brings them all rushing back.

I am addicted to her touch. After three weeks, she is all I can think about. Her skin. Her voice. The spicy scent of her underneath all those clothes. My *tante* notices my preoccupation and chides me for getting involved with an American when I am leaving for France so soon. I do not tell her that for this woman I am willing to stay another winter in this city, to be enfolded in the cocoon of her sweltering apartment and her even hotter embrace.

But she knows me and so she shakes her head. "Be careful, *ma fille*."

"I will." But I know it's too late for that. I go to her right after work, not even bothering to change or shower or have my own dinner. She's all the food I need.

"You're very cool," she says, greeting me with a long, slow kiss. Even before I am completely inside the apartment she is unbuttoning my blouse. I never see her nakedness, only the unveiling of her hands and sometimes, if I am lucky, the satin slickness of a slip over her heavy breasts. The dark nipples I can only imagine as they peak and harden under my hands and tongue, always through cloth. So it is her hands that inflame me. When I see her take off her gloves—to eat, to write, to fuck—I blush. Her fingers are long and thick, with clear pink nails that end just before her fingertips. They are unadorned and always accessible to me. She tosses my blouse aside, sees me staring at her gloved hands and smiles with the stretch of her voluptuary's lips and a sparkle of teeth.

"What would you like?" she asks, knowing I won't answer. But she gives me what I want anyway without the humiliation of begging, because she wants it too: the silk-on-silk tug on the end of each gloved finger. Then, as if clasping her fingers together in prayer, the leisurely pull of the glove until her fingers, then the entire hand, is bare. Repeat. Slowly, with the other hand, until my belly is trembling and aflame, my thighs clenching in anticipation of her touch.

"Is this what you want?" Her naked hands flutter over my collarbone and chest, then over the warm skin of my breasts that begs to be warmer still under her. She loosens my hair, my skirt, my thighs, and lays me across her bed. "I have something else for you."

The lamplight is lush over her skin, haloing its velvety darkness. She waits with her hands resting on her hips as I prop myself up in the bed against thick pillows. Under my eyes her skirt falls away first, the thick textured wool that I've felt against my naked flesh a dozen times. Then, with a quick flick of buttons and a shrug of shoulders, the jacket too is gone. Her slip, made of a coppery satin that makes her skin shimmer even more in the light, she quickly sweeps up and over her head.

Perfect. Pleasure. Perfection. Smiling face, arrogance itself, knowing that I find her beyond compare, hands once again on hips, waiting for me to speak. But I cannot. Instead I reach for her, pulling her blindly toward me onto the bed, touching her without barriers, tasting her naked skin for the first time. She is delicious. Berry ripe nipples, even darker than I'd imagined, salty sweet and thick. Her flesh, sweat-flavored and abundant, pulling taut under my hands, quivering. And, best of all, the musky scent of her pussy rising, unfettered, from between her legs. She laughs, gusty swells of mirth that stop only when my tongue has burrowed inside her and my hands hug the lyrical swells of her ass, then she sighs my name, offers praises to her god, cries out above me, her thighs trembling like wings. And when she comes I cannot stop. With her still gasping in surprise and delight, I drape myself over her, take her swollen nipples in my mouth, and sheathe my fingers inside her still-fluttering cunt.

"No…not yet," falls from her mouth, but I cannot hear. Her body quickens again despite her protest, and my mouth is ravenous. Her fingers stretch past the sheets to grip the smooth cherrywood of the headboard. The bedsprings sing vigorously as her gasping moans drown out Ethel's wails. My fingers are tireless. I could love her all night, touch her until our flesh rubs away and there's nothing but nerves and sensation, two raw naked beings, dripping, drenched, fused together by desire. Too soon she arches up in orgasm, a taut singing bow, then sags into the bed. I climb up her body, straddle her, wash her still-trembling flesh with the drip from mine—her thighs, hips, and shivering belly. A world of want shudders through me. She watches as I undulate slowly over the skin of her belly, then move up to take her hard nipple against me, rubbing my throbbing clit with its firm sweetness until she too moans with arousal. The nipple comes away wet and I want to lick it clean, but there is something else I want more. Her mouth.

I settle onto her face with a sigh. She cups me, spreads my lips wide and licks from ass to clit. Her naked flesh calls my hands; even in the lightning storm that fires my body I must touch her, feel the bare lushness of her that has been denied to me for so long. In the coming storm, her ship cradles me, rocking my body on the tumultuous waves as it shakes with tears and another kind of wet. My control is gone.

The inevitability of our parting is what has made this interlude so sweet. Today I leave, finally, for France. My sister lives there. Already she has a studio set up for me, a room and a garden. She says that I can paint there until I tire of it or of her. My lover has been good, but she grows restless and will soon leave. So I must go first. At the dock, she sees me off, tying a red and blue scarf around my throat. It smells of cocoa butter and almonds. As she does.

"I'll miss you," she says. A small lie. She's discovered something more exciting than love in her anthropology, something that will take her to a place where she needs to be, a place of complexity and reciprocal warmth and strangers to be awed by her. "Please come back when you've had enough of France. I'll write and let you know how I am. Without you all this is nothing. I hope you know that."

She lies so well. I open my mouth, about to tell her for once of my heart, but change my mind.

"Zora." My hands reach for hers.

"Djulie." My name floats above the last call for boarding. Our lips press together and it's the old fire again. My body ignites easily, but hers is already pulling away.

"Write me," I say, knowing that she will not.

As the ship pulls away from the dock I watch her from high on deck, the lone brown woman among the pale, waving throng. Her eyes find mine and she smiles. In that clear brown gaze for a moment I wish and I see those letters that she promised. I imagine her closing them with a kiss, and with her name and the love she did not speak of when she held my body in her hands. I wish for the impossible, I know. A foolish wish upon a lying star.

Marilyn

A. F. WADDELL

THROUGH THE HACIENDA WINDOW she viewed bougainvillea climbing wrought iron. In a beige silk robe she sat at the desk in her bedroom. She'd pinned up her hair; she wore horn-rimmed glasses. She yearningly opened a pictorial. The captions boasted of an American Camelot. The black-and-white photographs displayed images of a thin, elegant, loving mother; pampered, sun-kissed children; a wholesome, all-American man. Against backdrops of the Oval Office and the Atlantic Ocean he commandeered a desk, a sailboat. She knew Jack...

The beach house was a box of light above sparkling sand, against a night sky. Of stark design, its glass walls framed people dancing, drinking, and eating. Its deck faced the ocean. Inside, energies of jazz and laughter exploded through open doors and mingled with the sounds of the surf. The scent of sea air wafted through the sparsely furnished great room.

"Oh, I absolutely love negative ionization. It makes me high!"

Marilyn squealed. She wore a low-cut black silk dress and black heels. Her skin took the sun well. The tip of her nose had been shortened and narrowed; concavity below her cheekbones had been enhanced by the extraction of a few back teeth. Short platinum-blonde locks contrasted with tan skin, like vanilla frosting on a caramel cake. The mole on the left side of her face seemed an asymmetrical accent to her physical perfection.

"Marilyn, darling, are you sure it's not the margaritas?" laughed her small blond companion.

"Truman!"

"Would you believe who's here tonight? Am I hallucinating, or is that the president of the United States standing near the buffet table?"

She laughed. "Perhaps you are hallucinating…"

She looked across the room. It was him. He was surrounded, but towered over most others. Reddish-brown hair. Tanned, freckled skin. Intense, friendly eyes that beamed intelligence and energy. Guests were practically standing in line to see him. To touch him.

"I'll be back in a minute, Truman. You stay here. I won't have you teasing me in front of the president of the United States!"

She wove through gauntlets of guests. Hopeful eyes surveyed her. Everyone wanted a part of her, it seemed. She edged through the group of actresses, actors, writers, and hangers-on. She fixed her eyes on him; eye beams connected them. He watched her walk toward him. Her pink lips were pursed; she looked from right to left. Her high heels gave her body a lilt, a sway, as she walked. From sea to shining sea, her black silk-covered breasts glimmered under overhead lights. Her body was a country, he thought, filled with cities and states, plains and vineyards, desert and farmland. Roads and highways. Thigh-ways.

"Miss Monroe…"

"Call me Marilyn."

"Marilyn, it's wonderful to see you…er, meet you. I see all your movies."

"Hello, Mr. President…the feeling is mutual. I'm a happy constituent!"

He laughed. "Call me Jack."

"What brings you to California, Jack?"

"The fishing. The sailing. The parties."

She smiled at his broad Boston a.

"Let's get some fresh air, shall we?" He smiled. A few minutes apart, they left the room separately.

Truman stood on the deck, gazing at the shoreline to his left. The man and woman leaned into one another as they walked. He was a head taller than her, and broad-shouldered. Their voices lightly played against the slight roar of the surf. Their paths diverged as he walked toward a back entrance to the house. She walked to the shore, then climbed the steps to the deck.

"Darling, you have sand in your hair. On your dress. Where are your shoes?" Truman observed.

"Shit! Those were Feraud pumps. Damn."

"And what's that fragrance you're wearing, dear?"

"Semen by the Sea. Sperme auprès de la mer. *New from Givenchy."*

She put away the book of photographs. They sometimes met at Peter's beach house. Sometimes at her house. He'd given her a private phone number. She never knew when he might actually call her. Her film was on hiatus until October. The press had reported in typically negative mode: *"Marilyn Fired From Film Set!"* She'd never gotten used to her life being publicly misrepresented. In any case she could use the break from filming. Cukor often demanded seemingly unnecessary takes. The summer stretched before her; she could use the rest. And the play.

She picked up a volume of poetry, went to the bed and lay down on her stomach, pillow under her breasts, knees bent, calves up, ankles crossed, feet pointing. Reading in bed centered her; reading and eating in bed was even better. Few things she found more relaxing than quietly drifting through words and images.

The phone rang; she jumped. She lifted the receiver.

"Hello?"

"What do you have on?" he asked.

"The radio."

"Very funny."

"That's it. That's what I have on, Jack."

"Look, Marilyn…I don't have much time. Get a wiggle on."

" 'Get a wiggle on'? Another one of your New England colloquialisms, no doubt!"

"Marilyn…" he gripped his cock.

"OK…we're sitting on the shore…at our own personal clambake. I'm wearing a shirtwaist dress and pearls…you're wearing a sweater, cords, and dockers…"

"Dockahs, you mean..."

"We're eating butter-drenched clams...don't let the butter drip onto your sweater!"

"No, ma'am!"

"I unbutton and unzip you and pull out your cock...all eight inches of it. I tightly grip it and stroke it. My hand is slick with melted butter. It slides easily over and around you...over the head and down the shaft, over the head and down the shaft, over the head and down the shaft..."

"Mmmm..."

"Your cock is glistening in the sun, in the circlet of my hand. Gulls fly over and cry. The wind blows sand. Grains of sand stick to our buttery parts."

"Yes..."

"Social mavens are having a tea party on a nearby dune. One sees your cock and faints."

"Aaahhhh..."

"Now you're throbbing, pumping, spilling...you're coming onto your nice hand-knit cotton sweater! Bad!"

Her luminous skin was draped by a white-cotton sheet. Her sleep mask blocked filtering sun as she moaned, drifting into reality. A small white dog slept near. She slipped off her mask and lay staring up at the ceiling, its surface providing a backdrop, a screen, for replaying her dreams. She waded through images, rediscovering nocturnal stories and plays as they sequentially came to her.

She'd slept in a bra, a bra and nothing else. She got out of bed, opened the drapes, and stood before a full-length mirror. Her hair was mussed, her face slightly puffy. She slipped one bra strap, then the other, off her shoulders, then turned the harness around on her rib cage, unhooking it and letting it fall. In morning inventory, she cupped her breasts in her hands, lifted and looked at them. "How are my girls today?" They seemed in fine shape, round, soft, with pinkish-brown nipples looking up at her. She looked in the mirror. The mole on the left side of her face now seemed a bit lower. She sighed and dressed in a black silk robe. "Mafia! Maf! Come on, boy!" The small poodle bounced off the bed, energetically barked, and followed her from the bedroom, down the hall, and into the kitchen.

"Outside!" She opened the back door, the screen door, and Mafia trotted out into the backyard; she propped open the screen door. She gathered her newspapers from her front doorstep. In the kitchen she sat at the table and read. *"JFK Speaks On Nuclear Test Ban Treaty, Civil Rights."*

The housekeeper was off. She enjoyed the days when Eunice wasn't around. An empty house was a relief: no questions, no conflict, no colliding energies, just Marilyn and her dog. Mafia was a keenly intelligent, white ball of fluff, with eyes like shiny black olives.

After coffee and juice she dressed in a sleeveless checked cotton blouse, Capezio pants, and flats. She covered her hair with a scarf and put on shades. Going for a stroll, she found the neighborhood to be eye candy. The houses and lawns were surreally perfect and quiet. Her flats slapped the sidewalk as she walked west on Helena. She saw no other people. She imagined a *Twilight Zone* episode of a lone wanderer in a mysterious town, pondering the still, vacant landscape: immaculate lawns and homes, likely filled with mannequin people, or strangely evolving pod people.

She turned south, then east on the periphery of the country club. She thought of golf as men in ugly pants, whispering. Red-faced fashion-challenged golfers chatted, smiled, and drove their balls through air and grass and sand. It was time to do it: let loose Marilyn. Off came the scarf and sunglasses. Her posture straightened; her walk transformed. Like Jell-O on springs! she thought, recalling some film dialogue. A few men glanced her way, then displayed The Look: the sense of recognition that fixed their eyes upon Her. A nonverbal buzz went through the small group of men, as if primitive male vibrations connected and alerted them to a female on their territory. She walked and peripherally watched the men watch her, before turning north for home.

"Doll, you didn't wash your hair today, did you?"

"No."

In the kitchen Tony opened his case and spread his wares onto the table and counters: hair color and developer; palettes of cream foundation, concealer, blusher, lip color, eyeliner, eye shadow, and mascara; various brushes and sponges for application.

"Good. We need to do these roots." Marilyn sat. He mixed color and developer. With a small brush similar to a paintbrush, he stroked her dark roots. "OK. Twenty-five to thirty minutes and you're done. Then we can rinse and do your makeup. Who's shooting you today?"

"Nick Shea."

"Mmmm. Very nice."

Marilyn smiled. "Tony, sometimes I think I'd like to try a different look…but, I don't know…"

"Darling…I think you should stay with the platinum blonde. As a woman ages, she should always go lighter and brighter. Or, as in your case, stay with it. Why would you want to change? You look marvelous!"

"Well, thank you, Tony. It's interesting. Wavelength theory asserts that color is defined by the types and quantity of wavelength light reflection. White objects tend to equally reflect all types of light, and tend to reflect most of the light cast onto it. Light can be reflected or transmitted. When white light meets an object, the light's energy is absorbed by the object. Did you know that?" She smiled.

"Why…of course."

"So. In effect, light-blonde hair reflects, dazzles, and imparts energy into matter."

"I guess that you could say that." Tony smiled.

She sat and read a magazine. A knock at the door took her from her glossy-paper trance. She answered the door.

"Hello, Nick." She smiled. "Come in and get ready. I'll be right back!"

"Hi, Marilyn…" Nick entered and his puzzled gaze followed her as she rushed past him and out the door, through the wrought-iron gate, and down the walk. The rose, amber, and patchouli of Chanel No. 5 scented the flux of air. She turned right and ran past her neighbors' homes. Her bare feet met warm concrete. Was it her imagination or did faces peer from slightly opened drapes? *There she goes again,* they likely thought. A grown woman running, arms pumping, breasts bouncing under cotton, tan calves and ankles sprouting from cropped pants, bare feet slapping the sidewalk. She turned right to intersect the way home. She perspired lightly; she could feel energy and heat moving from deep inside to out, flushing her skin. She made the last turn onto her front walk, entered the gate, and opened the front door.

"Marilyn, where did you go?"

"Just around the block. I ran around the block! It gives me a glow." She smiled. Her eyes sparkled, her skin shone, energy surrounded her like a light. Her makeup suffered only minimal damage. Minor dabbing and smoothing would fix it.

"You look wonderful, Marilyn. When can we get started?"

"In just a minute. Be right back."

When she returned, she sat down on a cream-colored sofa. She wore a sleeveless beige silk blouse and black silk pants. Nick hovered with his Pentax, taking in hue, and form against form. Yes, this would be a subtle black-and-white work: a cream sofa, Marilyn's platinum hair against tanned skin; beige-covered globes atop black silk-covered hips and legs.

She placed her hands behind her head, crossed her ankles, and propped her bare feet on the coffee table.

"Marilyn, your feet are dirty!" Nick laughed. He reached and touched the sole of her left foot. "Hey!" She squealed and threw back her head, deeply laughing. His shutter repeatedly clicked as the images froze in his mind, angle to angle, frame to frame, her head going back back back, full shiny lips drawn back over pearly teeth, tiny nostrils flared, crinkled eyes half-shut, threatening to release moisture.

"Marilyn, I have an idea."

"What?"

"I'd love to get shots of you eating in bed."

Now wearing a gingham print blouse and jeans, she threw back the coverlet and top sheet, climbed into bed, leaned back into pillows, and balanced a food tray atop her lap. An apple, a carrot, a dish of yogurt, and a glass bottle of milk filled the tray.

"Do I really have to eat? I'm not very hungry."

"Come on…just a bite or two, for Nicky…OK?"

"Oh…OK. You're very sweet."

"Go!"

She put the glistening Red Delicious to her mouth and took a bite; her lips wrapped a spoon of thick yogurt; she drank a large swallow of milk. Her milk-kissed lips encircled a carrot. Her large, deep eyes signaled innocence; curiosity.

"Lovely!" Nick exclaimed.

Clean, hot, fragrant water was magical. As a child she'd dreamed of clean bathwater, water unused by others. It made her nauseous to think of the color and aroma of her childhood bathwater. Had the other kids spitefully spit and pissed in it? In a large household, the extremely frugal water gods had believed in conservation. She'd been designated lowest in the water-user hierarchy.

As she soaked, on her bath tray were Dom Perignon 1953 and a small yellow capsule. Steam glistened surfaces. The hot water purified her, obliterating nasty molecules and negative vibrations. She'd read about negative ionization and its soothing, healing effect. In a hot bath she were revived yet calmed. She felt one with the water, as if it was her liquid lover, dissolving boundaries.

She sipped champagne and swallowed her little yellow med. Her vigilant expression softened; she lay back her head; her gaze fixed upon the bathroom window, which framed lemon-laden trees; it seemed a wall painting. Her lips slackened and slightly parted. Her eyelids drooped and closed, she seemed caressed in a cotton-wool cloud, floating, floating...

He watched her walk down the hall; he closely followed. Her short robe was loose, open. Light filtered from the end of the hall, between skin and silk, outlining her arms, shoulders, waist, ass-cheeks. She wore tiny beige stilettos. Her calves curved and bulged. Her thighs tensed. Her buttocks moved in outward thrust.

Her panties and bras were scattered on the ceramic tile bedroom floor: black lacy things, red silky pieces, plain white cottons. Clothing was draped over the backs of chairs. Dirty dishes sat on her desk and nightstands. Books and magazines were haphazardly stacked. This definitely wasn't D.C. or Hyannisport.

"Marilyn, darling, what happened, did your housekeeper quit?"

"No. But sometimes I lock her out of my bedroom. Don't worry. The sheets are clean."

Splayed on the bed, Marilyn's legs, stiletto heels, were askew. Her robe opened over bare breasts. She was full and soft, he thought, unlike some semianorexic society wives. He wasn't boffing bones, he was sliding softness. The lifted hems of her robe showcased her cunt; she'd lightened the hair: blonde-yellow covered pink. *How very colorful,* he thought. *Looks like an Easter chick today – maybe it'll dispense little candy eggs.* He removed his suit jacket and pants and used a chair as a valet. She leaned forward from the bed, took hold of his tie, and pulled him close, bending her legs and pushing the tips of her stilettos into the front of his thighs. She pulled his mouth to hers.

"Mmmph…Marilyn…let me finish undressing."

By his silk-tie leash she pulled him lower, to her breasts. His hands danced their perimeters and cupped them. *They're all nice,* he thought, from the fit-in-a-champagne-glass size to apple to grapefruit to melon size. The other types he didn't know about, or didn't want to know about, or didn't remember from his being nursed. His mouth fastened onto one breast, ensconcing a nipple prong; his hand cupped the other. *Why do breasts smell and taste so good?* he wondered. *I could stay here for a while,* he thought, as Marilyn's hand centered the top of his head and pushed him downward.

"Marilyn…"

"Jack…"

He kneeled bedside, touching her belly and spread thighs. His hand lightly brushed her soft bush, his right index and middle finger traced the center of her. She was wet and slick. His fingers spread her. She rocked her hips. *I wonder if men ever break their fingers doing this?* he thought. She gripped his thick hair and pulled his face closer to her center. Hovering between her thighs, he studied her, her length and groove and concavity, her bruised-fruit slit. His tongue provoked, down to up, finessing her clitoris, melting into her. Heat arrows fired her circuitry, meeting, traveling a loop from clit to womb to breast. She moaned and rocked and pushed herself into him. His tongue pressed harder on her swollen clit; he went deeper. He felt he was drowning. *She reminds me of Camembert,* he thought. She moaned louder and rocked harder; she tried to pull him up. He moved up and kissed her lips. He stood and removed his tie, shirt, pants, and underwear.

His erect cock tested her, imposing, shallowly resting in her, like a slowly burrowing animal. She moaned and moved her hips; he felt himself warmly impelled through slick, grooved flesh. The cunt and cock seemed autonomous. From the back of his head synapsed wildness; a hot snake wrapped his spine. Force slammed his taut balls. Her clitoris channeled a high inner spot in wet pink concert; his cock filled her up and showered her; he watched her head go back back back, her loud mouth open, as in laughter, as in rapture, as in making love to the camera.

They lay still for a moment; Jack rolled off her, and lay beside her.

"Marilyn, it's getting late. I need to shower. My car will be here soon."

A bath, a bottle, a pill, a meal, a bed. The bath was tangy, milky, sweet: sea-salt, milk, and honey; the bottle was icy, crisp Smirnoff; the capsule was bright yellow; the meal was boiled eggs; the bed was remade.

She awoke in filtered sunlight, her brain on edge, as if there were slowly burning fuses wrapping her nerves, her pink flesh and gray lobes. Vexed by dreams of bicycles with no brakes and of Mafia loose in the street, her nocturnal being had been provoked; she'd felt as if on a rotisserie, turning, turning, on the sheets. Coffee would be a temporary antidote, before its chemistry tightened her springs.

In the kitchen Marilyn guzzled coffee and read the morning papers. "*JFK Conferences On Thalidomide*" said a headline.

"More coffee?" Eunice seemed to be banging every dish and pot and pan in the house.

"I'll take another cup. I'm going to my desk!"

She sat at her desk and dialed Jack. *The number that you dialed is no longer in service. If you think you dialed the number in error, please hang up and try again. The number that you dialed is no longer in service. If you think you dialed the number in error, please hang up and try again.*

She sipped her coffee, looked up a phone number, and dialed.

"Good afternoon. You've reached the White House. How may I direct your call?"

"Listen, this is Marilyn Monroe speaking and I need to talk to the president!"

"Ma'am, the president is unavailable. May I relay your message and phone number?"

"Goddamnit, this is important!"

"Ma'am, please..."

Marilyn slammed down the receiver.

Dear diary, goddamnit, what a day. Slept badly last night. I MUST sleep tonight. Eunice is here fussing about. I can't reach Jack. He's distancing from me. I'm in no mood for this. Had a session with Dr. Greenson, what a control freak!

"Marilyn!" Eunice called and knocked at the bedroom door. Marilyn sighed deeply. "Just a minute, be right there!"

She took her pills and got into bed, fumbled, and turned on the bed's vibrator. She dialed the telephone. She was rocking, rocking. Lying on her back, she felt warmth from above. Floating on the sea, she reclined nude on an oversized beach lounge chair: orange and yellow braided plastic strips centered and wrapped its aluminum frame. The chair-raft had large gaps between the woven plastic stripping. A docile, black-eyed Mafia floated adjacent in his doggy bed. "Stay, Maf! Stay in your bed, boy!" she cautioned. A roar from the sky pricked her ears. Her eyes focused on a Cessna that seemed to be skywriting. Behind the plane was tied the wooden structure of the Hollywood sign being towed across the sky. She took in her surroundings: adrift upon a lounge-chair raft, she must seem a speck in vast blue, a pink dot against orange. Clouds covered the sun; wind blew up small waves. She was lulled by rocking. Her skin was impressed by a sensation of gentle fluttering. Birds' wing pressure stroked her hair and face, breasts and belly and legs and feet. "Norma Jean…Norma Jean…" gave soft voices. Her skin and flesh and nerve and bone were infused with energy. She perceived light from her inside, out. Her hair blew in the wind and her eyes widened as she looked up, transfixed, as silhouettes lowered and hovered over her. Her head went back back back, full shiny lips drawn back over pearly teeth, tiny nostrils flared, eyes semiclosed, as in laughter, as in rapture, as in making love to the sky.

An Assassin's Tale

Gary Earl Ross

MAY 1901 – CLEVELAND

The woman on the compact speaker's platform at the front of the lecture hall was herself compact, short, and broad-shouldered. Her wavy brown hair was pulled back into a severe bun. She wore a pale-blue scarf around her neck, a white linen blouse, and a high-waisted gray skirt.

"Anarchism aims at a new and complete freedom. It strives to bring about the freedom which is not only freedom from within, but freedom from without...." She held out her right hand, palm up as if offering her ideas on a tray. "Freedom from without."

From where he sat near the back, Leon was unable to tell whether the eyes that flashed behind the woman's pince-nez matched her scarf or her skirt. In either case, they were striking. Dressed in his old gray suit and smelling of Doctor Ray's hair oil, he gazed at her with awe. Apart from a few whores and Magda, a widowed seamstress he'd met at a socialist gathering, Leon had known few women: his late mother, whose ringed eyes were striking only for their sadness; his two sisters, whose faces already showed the same depletions as their mother's; and his bitch-viper stepmother, who had slithered between his father's sheets before his mother was cold. None of them had even a sliver of the dynamism that powered Emma Goldman. Compared to his father's thick Polish and abandoned attempts at English, Miss Goldman's Russian accent was almost musical. The more she spoke, the more deeply her words resonated within him. If God were, for him, still alive, Leon might have thought a divine hand had directed him to the Franklin Liberal Club, to this woman with whom he felt an immediate kinship.

"We do not favor the socialist idea of converting men and women into mere producing machines under the eye of a paternal government." She shook her head emphatically. "We go to the opposite extreme and demand—" She slapped a palm down on the lectern. "We demand the fullest and most complete liberty for each and every person to work out his own salvation. The degrading notions of men and women as breeding machines are far from our ideals of life." She removed her pince-nez. "The joys of sex without breeding are the subject, I think, of another lecture."

Soft laughter rippled through the audience.

Emma Goldman smiled and replaced her spectacles. Then she recited a litany of actions inspired by the indifference of fat industrialists to ill-fed workers, of rich governments to poor citizens. She spoke of the Haymarket Riot and how bravely its martyrs faced the gallows, of the workers killed by private police during the Homestead steel strike and the subsequent attack on industrialist Henry Frick. The failed attempt on Frick she likened to the assassination of King Umberto I: "Sasha Berkman and Gaetano Bresci, both sensitive men, men keenly pained by the misery of their brethren..."

At the mention of Bresci, Leon sat up straighter. Bresci's tracking and shooting of the Italian king last July was an act of courage with which Leon was quite familiar. A newspaper account was in his wallet at this very moment. Feeling that destiny was at work, he exhaled slowly, overwhelmed.

When she finished, applause filled the hall. Newspaper reporters snapped notebooks shut and dashed out. Policemen stiffened as if expecting a riot. But most of the audience filed toward the exits quietly. A crowd gathered around the speaker's platform and the table of books beside it. Emma Goldman stepped down, shaking hands and smiling.

Leon remained in his seat until the crowd around her thinned. Then he stood, ran a hand through his dark blond curls, and started down the aisle. When he reached her, she was talking to a big man with the callused hands of a laborer. Those hands brought back memories of Leon's own days at the wire mill, where he'd worked as a winder, sometimes with a bloody froth in his gloves. He still hated that job, especially when he looked into a mirror and remembered the night the wire snapped and whiplashed his cheek. Of course, mill work was better than his earlier job as a forker in the hell-hot air of a glass factory....

When Miss Goldman's conversation ended, Leon offered his hand. She took it in both of hers, fingertips probing its roughness, palms gently closing off his skin from the air it breathed and feeding it instead of the electricity she generated. He struggled against the tingle that ran through him, afraid to let her see he was shaking with excitement, that his loins were stirring. If only he were important enough to provoke such feelings in a woman like her.... Gently, he withdrew his hand and asked, almost in a whisper, "Will you suggest something for me to read?" He looked into her eyes.

Blue, like mine.

"I would be glad to." She studied him a moment. "Such sensitive features. The eyes of a man who sees past the suffering of the present to the freedom of the future." Her smile widened. "Perhaps you would like to join a few of us for a discussion?"

Leon hesitated. "I can't stay." He stared at the floor. Despite their kinship, he felt small in her presence, unimportant. Unimportant enough to lie. "I must work tomorrow...at the cheese factory in Akron." He raised his eyes, as if in apology. "I must get back tonight."

"Of course," Emma Goldman said. "Any one of these books—" She gestured toward the display.

"I...I have no money tonight," he said quietly.

"I understand." She gathered several pamphlets and handed them to him. "These explain our purpose and vision. Perhaps you can read the books later."

Leon said, "Thank you, Miss Goldman."

"You're very welcome, Mister...?"

Importance must be earned, he thought.

He waved her question aside even as he started to back away from her. "I am no one," he said, with the self-deprecating half smile of the timid. "No one at all."

June 1901 — Cleveland

In the loft of the barn behind the boarding house in which she lived, Magda lifted her skirts and exposed her hairy slit to Leon. "Enough already about bosses and workers and the poor," she said. "I don't bring you up here to talk about your theories. I bring you up here to fuck me."

Trousers and braces down around his boots, Leon knelt between Magda's bony thighs and tried to work his penis into her cunt, but he was just not hard enough. He stroked and squeezed himself, tried to choke his manhood off at the base to make the tip thick enough to part her nether lips. She kissed him, deeply, and reached for him with fingertips toughened by years of needle pricks. Massaging him, she tried to make him harder. But nothing worked, and Leon sat back on his haunches, apologizing.

Magda's eyes filled. "You don't find me beautiful anymore," she said.

"No," Leon said, then stammered, "I mean, that's not it." He looked away from her eyes so lying would be easier. "You are beautiful. It is just that I...I haven't been myself of late."

The truth was, Magda was anything but beautiful. She was stick-thin, with drawn features and brittle blonde hair, and she was more than a dozen years Leon's senior — nearly forty! When they had met some months ago, he thought he had found a kindred spirit, someone with whom he could discuss the woes of workers and the plight of the poor. At first interested in what he had to say, Magda had shown her true intentions two Sunday afternoons ago, after their last coupling in this very same loft. He had asked why in the seven or eight times they had made love in the past few months she had never let him see her completely naked. In none of their encounters had she ever shown the slightest shame at having her skirts up about her waist, her knickers off, and her shoes unbuttoned. In fact, as a barren widow, she had said more than once, she missed the male member, missed feeling it throb inside her. But she had never removed all her clothing, never let him touch or kiss her bare breasts. She had reddened at his question and looked away and said, "Only a husband will see me completely undressed." When she turned back to him, the color had left her cheeks and her eyes fixed on him with an intent he began to understand only after they had parted company. She had moved in socialist circles not out of sympathy for the oppressed but in search of free thinkers whose ideas of free love would let them fill her emptiness until she could find another husband. Though he had come back to the loft today in the hope that he had been mistaken, one look into Magda's eyes told him he was right. Clearly, she hoped he would ask her to marry him. Leon shriveled at the thought of spending every day with someone who shared only a shallow interest in his passions.

"What do you mean you haven't been yourself?" she said now, her eyes close to spilling. "You're the same Leon I met in February, always going on about the factories and the—"

"No," he said. "I am different."

"How, except that your meat is of no use to me?"

"I am different. I have a purpose and a destiny. A role in the revolution that you cannot understand." He was silent a moment, then whispered, "A role not here, not with you."

She looked confused as well as hurt. "Leon, what are you talking about?"

He stood, buttoning his drawers, pulling up his trousers and sliding his arms through his braces. "I must go," he said. As he climbed down the wooden ladder he could hear her weeping above, but he didn't care. Some things were more important than the tears of a foolish woman.

August 1901—Buffalo

There she is!

Leon had stopped for a Duffy's apple cider when he spotted her seated between two men at the East Esplanade Fountain. Emma Goldman wore a pale-green summer skirt beneath a simple white blouse and a straw sun hat cocked to one side. She appeared deep in conversation, smiling as she turned from one of her companions to the other. The men were like bookends—scuffed shoes, light-gray suits and waistcoats, beards, spectacles, slouch hats. The only difference between them was that the one on Miss Goldman's right was older, heavier.

Leon moved away from the refreshment stand toward a line of trees that led to the Court of Cypresses behind the Ethnology Building. He stood behind an evergreen and brought the cider bottle to his lips. He parted branches with his free hand and peered across the busy walkway at Emma Goldman. He watched her for a long time but was too far away to hear what she was saying.

He gulped more cider, swished it through his cheeks, and let it sting his tongue for a few seconds before swallowing.

After telling his family he was taking his share of the farm money and heading west to find work, Leon had come northeast and taken a room in a town near Buffalo. Spending carefully in the absence of a job, he moved through his days in a sleepwalk of faith that sooner or later his true purpose would unfold and he would know what he was supposed to do. As if called by an unseen force, he had taken the train into Buffalo today, to come to the Pan-American Exposition. Perhaps the same force had summoned Emma Goldman to the grand fair as well so she could explain everything, help him see what he sensed, that his was a pivotal role in the revolution. If only he could manage to speak to her alone....

In their two brief conversations after he first met her in Cleveland, they had established a bond, he thought, a recognition their futures might be linked. She was intellect. He was action, or would be action as soon as idea and opportunity presented themselves. When he had last seen her, she was bound for Rochester. Only through one of her associates had he learned she would visit Buffalo too. Leon felt a prick of betrayal in his belly. She herself should have mentioned she was headed elsewhere. What if he had needed to meet with her, for comfort or inspiration? What if something she'd said, or would say, held the key to his destiny? Why was she with those dry excuses for men when she could be in the company of someone younger, more dynamic?

He ached to have her gaze upon him as she did these other men. After watching them for several minutes he saw that she smiled more often at the older man, that she touched his knee with unseemly familiarity. At one point she inclined her head so close to his that Leon feared they might actually kiss in public.

Leon let the branches close and pressed the bottle against his forehead, to cool his brow, to calm himself, to think. Eyes shut tight, he struggled to free his mind of an image that made him seethe: Miss Goldman in an intimate embrace with the older man. But the picture persisted, the man's flaccid buttocks working between Miss Goldman's thighs, his manhood limp and dripping when he finished his business with her. If he had a gun, Leon thought, he would stroll up to this man, in full view of Miss Goldman, and reveal him for the useless antique he really was by putting a bullet into his eye.

Then Leon inhaled sharply. He was a victim, he realized with sudden certainty, of his own mistake. In their second meeting he had introduced himself to her as Nieman, partly because he was by nature secretive and partly because he believed the name suited a common laborer like himself, a faceless drone toiling in the service of capitalists who spent more in a minute than men like him earned in a year. What a fool he had been! How could he have expected to command the notice of someone like Emma Goldman when he went by a German name that in translation meant *nobody*?

Leon made his way through the crowd toward the U.S. Government Building, his brain throbbing against the constriction of his old brown hat. The early-afternoon sun was high behind him. The statue atop the building's massive white dome burned bright gold against the blue sky. Leon stopped to look up at the dome. According to his guidebook, the statue was a re-creation of the famous *Winged Victory*. But Leon ground his teeth, because from this distance the sculpture reminded him of nothing as much as it did a crown, a king's crown. Entering the building between thick double columns, he thought of Bresci and Umberto and the correctness of the assertion that kings must die for men to be free.

Then, before he could move more than a few paces inside, he found himself staring up at a large portrait of President William McKinley.

September 1901—Buffalo

"Mr. Nowak?"

The man behind the bar was thickset and dough-faced, with short gray hair and a ragged mustache. Despite a barkeep's simple apron and shirtsleeves banded at the biceps, the way he was resting his forearms on the burnished walnut surface left no doubt that the eastside hotel called J. Nowak's belonged to him. Nowak looked up from his newspaper and straightened to his full height.

"I'd like a room," Leon said. He smiled.

Nowak's eyes were heavy-lidded but cold and penetrating. "Thirty cents a day or two dollars a week. Payable up front."

Leon pulled a roll of paper money from inside his suit coat and peeled off a two-dollar silver certificate and slid it face up to Nowak, who swept it into a drawer underneath and took out a black receipt book. "Hey, Frank," he called over his shoulder. "Somebody needs to go upstairs."

A door opened behind the bar. A young man in shirtsleeves and wire spectacles emerged as Nowak bent over the bar, pen poised above the receipt book. "Now, what name do I put on your receipt?"

"John Doe."

Nowak looked up again, and Leon continued to smile benignly. "John Doe it is, then." He signed the receipt and handed it to Leon. "Frank, take Mr. Doe here to Number Five."

The young man led Leon to the far end of the barroom, past a lone patron lining up his next shot on the pool table, and up a flight of stairs covered with worn carnelian carpeting. On the landing, Frank turned to him. "What made you say John Doe? I'm studying law. Nobody's called John Doe."

Leon tapped his hat against his chest. "I'm a Polish Jew. If I tell him my real name, he might not let me stay here."

"So what is your real name?"

"Nieman, Fred C. Nieman. I'm here to sell souvenirs at the Exposition."

Number Five was narrow and dingy, with a small bed on one side and a porcelain washbasin atop a scarfless dresser on the other. A shaving mirror hung above the washbasin. The walls were yellowed and peeling, the seams between the floor planks packed tight with walked-down dirt. A single window with a once-white curtain was opposite the door. Frank struck a match and fired the gaslight beside the shaving mirror. Then he sidled past, as Leon laid his hat and valise on the bed, and opened the window. A faintly sour smell from the alley below wafted into the room. Turning, Frank told Leon the lavatory was at the end of the hall and asked if he needed anything else.

"Directions, if it would not be too much trouble."

"Of course," Frank said. "We're on Broadway, a couple miles east of Main Street. To get to the Exposition from here—"

Still smiling, Leon held up his hand and shook his head. "Not the Exposition, not tonight. Monday I will go there and find the man who has hired me to sell souvenirs." He gestured toward the window. "This is Saturday night. There is a place in every city where a man can find certain kinds of…entertainment."

Frank reddened, and Leon enjoyed seeing the boy's wonderment at what kind of Jew sought a whore at the close of his Sabbath.

When at last he was alone, Leon closed the door and unpacked, laying his undergarments and socks in the top drawer and hanging his spare shirt on the door hook. His Gem shaving paste and folding razor, Sozodont tooth powder and toothbrush, and Doctor Ray's hair oil and brush he placed beside the washbasin. The last thing he removed from his valise was a wooden box that bore the imprint of the Walbridge Company. He had stood in the sporting goods department not three hours earlier. Lifting the lid, he recalled the moment, the eagerness of the clerk to make the sale, recalled that his fingers were steady as he passed a pair of two-dollar bills and a half-dollar piece to the clerk, steadier still as they closed around the rubber-covered grip. Now he removed the nickel-plated .32 caliber double-action Iver Johnson revolver from its bed. He examined it lovingly, running a finger along the barrel, down the backstrap, over the black grip. He turned it this way and that, breaking open its hinged frame and listening to each click as he turned the cylinder. He read the number—463344—but made no mental note of it. Closing the frame and sliding his finger into the trigger guard, he knew only one thing.

This gun felt perfect in his hand.

Leon followed Frank's directions to a building a few blocks away. He knocked three times at a side door in a dingy brick alley. The door swung in, and a large bearded man in a derby led him upstairs, puffing as he climbed. "Girls waiting for nice fellow like you." His accent was thick, familiar.

The door at the top opened onto a small gaslit parlor with wine-colored wallpaper and heavily curtained windows. Six stuffed chairs were crowded against the walls, three occupied by women in once-fancy dresses. The man quoted a price, accepted Leon's money, and withdrew, leaving him alone with the women. The nearest one rose and came near, her dress whispering across the carpet. She was older than Leon, with black hair, a pinched nose, and too much face paint. Her breath reeked of beer and sausages, her body of perfume diffused by summer sweat. He shifted his gaze to each of her sister whores and found neither more appealing. He was about to take the first's hand—what did it matter who?—when a rear door creaked open and a fourth woman appeared.

This whore was younger than the others, shorter, more compact. She had glittering eyes and wavy brown hair and carried herself with surprising dignity. Whatever had taken place on the other side of the door, she had reassembled herself much more decorously than the young lout who followed her out. His waistcoat was still undone, his tie hanging open, his straw boater perched at a ridiculous angle on his head. He teetered as if he had drunk too much. She smiled and pulled away when he bent to kiss her cheek, deftly steering him toward the door. He sighed, "Ah, Petra, I do so love you," but she said nothing until she had shut the door behind him and waited for him to descend the stairs.

"Horse's ass," Petra said finally. "No other horse parts, just ass." The women giggled.

Leon felt a catch in his throat. Part of him wanted to go after the young man and beat him senseless for daring to come to this place. Perhaps it was that meticulously waxed mustache or those polished boots or that olive-colored summer suit and silk tie in the presence of simple folk who could eat for a month on what such vanities cost. Perhaps it was the affinity Leon felt for these women, a kinship born of common beginnings half a world away. Perhaps it was just that if Petra donned a pince-nez and mounted a speaker's platform…

"You no like Anya?" the first woman said, aware of his shift in attention.

Leon said nothing but looked at Petra.

Anya threw up her hands and stomped to her seat, calling him something in Polish that in the anxiety of the moment he took an extra heartbeat to understand: *sodomite*. All the women laughed, and Leon bristled. Then Anya told him they were fresh out of boys for the moment but expected new arrivals tomorrow. Again the women laughed.

"Nie!" he said, his own Polish startling them. To Anya he spat, *"Brzydki prostytutka!"*

His mother was the ugly whore, she said, and he had nothing but limp meat. *"Maly!"* she said, holding up her thumb and forefinger with less than an inch between them.

Before Leon could reply, the bearded man lumbered back into the room. His gray beard clung to his reddening face like ash to an ember. The whores' sudden silence made Leon wonder if the man was their father. He looked from one woman to another, his eyes shiny black pebbles. "Is trouble?"

Petra shrugged and nodded toward Leon. "He no like Anya."

"Bezsilny," Anya said. *"Obwisly."*

The man glared at her. "Your job to make him hard!" He turned to Leon. "Who you like?"

"Petra," Leon answered, pointing.

The old man grunted with a weariness that told Leon this was not the first time someone's preference for Petra had led to such conflict. But none of that mattered when she took his hand and led him to a dimly lit back room.

The girl shed her dress and slips and Leon could see she wore no corset. In her remaining underthings she knelt on a horsehair mattress on the floor. She shook down her hair and curled a finger toward Leon, who hastened out of his suit and shirt and left them piled beside the mattress. He knelt before her, and she undid the buttons of his underthings. Her hands were dry, her fingers thick, but when she took hold of him he shuddered and stiffened immediately, the head of his penis emerging from the foreskin like a snake from its hole. With her free hand she worked his underclothes off his shoulders and over his erection and buttocks and garters. Then she urged him onto his back and pushed his knees apart. Arranging herself between his legs, she lowered her face to his middle.

Leon swallowed, anticipating that she would place him in her mouth. Another whore had done that to him once, and he had been amazed at the warmth of her spit and her tongue. Surely, he had thought then, she would not let him spend in her mouth. But she had, gulping down every drop and moaning as she did so, as if his essence itself were enough to satisfy her. No one else had ever permitted his penis past her lips, even though he had asked. Sometimes, with Magda, he had closed his eyes and remembered the whore's wonderful mouth, imagining Magda's cunt with thicker lips and a dancing tongue. Now Petra, who looked so...*ideal,* was going to do the same thing to him, would perhaps swallow his juice as hungrily as the earlier whore had done. But she didn't, and he realized with a tremor of disappointment that she must be looking at his swollen member, inspecting him for the pox or parasites. She needn't have worried. His last episode of the pox had been years ago. If she had asked, he could have told her.

When she was satisfied that he was clean, she raised her head and smiled at him and began to undo her chemise. "You handsome man," she said, her small, full breasts swinging free. As she lay naked beside him and turned onto her back to offer herself to him, Leon didn't hear himself say she was beautiful. In fact, as she said "How you like?" he heard nothing but the pounding in his temples, the pounding that pushed out his momentary disappointment and left him dizzy. For a few seconds he looked at her rounded body and hesitated, as if afraid touching her would damage her or desecrate her. In the flickering gaslight he saw no pimples or imperfections, no birthmarks or life-marks like scars or rough skin. He saw only the smooth terrain of an angel in waiting. When he blinked and swallowed he saw only her smile, wide and welcoming, and the tiny creases at the corners of her striking blue eyes. She slid her tongue over her upper lip, perhaps to prod him into action. So he rolled onto her, more clumsily than he would have liked, and pushed his own tongue deep into her mouth. Her tongue was small and yielding, widening and relaxing as his tongue pressed against it. Holding her as if she were his last anchor to the world, he saw bursts of light behind his closed eyelids and had no doubts about the sacredness of the moment. This woman was special, destined to be his inspiration. Gasping, he broke the kiss and burrowed his face between her breasts and then licked until, shivering, he came to a nipple. He took the bud into his mouth and sucked until it thickened and her breath quickened. How he had missed the feel of a woman's unclothed breast! She wriggled beneath him, spreading her legs and whispering, "Put in cock. Put in cock." But he continued to suck, as if he hadn't heard, and she reached for him, bringing the tip of his penis to the edge of her slit. "Put in cock now." When he shifted and his lips left her breast, she slid back his foreskin and inserted just the head. Eyes now open, Leon arched his back as if she were pulling him into her and the breath escaped his chest as if it were being forced out. For an instant they were frozen, his manhood buried to the base in her wetness. Then he began to move, crying out as he did so, almost crying tears. Sounds now filled his ears—English, Polish, pants, gasps, whispers, whimpers—but he could make sense of nothing. Only when he peaked, in the seconds before his climax, did he become aware of the perfection of their coupling. Only after he began to spend, endlessly, and his head started to spin did he realize where he was and with whom. But he lost touch with everything moments later when she did take him into her mouth. She licked and sucked until his hardness returned. Then he took her a second time, spilled into her a second time, and the world, between the clock strokes of destiny, meant everything and nothing.

Afterward Leon slid into a brief sleep. He woke to the feel of a finger on the tip of his nose, saw Petra's eyes above him, hair cascading about her face in the soft gaslight. He smiled up at her, even as she said it was time for him to go. She hurried him out of bed, drew the blanket around her shoulders, and squatted over a basin in the corner, her back toward him. Pulling on his clothes, Leon heard splashing sounds, as if she were washing him off her. Waiting until she had finished, he asked if he could come back another night. He was unsure which night, but he wanted to see her again, to be with her again. He was on a mission, he said, and had very little time left. Some of it he wanted to spend with her.

"Yes," she said, after a moment. Suddenly, she whirled to face him, the blanket flying open, exposing blemishes and rough patches of skin on her plump young body. She pursed her lips like a pouting child. "But you call me right, or no come back."

Leon was confused. "I don't understand."

"You call me right." With her thumb she tapped the bone between her already sagging breasts. "Petra," she said firmly. "No Emma, Petra."

Days later, in line behind a swarthy Italian and in front of a gigantic Negro, Leon stepped inside the Temple of Music at the Pan-

American Exposition and felt the temperature drop ten degrees. Relieved to be out of the scorching afternoon sun, he moved forward, the sound of his footsteps lost amid the shuffling of hundreds of other feet and the murmur of voices. Somewhere up ahead an organist played soft music, a fancy piece Leon had never heard before. No doubt it was a tune written by a capitalist lackey, but Leon found he liked its peaceful rhythm. Placing one foot in front of the other almost in time to it, he kept his right arm pressed against his abdomen, the hand wrapped in a white handkerchief as if injured. He could see that he was six heads away from his objective. Then five, four, three.... Suddenly, the Italian in front of him was stopped, searched, and finally waved ahead. Then, at last, Leon was face to face with a genial, silver-haired fat man in a black frock coat and white waistcoat. Seeing Leon's right hand was injured, William McKinley, President of the United States, reached out with both hands to shake his left. In that instant, Leon thrust his wrapped hand toward McKinley's ample abdomen and squeezed the trigger. The handkerchief covering the gun caught fire and began to spiral to the floor as he fired a second time. Leon sank to one knee, lining up a third shot, but out of the corner of his eye he glimpsed a giant Negro fist arcing toward his head. Then the soldiers and policemen, tools of the oppressors, were on him, beating and kicking and cursing him. Amid the screams and confusion and pain of the next several minutes, he heard the man he had just shot say, "Be easy with him, boys."

Not dead yet, Leon thought, as he was hauled to his feet. *But soon.*

October 1901—Auburn, New York

At Auburn Prison, on the morning of Tuesday, October 29, Leon Czolgosz put up no resistance as he was eased into a wooden chair mounted atop a rubber-sheathed platform about four inches off the floor. Eight or nine men were gathered about him—the warden, several guards in dark uniforms, doctors, a man whose purpose he did not know. He was glad he had refused those damned priests but still wished more people had come. He didn't wish to waste his last words on turnkeys, prison sawbones, and newspaper hacks who would twist everything he said.

The men went to work on him at once, as if he were a thing

under construction. He began to flinch when they touched him. Someone strapped his wrists to the arms of the chair, his torso to the back. Another man lowered some kind of ill-fitting cap onto his head and dripped water through a hole in the top. Leon shuddered as his right trouser leg was rolled up and something cold was tied around his calf. A leather strap was slipped over his eyes, bit into the skin above his eyebrows. The darkness unnerved him. "I am not sorry," he called out, as much to steady himself as to show contempt for his murderers. "I killed the president because he was the enemy of the people, the good working people." He swallowed. "My only regret is that I haven't been able to see…my father." But instead of his father it was Petra who swam into view against the stiff leather that blinded him to the busyness around him. He tried to smile, to apologize for failing to return to her bed, but another leather strap was placed over his mouth, and his tongue tasted the residue of tannin. He imagined it was Petra's tongue, that she was holding him fast and kissing him good-bye. When she pulled away from him to smile, she became Emma, spectacles abandoned and hair in disarray against a pillow. "Look past the suffering of the present to the freedom of the future," she said. "I am with you." And she was with him, in the death chamber, kneeling before his chair, undoing the buttons of his prison trousers, smiling up at him until he felt himself stirring. Apart from the rasp of his own breathing as, in his mind, Emma Goldman skinned him back and closed her warm, wet mouth around his thickening manhood, the last sound Leon heard was the squeak of a switch closing somewhere in the room.

Then he began to spend, hotter than he had ever spent before.

And continued to do so for forty-five seconds.

god's-eye view

TULSA BROWN

PABLO HAD A PROBLEM WITH WOMEN. Or rather, *I* had a problem with Pablo's women. Every chemise left behind, every knowing, feminine smile in the market was a knife in my ribs. Sometimes I walked into our apartment, a studio with a bedroom and a stove, and still smelled perfume meandering lazily through the odor of paint. Pablo didn't deny it; he was quite baffled by my anger.

"But Fernande—I am Spanish."

"And I am only twenty-five! No woman forgives affairs while she is still young and beautiful, not even in Paris."

Yet I did forgive him, time and again. I forgave and made up, bent into a glorious *L*, my ankles on either side of his handsome face while he bucked into me, a fiery horse galloping, riding me to bliss. I hung onto his muscled thighs and he turned his head, opened his wet mouth on my foot. The pleasure cascaded down my leg and splashed into my sex, sailing me away.

Pablo Picasso was twenty-six, and the most exciting man I'd ever known. Short, wiry, with black hair that tumbled over his forehead, he had a bullfighter's gift of being quick and still at the same time. When he gazed on something, he devoured it. When he painted, the new work seemed to roll out in a low thunder from his belly.

Were they good paintings? I didn't know. In the spring of 1907 the art dealer Ambrose Vollard paid two thousand gold francs for a bundle of canvases, and that meant we finally had wood for the stove again, and could eat somewhere besides the kitchens of our friends. That made them good paintings to me.

By summer, Pablo had finished with the harlequins—forever, he said. He began to paint horses and men, in terra-cotta and gray. In the haunches of the horses I saw the sway of my own full hips; their dark, almond eyes were the same ones that looked back at me in the mirror. It was all right to be a horse, I told myself. As long as I was the only one.

Then, August. I arrived home late in the afternoon to find the studio an empty oven, brushes baking, uncleaned. Every surface glimmered with golden light, a canvas seemed abandoned on the easel. I hesitated, dizzy with the heat and mystery. A squeal cut through the air like a finger of winter.

The bastard!

I charged into the other room, the bedroom. Pablo was already on his feet, erection swaying, an alluring shock of ruddy flesh. Sweat sheened on his upper lip, fear or lust.

"Fernande, look what I brought home. We can share."

In our bed was the girl from *la patisserie,* copper hair and luminous skin. Her buttocks rose from the sheets like fresh buns, her shoulder was a creamy *petit four*. The scent of the bakery still lingered on her abandoned clothes, filled the room with the ripe smell of yeast and warm flour.

My thoughts whirled, grief and anger, then a strange, curling…vengeance. Would he like to see how it was? Really?

I withdrew the pins from my dark hair and it fell, some strands clinging to my damp neck. I began to unbutton my blouse. "Pull back the sheet, or we will all melt," I said.

Pablo straightened, lips parted, the girl's ginger eyebrow arched. Despite the invitation, neither of them had truly expected this.

I sounded braver than I was. I had heard of these things, women together, *la vie bohème*. But it was a big step from thinking to doing. My insides trembled as I slipped in between the two of them.

Her kiss startled me. In Paris, women always kissed hello and good-bye. But this was different, a hungry searching more intent than her demure smile had been. She opened me with her tongue, and the warm surprise rippled down to my sex, called the bud of my clitoris forward.

It made me daring. I stroked her breasts, rolled the nipples between my fingertips until they were firm, wondering at the triumph it gave me. I had breasts of my own, but on another woman they felt like something new. I cradled the pliant weight and fastened my mouth on one. She sighed and her nipple hardened more, until it was an abrupt little head against my tongue. Ancient memory stirred, moisture welled and simmered between my legs. I sucked like a greedy infant.

Pablo's cock prodded me from behind, a thick, unexpected hardness. I'd turned my back to him at first, determined to make him jealous. Then I'd simply forgotten, caught up in my soft discoveries. For an instant I was irritated by his intrusion, then the ripe plum head spread open my slickness, shouldered its way up to nudge the pulsing sweet spot. The encouragement made it thicken, rear up. *Mon Dieu!* With a breast in my mouth, I felt I had a penis of my own. I wanted to unlock and enter her, fuck her, and at the same time I wanted to be cleaved, rent open by the beast at my back.

Somehow she knew this. With a gentle but firm grasp she removed me from her breast and guided my face down between her legs. Pablo rustled clumsily over the bedclothes, repositioning. My eyes were riveted on the wonder suddenly before me, the russet-brown forest and cerise folds glistening with invitation. I'd seen many women naked, artists' models, but that wasn't the same as one laid out *for* me, legs spread. How would this be?

Not sweet, not salt, not exactly. The scent was like the edge of the ocean. I closed my eyes and licked gingerly, a shy explorer. I felt Pablo's strong hands grip my hips and he entered me from behind, a slow surge that pushed my raw female voice up from my belly. It also thrust me forward and my tongue spread her plump lips suddenly, lapped hard over the tight knot of her clit.

She squealed, a long ribbon of delight, and the revelation made me tingle. So this was what he'd been doing! Instead of anger, though, I felt a rush of ambition. I wanted to possess that sound, create it for my own. I leaned into her earnestly. Pablo began to buck, his animal breath ignited. Swells of sensation opened inside me and I passed them along, lavishing my tongue on the sex that rose to meet me. The pleasure unfurled through us, one to the next, joy sweeping out like a blanket over the grass.

"Do you see?" Pablo said much later, when we were alone and the blessed cool night had crept through the windows. "It wasn't dangerous. It wasn't love."

Dangerous. Love. His summer words returned to haunt me that autumn. I realized what a fool I'd been, distracted by such pastries, while the real threat was rising, swelling like a shadowy hill in the landscape.

We had known the Americans for some time. They were a brother and sister, Leo and Gertrude Stein, and they'd been the first to buy Pablo's paintings, or at least hang them in their house at 27 rue de Fleurus. Pablo was so pleased to have his harlequins among his friends' work, proud to keep company with Cézanne, Monet, Matisse, Braque. Art dealers and critics came to the Saturday salons, and sometimes paintings were sold, although rarely Pablo's.

It made him grin. "Leo Stein is the best-loved mistress in Paris, but he is not mine."

I loathed the man. He was tall and affected, grew a beard and tried to cut it like Matisse's. He painted a little, wrote a little, and spouted endless opinions.

"Ah, Fernande," he said once. "The woman who can talk of all that she knows in a single night: clothes, perfume, and poodles."

After that I sat in the kitchen with the wives, or studied the paintings without a word.

The other person who hardly dared speak in Leo's presence was his sister, Gertrude. At thirty, she looked like a Buddha in brown corduroy, two hundred pounds that had never known a corset. She wore socks and sandals, and walked with a soldier's stride. Yet at the Saturday salons, she only leaned forward in her chair, plump, feminine hands clasped, brown eyes luminous with interest. Silent.

Gertrude Stein said she was a writer. I wasn't sure. She'd given me some of her work to read and after a page, I felt dazed.

The words seemed to tumble out in a bright waterfall, beautiful but bewildering. Reading Gertrude was like trying to study one of Monet's paintings with my nose against the canvas.

She loved Pablo's work, and that was enough for me. Whenever we were truly desperate, Gertrude managed to sell a drawing for us, wrung a hundred francs out of a friend or a stranger, sometimes on pity alone. When Pablo began her portrait, I believed it was from gratitude.

It never occurred to me to be jealous, not even as the sittings stretched from spring to summer. Gertrude wasn't Pablo's taste in "pastry," or any man's, I thought. Besides, all they did was talk. I knew this because one afternoon I pretended to leave, then sat outside the door in the airless stairwell that smelled of dogs and cooked cabbage. For nearly two hours I listened, lulled to the edge of dreaming by the continuous stream of words: Pablo's quick Spanish lilt and Gertrude's rolling contralto, a sound so rich it seemed like two voices. I hardly understood any of it.

They talked of painting and writing and art, of the need to tear things apart to see them clearly. Pablo spoke excitedly of splitting a thing open to show all its sides.

"All dimensions at once," he exclaimed. "God's-eye view!"

I felt strange at that moment, as if I'd heard something blasphemous, or terribly intimate. I hugged my knees, feeling small, an outsider. At least, I thought, they're not in bed.

The portrait was finally finished in the autumn of 1907, and it was unlike anything he'd painted before, unlike anything I'd ever seen. Gertrude's face resembled an African mask; her body seemed to be made of brown stone. She was a monolith leaning forward in the chair, an idol. I hoped Pablo would put it away. Instead he gave it to her as a gift, and from the wall at 27 rue de Fleurus she gazed down on me, on everyone, a conquering goddess.

I was pierced.

"Admit it," I demanded. "You love her!"

"Of course I do. We're family—artists." Pablo's smile was crumpled. "Gertrude and I are brothers. Stop worrying, Fernande."

I couldn't. There was something about the two of them now, a silent language that hummed in every glance. And Pablo had taken another turn. Gone were the horses—my hips, my eyes.

Pablo met often with Georges Braque and the two of them talked and drank late into the night. In the morning, Pablo was up at dawn and painted ferociously throughout the day, his resolute eyes searing the canvas. Soon many new pictures leaned against the wall, strange, primitive shapes, women split open and laid flat, sometimes in pieces. God's-eye view, I remembered with a stabbing pang. It was hard for me to care for any child that had been nurtured by Gertrude Stein.

She came more often now and the two of them sat knee to knee, talking in half sentences, the familiarity of lovers. I didn't dare leave the apartment; the air seemed ready to ignite. Worst of all, I could sense the low thunder in his body, the powerful thing uncurling, spreading outward, unstoppable. And it rolled toward her.

"Genius," Gertrude said.

"Genius," Pablo answered, eyes glowing.

I was distraught. I looked in the mirror, at the face he'd called beautiful. What was no longer there? How could I stop the unstoppable?

And then—a woman appeared at the Saturday salons. She was in her mid-twenties, and not especially beautiful: slight and dark, a straight-backed shadow with a Roman nose and bright, birdlike eyes. Pablo said there was something gypsyish about her, with her tiny hands and feet, and gold earrings. I knew in a glance she came from the country of Proper, layered with underwear, tied and buttoned. In truth she was an American, from San Francisco. Her name was Alice Toklas.

The salons were always a swirl of new faces; I'm not sure why Miss Alice caught my attention, and held it. Perhaps it was because she was the only person whose eyes followed Gertrude Stein as closely as mine did.

On the third Saturday, I cornered her and asked what she thought of the paintings.

"Oh!" She seemed surprised anyone would speak to her, especially in English. "They're beautiful, they're confusing. I've never seen anything like them."

"What do you know about art?"

"Nothing." The word was sincere. "But now I can recognize a Matisse, and a Picasso." Her eyes lifted up to the large, brown portrait of Gertrude and lingered there, a gaze that was half reverence, half butter.

I felt the first quickening of hope about Pablo's "brother."

Miss Toklas turned up again and again at 27 rue de Fleurus. I saw her and Gertrude walking through the Luxembourg Gardens, Alice trying to keep up with the large woman's long strides, a dark sparrow fluttering devotedly along.

But not fast enough. Gertrude turned often to speak to her, the way one turns to the hearth on a cold afternoon, yet there was a polite formality between them. They were still only friends. Somehow I'd known this would be a problem, from the first glimpse of Alice's tightly buttoned dress. Her homeland still bound her, thousands of miles away.

"Come to the studio," I encouraged them both. "Alice should see all the paintings."

They did, on a golden autumn afternoon. Alice walked through the door, twinkling as she always did in Gertrude's presence. Then the monolith and the bullfighter sat down together and the rest of the world fell away from them.

"Pablo." His name was a caress on her lips.

"Gertrude," Pablo said, and squeezed her hand.

Alice looked at me, stricken. At last, I thought, we are on the same page.

"Miss Toklas must have French lessons," I said, "if she wants to stay in Paris." I lowered my voice. "I'll be glad to give them to her."

She came two days later on a blustery afternoon, when rain whipped the streets and pared the golden trees, dashed their fine garments to the pavement. Alice wore a long gray dress, starched white lace at the collar and cuffs, twenty-four black buttons down the bodice. She seemed surprised that I answered the door in a Chinese dressing gown, tied only with a sash. I locked the bolt behind her.

"Are the thieves so bold they'd try to rob us in broad daylight?"

I turned. "The only thief that worries me is time. Tell me quickly—do you love her?"

Alice flushed, a swift bloom of pink between her white collar and dark hair.

"Quickly," I insisted. "Yes or no?"

"Yes!" The confession was breathless with fear, but flung defiantly, an ardent little gust in the chilly room.

I smiled. "All right. Then this is your first lesson, the most important one." I loosened the sash, let the brocade ease open. The cool air licked my naked body in a shaft, and I shivered. "Repeat after me: *C'est ce que je dois faire.*"

Alice stared, eyes riveted on the opening of my robe. I started toward her, a loose, swaying walk that made the heavy fabric swing. "Come, come, Alice. *Repeter: C'est ce que…"*

She obeyed in a faltering whisper. "What did I just say?"

"You said, 'This is what I must do.' And it is." I slipped the robe from my shoulders, let it fall to the floor in a silky puddle of red and gold, dragons and cranes. Alice inhaled, her lips pursed, but her eyes skimmed over me again and again, tasting.

The storm had unbound her hair, filaments spiraled down in tangled ringlets. Her dress smelled of wet wool. She looked like a bedraggled kitten, rescued but uncertain. It made me think of another cat, a languid marmalade, who'd kissed me so brazenly, then mewed under my tongue.

I stepped in close, so close that my nipples grazed the stiff gray fabric. I could hear her rapid breaths, sense her trembling. I was just as nervous, yet I knew this was what *I* had to do, too. I embraced her with one arm and laid my warm cheek against her cold one.

"This is Paris. If you love Gertrude, you must *love* her, be her eager bride." I caught her hand and lifted it to my breast. "Like this."

She cupped me cautiously at first, then began to stroke and play, entranced by the soft, jiggling weight.

"Say her name as you feel it," I whispered. "Speak to her through my ear."

"Gertrude," Alice said, and the sound was an oboe, deeper than I'd ever heard her speak. My nipple hardened against her palm. Alice's breath stroked my shoulder, light, feathery, aroused.

I didn't undress her, I unwrapped her like a present: twenty-four little black buttons, two sets of clasps on her old-fashioned, voluminous skirt. I foraged through layers of scalloped lace, unbound the strings of her pantaloons and corset. When this last was released, she couldn't stop the relieved murmur. I traced the marks the whalebone stays had left in her soft flesh. The gentle undulation of her belly, the curve of her pale buttocks kindled me.

I caught her chin. "Show me how you'd kiss her."

And she did, a flash of force and heat I'd never have expected from such a dainty creature. My clitoris rose like a tiny cock; my hips and breasts seemed to swell, plump and eager—the body of the goddess. I felt like a new creation, Pablo *and* Gertrude rolled into a single being.

I steered her to the bed with a determined swagger, laid her onto the unmade sheets. Rain lashed the window above us, like a blustery scolding from far away. But the country of Proper no longer existed. I coaxed Alice's thighs open, and stroked the wet, satiny folds of her sex, gently nudged the rising bud. Her chirping noises softened and deepened into a crooning song, a woodwind lullaby.

"*Repeter,* Alice," I teased her.

"*C'est...c'est...*oh."

I had much to show her, but I was hungry, too. It occurred to me there was a way to do both. When I removed my hand from between her legs, Alice opened her eyes, disappointed. I slithered around, tugged her onto her side, and burrowed my face between her thighs. There was nowhere for her face to go but between mine. She stiffened, her breath ruffling my pubic hair in warm, excited puffs.

The scent was as I remembered it: the ocean's edge. It was the smell of adventure.

"Like this, Alice," I said. "Like a cat."

I craned my neck and slipped into her with my tongue. The heat of that cleft woke me again. Never mind where my hand had just been, this was new, raw. Exhilaration shimmered in a buttery trail from my mouth to my own cunt. As if from a distance, I heard Alice moan, felt her fingers press hard into my thighs. She was lost in the dream of mysterious sensation. I lifted my head, my mouth smeared like a child's.

"Lick," I commanded, and spread my legs wider.

She did. Her timid, teasing tongue made me bend and twist, chasing the exquisite flickers. But she soon learned to mimic me: when I lapped in smooth strokes, so did she. When I sought out the pearl of her flesh and began to nurse on it, she shuddered and moaned, an animal rumble larger than her delicate body. At last her lips formed a soft sucking kiss around my clit and I felt my whole being curl into that sweetness.

Yes. Splendid. More, please, and more.

Alice's thighs hugged my head in a tight embrace; I knew I was squeezing hers. We sucked and squirmed as if wriggling through the same tight space. Then I felt her hips twitch, the body's bloom, a leap of freedom. I was so pleased, my own coming caught me by surprise. I was lifted in an unexpected billow, then again, rode silky whitecaps of triumph and loveliness.

"Oh," Alice gasped a moment later, her voice frayed. "Oh, my."

We didn't linger in the downy moments; Pablo would be home soon. I helped Alice dress. She seemed lightheaded, still sailing, features soft and mouth plump. She picked up her corset as if it were some strange and disagreeable thing that had washed up on the shore.

"I'll get you a satchel to carry it home," I said.

At the door, she caught my wrist. "Fernande, how do I begin?"

"Everything begins—and ends—with a kiss." I leaned over and placed one on her cheek, a sisterly benediction. Alice's smile was a bit wistful.

Pablo arrived home at dusk, smelling of rain, carrying wine.

"Are you going to see Georges tonight?" I said.

He looked at me in my Chinese robe. Dark tendrils clung to his wet forehead. Even by candlelight his eyes flashed, probed, entered.

He grinned. "It depends."

When he kissed me, I opened his mouth and sucked his tongue inside; the memory of the goddess and bullfighter I'd been today was hard to relinquish. My audacity fired Pablo. He liked the scent of another woman's sex on me, too, although I don't think it registered exactly. He burrowed hungrily into my clothes, my hair, his cock rising against my thigh. I tugged open his pants and he laughed, happy and eager, a Spanish highwayman ready to pick my every pocket. That night, *I* was the woman split open and pressed flat against the canvas of our bed, God's-eye view of euphoria.

The Steins traveled to Florence with friends, including Alice; we didn't see them for weeks and weeks. If Pablo mourned

Gertrude, he hid it. He had his pride and his work, and a new distraction: Ambrose Vollard had arranged an exhibition for him, and the critics had much to say.

"Madman!" Pablo roared, half in fury, half in delight. "I've hardly begun. I'll show them a madman yet."

Bless you, Vollard, I thought.

Finally, the Steins returned and a salon was arranged. I was enchanted by Alice's new batik gown, a simple, loose cut, rich with embellishments. She no longer fluttered in Gertrude's wake, she floated in it with a regal, contented air. Bride. Our eyes met and I squeezed her hand, happy for her, for all of us.

The large woman turned to me purposefully, and my heart jumped. What did she suspect? Before she could speak, though, her brother cut into our group.

"Fernande, you're a terrible teacher," he said. "Miss Toklas does not know enough French to order a decent piece of fish at the market."

"Leo," Gertrude's voice rang loudly through the crowded room for the first time, not a bell but a golden thunderclap. "There is more to life than fish."

The pompous windbag was struck dumb for thirty glorious seconds, and I fell in love with Gertrude forever.

Eva Braun's Last Tragic Abortion

Lynda Schor

EVA LIES IN THE MOTHER-OF-PEARL TUB staring at the green tarnish bleeding from the carved copper faucets into the bathwater. She raises the hand mirror she'd brought with her into the bath, which, like the faucets, is carved with Aries rams just at the point of being transformed into Taurean bulls—Adolph's sun signs. Used to picturing herself as Adolph sees her, she peers at her face as if to recall herself, whatever that is. Or perhaps to catch a glimpse of a new possibility. She feels (perhaps it's the water, the sensation of floating) unmoored, as if she could, like a turn of a faucet, find herself beautiful one moment, ugly the next. She moves the small mirror from her face, flushed, surrounded by an aureole of fine curls, downward toward one breast, which, as she's just six weeks pregnant, is tender, swollen, nipple rounder than usual, areola rosy. She enjoys the sensation of prickly cool on her face and shoulders, the rest of her submerged in water almost unbearably hot. She moves the mirror along to her belly, just slightly more rounded than usual, an almost undetectable convexity between diminutive pelvic bones which stand out of the murky bathwater like small sails softened by mist. It's exciting to see each small portion of her body at one time, magnified, as if it's foreign terrain. Raising her hips, she feels the slight tickle of the water's edge, above which she's flushed pink. The portions of her still in the water appear dead white, buttery, and unarticulated. Sexual arousal was the only time Eva could stand feeling the least bit vague, her boundaries undefined. The image in the mirror of her stomach, then her pubic hair, excites her, then the pictures in her mind superimposed, then the warm excitement she feels, then those sensations in her mind, then the image in the mirror—she's tempted to carefully deconstruct passion, but finds she no longer wishes to think. She lays the mirror across the marble ledge and closes her eyes and listens to her breathing.

Eva imagines she can hear similar breathing from Adolph's room, on the other side of the bath. She would like to think they are doing the same thing, separately, and toys with the idea of climbing out and trying his door. She jumps when Adolph, in his brown, beige, and gold flannel robe, barges in without knocking. Timid about his aging body, he pulls on an already tight belt. Eva looks into his eyes and sees herself anew in the lust reflected there.

He stands looking at her for a moment, glassy-eyed and peaked, and Eva senses his whirling galvanism, his inability to remain immobile, or placid. She watches him and imagines how he sees her lovely hair, pulled up in back except for the long, damp tendrils which hang down around the sides of her narrow face and delineate her small, moist ears, rounded cheekbones, and, under a wide chin, her surprisingly slender neck.

"Your wide, smooth forehead reminds me of Franklin Delano Roosevelt, the greatest war criminal of all time," he says in a tired voice, while laying his chenille robe over the gilt stool. He sits on the edge of the tub, one patent-leather scuff hanging precariously from the toes of the foot he has resting on his other knee.

Eva stares at the pale flesh of his abdomen. He's not at all fat, but there's a looseness to his flesh nowadays. His white calf, crossed over his thigh, is slightly freckled, like freshly poured pancake batter with raisins. How ugly he is, she thinks.

"What are you thinking?" he asks.

Slightly flustered, she says, "Nothing."

"That you find me repulsive and ugly because I'm so much older than you?"

"I don't find you ugly," says Eva, upset to be caught at a rare moment when she saw him clearly as one would see a stranger, or an object. "I feel our spirits meeting," she says, observing how his eye sockets resemble miniature anuses.

Adolph leans over the edge of the tub and dips his hand into the water. He fondles Eva's ass slowly, feeling, and picturing, her lovely curves, then, reaching under her, inserts his finger with its square nail into her anus. As he pushes he describes the smoothness he feels as "a road, fish entrails, a muddy trench, a shiny train track, the inside of a cheek." Eva responds to his descriptions. She's always turned on by him. She listens to his monologues for hours. She's especially moved by Adolph in his uniforms. He has charisma.

"I believe," says Adolph, "in ending life in a clear-cut manner. No use being so in love with it, so dependent upon it, to wish to prolong the pain of it. It can be so neat if our relationship with life is broken cleanly, when we make the decision to end it. I can't stomach passivity. I'm in love with free choice."

"Why are you thinking about ending your life?" Eva asks. "Do you think it's fair of you to end a life that expends so much in the service of others?" She studies his buttocks hanging further over the water. His passion for order and cleanliness seems to be growing daily. She wonders about "free choice."

Adolph abstractedly rubs his forefinger in the moist bar of soap near his thigh, and rubs the foam into his skin for a moment. Then he slips out of his patent-leather scuffs, the only shoes he wears now in the bunker, even when dressed in suits and uniforms, and gingerly enters the tub, facing Eva, careful not to scrape his back on the copper fixtures. He peers over his knees, folded nearly to his chin. Eva's legs wrap around him, her calves circling his buttocks underwater.

Eva feels uneasy, but says nothing. She can't help recalling her pain when Adolph continued his relationship with the beautiful, buxom Geli Raubal, lying to both her and Eva, unable to break off with either one until Geli made the choice by killing herself.

"What about Geli? Were you so strong then?"

"I didn't miss her," says Adolph, misunderstanding. "I was enraged that she found a way to counteract my will."

"Geli lives with us always," cries Eva. "She still lives in us both." Perspiration drips down her face and neck, reddened more now by suppressed anger. The heat of the room, the water, is suddenly unbearable. She focuses on the spot where her calf touches Adolph's thigh until she loses any sensation of the contact.

Eva recalls the funeral, Geli perfectly beautiful, perfectly frozen, embalmed in the best Egyptian technique, worthy receptacle of the costly scientific studies of the Third Reich. Even then Eva envied Geli as she lay there, peaceful, her white hands across her breasts, clutching dried baby's breath. Her dark hair was pulled back around her heart-shaped forehead, so different from Eva's. The deep blue color of the clingy jersey dress chosen by Eva accentuated the clarity of her eyes, a shade of blue quite different from Eva's and Adolph's light ones, her skin pure white, cheeks rosy with rouge. Eva recalls seeing Adolph lift Geli's dress. Her thighs, close, made a heart shape, outlined by the top edge of her black underpants. He gazed into her eyes, which stared dumbly, willfully, into space.

Adolph suddenly looks meek. He lowers his eyes, seeming to watch the scummy water.

"She still is the master of your moods," Eva continues. "That's why you're always so sad. And I think about her all the time too. You're lying on your bed, arms out, naked. 'Eat me,' you order. 'I'm not in the mood,' I say. 'Then Geli will do it,' you say. You turn your head. Geli is kneeling, hair shiny and disordered, light trapped in the tangles like fireflies, straight-cut bob just brushing the silk sheet. Her large, firm breasts rest arrogantly over her wide rib cage, and the small, dark birthmark between her heavy mounds disturbs me. She bends over you lingeringly, letting you feel her hot breath on your groin. I lean tensely against the chill wall and watch, pulling the peach silk cover sheet over my small breasts. After a moment you lift her hair in your hand, exposing a portion of the back of her neck, which is thin and childlike in contrast with her voluptuousness, and which, though resembling my own, is somehow hateful to me. I restrain an urge to smack her, even though it might cause her to bite down hard on your prick. Geli looks at me, her eyes pulled by your clutching of her hair. Within my jealous hatred, a bubble of compassion grows. Only then can I gently kiss the soft hairs at the nape of her neck also, while I whisper to her with love and envy, 'How can you be such a masochist?' "

"Don't talk to me like that," Adolph says, but meekly. He is forgetting all he'd meant to tell her about his depression, caused by events presently occurring in the German Nation, and everyone either against him or after his ass.

"You can't make a commitment to me," Eva says, watching his soft penis move in the water like a slug.

"Can't you get over it?" Adolph asks. "I needed emotional security from both of you."

"Don't you think I need emotional security?" Eva screams.

Adolph covers his ears with his hands. "Don't scream like that. It reminds me of my mother."

Eva feels the wrenching of tears in the back of her throat. Adolph places his fingers on her breast, but she only cries harder.

"It's strange about the mind and the body," Adolph says. "Without the mind, the body is an animal. The mind is God and religion. The body of Eva won't respond when her mind is upset and angry. This is Eva's integrity." He pauses. "My own body, on the other hand, tends to respond to the physical under any mental conditions. It therefore follows that my mind has more integrity than my body."

"If your body has no integrity, neither does your mind," Eva says. "Mind and body are one."

Adolph is aware that he's sweating. Eva has never spoken to him like this. It reminds him that there's no time.

"Listen," Adolph says, "I don't bother about your past, why harp on mine?" He recalls that they are practically buried alive underneath the rubble of the destroyed city.

"It's our past. Our past was connected. Should have been connected. Except all the parts you didn't share," Eva says. *I've lived with you so long*, she thinks, *and have been so alone*.

"Nothing like that matters any more. Today's the day I make a clear commitment to you. We're getting married," Adolph says.

"Only because today's the day you're making a clear severance with your relationship with life," Eva says, pouting.

"Sarcasm is unbecoming in women," Adolph says, rubbing his chest against Eva's. His excitement has the quality of desperation.

"Do you hate me?" he asks, holding his penis as if it's something to grasp for security.

"No, no," Eva says, nearly inaudibly. She feels triumphant, yet sorry for him.

He stares at her, supplicating, as if she can give him self-esteem like a gift. "Hit me, oh, hit me, Eva," he sputters, churning in the water in what seems like an attempt to become smaller, something lower on the evolutionary scale. "I feel I'm nothing. A piece of slime. I can't bear it. Hit me hard. Put your finger in me," he begs, on his knees in the water. Then, sinking down, beginning actually to look like slime—white, flabby, shrinking, he becomes another creature, a pulsing sea anemone, a mudpuppy, so light that he moves with the oscillating water.

Feeling powerful, Eva raises herself to gain leverage, and smacks Adolph really hard. He glances at her with a mixture of love, gratitude, and supplication. Placing his hands above his own head as if they're tied there, he writhes, whispering unintelligibly.

Eva doesn't know what fantasies he disappears into. Yet she adores his strength. She loves that he allows her to hate him without fearing the loss of her love. She gladly would have pretended to untie his wrists and feet if only he'd told her about their being tied. Squatting with her back toward him, she moves over him, lowering herself on him and watching his feet turn in and caress each other, toes curling under, then out.

Adolph moans. "Now, baby, now."

Eva knows what he wants. Relaxing her muscles, she urinates around his penis, imagining a mountain stream. The warm liquid and sense of abandon excite her too.

"Let's pretend," Adolph says breathlessly, "that you're a massacred Oglalla Sioux Indian, beautiful, and oh so wounded."

Eva nearly loses her balance as she feels her hair being pulled back by Adolph. She can almost sense the location of each hair on her head. Her mouth is long, her eyes pulled slanty.

"Boy of the Loups," Adolph says, "the scalp of a mighty Dakota shall never dry in Pawnee smoke."

"What?" asks Eva.

"It's from *The Prairie*, by James Fenimore Cooper, who copied it from our Karl May." Adolph stares at Eva's throat, trying to imagine blood there. He keeps his hold on her hair. "The fickle

Indian gives up his wife for a white woman. But shaking off the grateful sentiment like one who would gladly be rid of any painful, because reproachful, emotion he laid his hand calmly on the arm of his wife and led her directly in front of Inez."

Adolph presses his penis back and forth along his own thigh, eyes closed, concentrating. Eva is surprised by his erudition.

"You be the discarded Indian wife," Adolph suggests feverishly, "and after my battle scene I ravish you.

" 'Fool, die with empty hands,' Mahtoree exclaimed, setting an arrow to his bow and sending it, with a sudden and deadly aim, full at the naked bosom of his generous and confiding woman…"

Eva no longer hears his words. He is sweating. Ripples generated by his hand drilling on his own penis seem like volcanic waves. She feels as if she's drowning. She can feel each minute body hair as live coral or seaweed pushed back and forth by the stormy waves.

"I admire your control," Eva whispers.

"Shh," Adolph says, one hand on his lips, the other still holding himself, but absolutely still now. "You're lying on the bloody sand. Both of us are wounded." He breathes in and begins stroking his hand up and down along himself again.

"This is wonderful. You're letting me share your fantasies," Eva cries.

Adolph moves his hand faster, then stops and holds his breath. Eva watches the three creamy spurts as they land on his stomach, then slowly dissipate like smoke in the water.

Adolph lies there exhausted, crumpled and infantlike, his hand curled next to Eva's breast. He rubs her nipple halfheartedly, as if he wants to try to satisfy her.

"I feel good," he says, tracing a finger lightly over her round breast. "I'd love for you to have my baby."

Eva knows he only says this because it's probably their last night alive. She hates him for this deception, yet looks hopefully into his eyes wondering whether to reveal that she's pregnant.

"Imagine a baby of the Führer. It would be such a grand baby. With such beautiful blue eyes." Tears moisten his own pale eyes, now framed in pink.

Eva recalls all the abortions he'd insisted upon, and her unsuccessful attempts at suicide, which she knows full well were desperate demands for attention and fulfillment of needs he was simply incapable of fulfilling. Staring at Adolph, she sees him as an infant. His cheeks are fat and rosy, and when he squeezes his small lips into a rosette, the bluish vein on his white forehead becomes even more apparent. His curls are soft and blond.

Water drips, echoing in the silence as in a tunnel. Blue-green stains run down like blood on the tiles where the faucet drips. For the moment, Adolph is still. They face each other in the tub. Eva sees herself as she looks at Adolph. Both are now wet-haired, bedraggled creatures, pale and limp. She feels a rush of hatred, yet her belly and thighs feel heavy with desire.

Adolph gazes innocently into her pale blue eyes. "I really want to be your only baby," he says.

The Great Masturbator

K. L. Gillespie

THE NAKED WOMAN WHO LANGUISHED IN THE SUN on the far side of the cove had already been dead for several days. The ravages of death had played havoc with her looks, but to the young boy transfixed in her shadow she was the most beautiful thing he had ever laid eyes on. It was the first time he had seen a dead body or a naked woman, and he was aroused and repulsed in equal measure as the two things inextricably merged in his mind. He wanted to run away, frightened that the corpse would topple and consume him, but he was mesmerized, and as the blood in his veins congealed and the wind died down and the waves stopped rolling, he knew that this image would haunt him for the rest of his life.

The rotting carcass was on the verge of collapse when Dalí's hand appeared in the painting, invading and pillaging its two-dimensional reality with his ruthless brushstrokes. He applied the finishing touches to his childhood memory like a marauding invader armed with a sable paintbrush, and the wet paint glistened in the sunlight as it streamed into his studio.

Dalí sat back on his stool and studied his latest masterpiece. Instinct told him that there was still something missing, and his hand hesitated in front of the canvas, digits twitching, while he delved deeper and deeper into his subconscious until…like a bolt of lightning, inspiration hit him and he started to paint two crutches, propping the corpse upright for eternity.

"After all, everyone needs a crutch," Dalí proclaimed as he leaned back, adjusted his moustache, and admired the stroke of genius he had just given birth to. Now he was happy, and with his painting finished he could turn his mind to other things. He had not masturbated in weeks to achieve the heightened sense of creativity he needed to work, and now that "The Spectre of Sex Appeal" was finished he intended to become a pleasure-seeking Narcissus.

He knew Gala would not be home for a while, so he wiped his paintbrush on a well-used rag and began to undress in front of his easel. He ripped off his ruffled shirt and threw it to the floor, never taking his eyes off the painting in front of him until he was naked. Dalí swung around to face himself in a panoramic, rococo mirror that filled one wall of his studio and he hungrily admired his taut, tanned reflection. His waxed black moustache quivered as he allowed his eyes to caress every inch of his body, permitting himself time to linger over the majestic beauty of his budding erection. Soon his desire was leading him toward the upholstered pink curves of his iconic sofa and with a clear view of himself in the mirror he murmured, "I truly am madly in love with myself."

Dalí sank down into the soft, satin sofa and drifted toward the world of fantasy he craved, until a car horn reverberated through the air, splitting Dalí's lucid dream in two with its intrusively relentless *beep-beep, beep-beep*. He knew it was Gala and he rushed to the window without dressing, peeping outside just in time to catch a tantalizing glimpse of his wife's stocking-top as she climbed out of the car. The other door opened and a young fisherman from the village clambered out; he was beautiful, just Gala's type, and she beckoned him toward her hungrily and kissed him. Her lips parted and her tongue sought out every nook and cranny of her new lover's mouth. She knew she had an audience, and she scanned the windows of her house until she met Dalí's gaze. When she found him she pulled away from the fisherman and blew her husband a kiss before leading her lover into the house.

"Oh, my sweet Gala; my fantasy made flesh; my crutch," murmured Dalí breathlessly as he gripped a nearby curtain in his fist and pushed the heavy velvet into his mouth to suppress his uncontrollable excitement. He squirmed with anticipation and reached for an antique gilded chair to support his slender frame. His fingers explored the coils and twists of its woodwork and he enjoyed the cool complications of the carved flowers beneath his skin. His senses were working overtime and he was helpless as he fell to the floor behind the chair and passionately traced the contours of its legs with his tongue. He became lost in his own world of desire and forgot all about Gala as reality faded into the background.

Click-clack…Click-clack…Click-clack….

Dalí was jolted back to his senses by the sound of Gala's heels on the stairs; their crisp call to arms echoed through the house, bouncing off the tiles in all directions. His ears sucked in the sound and within seconds he was alert and on his feet, darting across the room toward the welcoming curves of the sofa, eyes wide like a primeval hunter with food on his mind. He removed a painting from the wall and revealed two peepholes into the next room. Then he listened patiently until he heard laughter in the corridor. His breathing quickened and his pulse raced as the blood rushed from his head. He took a deep breath and steadied himself against the wall, then turned his eyes to the peepholes just in time to see the door open.

Gala led the fisherman into her bedroom and Dalí gasped as he allowed his eyes to drink in her beauty. He lingered on her breasts, which tantalized him from beneath a sheath of wispy scarlet silk, and, as she unzipped her skirt and let it fall to the ground, she revealed the full splendor of her nylon-clad legs, like celestial ladders leading to heaven. Gala wore her sexuality like a translucent veil—Dalí defied any man not to come under her spell. She was elemental. As he watched her unclip her suspender belt and roll down her stockings with the graceful arched animation of a Carpaccio figure, he felt as if he would be wholly consumed by the passion she aroused in him.

Gala sensed Dalí's presence, and the thought thrilled her as she ran her fingertips over her young lover's body. "Take your clothes off," she demanded, and the fisherman dutifully obliged. He was naked beneath his waxed overalls, and Gala's eyes hungrily absorbed every muscular contour his body had to offer.

Dalí could feel the blood coursing through his body as he watched, forcing itself into the blossoming erection that swelled up in front of him, and he stroked himself tenderly, enjoying every detail of his sexual becoming, inch by inch. He struggled to keep quiet, eager not to give himself away, but he was a tightly coiled spring, a viper ready to strike; and the temptation to submit to his urges was overwhelming as he watched his wife parading her naked plaything around the room.

Gala led her lover to the bed; she desperately wanted to feel his rough fingers caressing her from every angle, and she tossed her head back in delight as he clutched her breasts with his callused hands and covered her with passionate kisses. She ran her hand over his broad, strong back and with her other hand she guided him between her thighs. As the fisherman entered her she flung her arms and legs around him, embracing him in a vicelike grip so tight that his every move became Gala's reason to live. "Harder," she urged, and he dug his fingers deeper into her flesh, planting the seeds for the riot of bruises that would dance over her skin the next morning.

Dalí was fast approaching the limits of dementia as he eagerly reached down to his rigid phallus and began sliding his hand backward and forward, up and down its shaft, matching the fisherman stroke for stroke until all three of them were unified in their joint quest for pleasure.

Unable to control himself any longer, Dalí flung himself to the ground in a Bacchic frenzy as a surge of erotic hallucinations swept over him. His reflection morphed hypnagogically in the mirror, taunting him with its pulsating reality. When he could take it no more, he closed his eyes and a mysterious oak paneled door presented itself in his mind's eye.

"My hairspring tells me it's just a matter of time, just a matter of time," Dalí muttered as he reached out for the brass doorknob in front of him. His right hand reflected back from its convex curves, warped beyond recognition; swollen and distorted, it seemed to mock him, but there was no going back now.

The door slammed shut behind him and Dalí found himself standing on a long, familiar beach. The sun was beating down and the horizon stretched out forever, until he could no longer tell where the sky ended and the sea began. He felt as though he were the only man on earth, but instinct told him he was not alone, and he scanned the vast, flat plains in front of him until he spotted a lion prowling across the hot sand. As Dalí watched it swing toward him, it rose to walk on two legs and its fur fell away to reveal the voluptuous curves of a naked woman.

The lion-woman beckoned Dalí toward her with the knife she carried in her right hand, and as he approached she ordered him to kneel at her feet. Dalí fell to the ground obediently and started kissing her toes while she smiled down at him like a marble Madonna.

"I am here to bring you pleasure, Salvador," she murmured, as she placed the knife under Dalí's chin and used it to raise him to his feet. She knelt in front of him and his passion surged through his body like a lightning strike as she pulled him toward her. Dalí groaned in delight as she took him in her mouth and wound her tongue around his glans. He could feel the blade of her knife dragging his skin as she toyed with him and the pressure welled up deep inside. He could feel his hairspring tightening as he rocked his hips toward her bloodred lips, and every atom of his being threatened to explode with pleasure until he looked into her eyes and saw his own reflection staring back at him.

Dalí dragged his eyes away from the studio mirror and drew his body back up to the peepholes. Gala was now astride the young fisherman and her head was thrown back in abandon as she writhed on top of him. Her breasts strained against his cupped hands and she was lost in her own world. Dalí closed his eyes and reclined on the sofa, squeezing his wilting erection in his hand, desperately willing it back to life.

When he opened his eyes again, he was alone on the beach and the woman with the knife had disappeared. Not knowing what else to do, he started walking toward the sun. He covered miles of sand in a single step until something caught his eye in the distance. A convoy of grotesquely deformed elephants was heading toward him, but Dalí was more interested in its exquisite cargo. Squinting against the sun, his eyes passed over the elongated animals to settle on the beautiful, naked women who balanced precariously on their backs. Their heads were lost in the clouds and they were so absorbed in the intricacies of their own delightful bodies that they were oblivious to Dalí's presence. He fervently watched them as they approached.

The monstrous animals, lead by a zealous white stallion, struck fear into Dalí's heart, but a carnal fervor gripped him so tightly that his desire to get a closer look at the cumulous beauties that rode on their backs outweighed his survival instinct. He threw himself to his knees to welcome them with open arms and a hopeful erection, convinced he would be able to watch the procession pass him by without being noticed, but he could not hold back in the face of such temptation. He took his throbbing penis in his hand and began to jerk it slowly backward and forward, building up speed until he was thrashing around in the sand like a fish.

Dalí's self-copulating waltz inevitably incurred the wrath of the high-strung white stallion, which raced toward him baying for blood and threatening him with its thundering, outstretched hooves. Within seconds the animal was bearing down on him and he could feel its malodorous breath on his face. Dalí knew there was no escape as it reared up onto its hind legs, and his life flashed before him in the split second it took for the hooves to come crashing down. He prepared to face his death, but suddenly spotted a familiar brass door handle nestling in the sand. He flung his arm toward it and wrenched it open.

A staircase lay hidden beneath the trap door, and Dalí knew it was his only chance of escape. He threw himself through the opening and plummeted down the steps at such a pace that he lost his footing and tumbled unceremoniously into a never-ending corridor carved out of the stone. Still desperate to escape his attacker, he hurled himself forward as if propelled by some mysterious force. He ran and ran and ran until he eventually tripped over a copulating couple draped across the passageway. When his eyes adjusted to the dark, he could make out more and more bodies leading to a central cavern where the whole floor heaved in orgiastic delight. There were dozens of beautiful young strangers scattered about, their rich black hair sparkling like gemstones as they frolicked naked in the flaming torchlight. Dalí's fear began to subside.

Soon every pair of eyes in the room was riveted on him, and he preened and tweaked his black, gravity-defying moustache as he allowed his gaze to wander hungrily over their stripped bodies. Everywhere he looked, arms and legs were intertwined, pulsating wildly as the revelers split, doubled, multiplied, evaporated, condensed, and dispersed simultaneously before Dalí's eyes.

A beautiful young woman broke away from the crowd and rubbed her body against Dalí. He took her breasts in his hands and ran his tongue along their expanse, squeezing them and biting their strawberry tips with his teeth. He wanted more but she pulled away, leading him by the hand toward the others. Dalí was unable to resist any longer, and he plunged into the writhing mass of bodies. Straightaway he could feel a hundred hands caressing his body and a thousand fingers probing his flesh. A dozen anonymous lips kissed his skin, and Dalí gave himself over, body and soul, to the pursuit of pleasure. Once again he could feel himself approaching the pinnacle he had been searching for, as one beautiful stranger after another engaged him in passionate clinches and introduced him to sensations he had never dared imagine before. He could feel his hairspring revving up again, but he was haunted by the familiar dread that all this would be torn away from him at any second.

As soon as this thought crossed his mind, the floor started to shift and the walls started to close in. Everyone ran for their lives, but Dalí lost his footing and fell to the floor. By the time he scrambled to his feet the exit had been blocked and the water level had started to rise. Dalí began to panic, realizing he was all alone, and as the ceiling threatened to squash him he was plunged into darkness. "Help," he gasped, as he struggled to stay afloat. "Help me, I can't breathe."

The fisherman looked around sharply. Gala had heard it too but she convinced her lover that he had imagined it and as she pulled him back toward her he soon forgot all about it.

Meanwhile, Dalí was crouched in the fetal position on the floor beside the sofa. He was blue in the face and gasping for air, but he did not miss a single stroke as he encouraged his drooping erection back to life. When the rigidity began to return he took a deep breath and closed his eyes.

Dalí was drowning in a sea of albumen, the viscous liquid filling his lungs so he could not breathe. He had to escape, sooner rather than later, so he summoned all his strength and punched through the solid rock bearing down on him. He tore at the material with his bare hands, expecting its sharp edges to slice through his skin, but the rock was soft and yielded to the force of his arm, like well-tempered flesh.

At length he climbed out of a giant egg, coughing and sputtering, and wiped the slime from his eyes. He was already cold and wet, and when he looked around him his heart sank. The snow on the ground was a foot deep and he was surrounded by the twisted torsos of ancient trees. There was no color to be seen, just the black and white of the snow and its shadows for miles around. Dalí felt drained and was about to give up when he spotted a little Russian girl dressed in white furs and sitting in a three-horse sleigh. She resembled a small wild animal and Dalí recognized her immediately. It was Gala.

"We've been waiting forever, Salvador," she whispered before setting off through the trees in her sleigh. Dalí followed her, running naked through the snow to keep up, and she eventually led him to a brightly painted red door in the middle of the forest. She ran through the doorway and Dalí followed her.

There was no sign of the child on the other side of the door, but Gala was waiting for him, asleep and naked but mysteriously suspended inches above the ground. A giant pomegranate hung ominously above her, spilling its ruby-red seeds into her inanimate lap, and a pair of tigers prowled the sky above her. Dalí immediately feared for her safety and tried to wake her. He shook her and called her name, but it was as if she were dead. Dalí was hopelessly excited by her lifelessness. He fell to his knees and, driven by an uncontrollable urge to vanquish his desire, took hold of his erection in his right hand, building up a rhythm and losing himself in a gamut of sensations and emotions.

At last Dalí could feel the root of his desire rumbling in his feet. It rose up his body, encircling each leg in its delicious embrace, caressing his buttocks, urging him on with its sublime encouragement. His breathing intensified and his body started quivering as his hairspring prepared to give. His whole body felt as if it were being turned inside out as the beginning of the end manifested itself in the base of his penis. A tsunami of energy welled up in his groin, and he clung to every precious moment of ecstasy that remained. Finally he wrenched out the ultimate pleasure with all the animal force of his clenched fist, and his cherished life force was sweeter than honey as it spilled like microscopic angels into his outstretched hand. Somewhere in the distance he could hear Gala crying out his name.

Gala threw back her head as wave after wave of euphoria washed over her and one climax chased another. She clenched her fists and gritted her teeth as every cell in her body blossomed in delight. Finally, unable to take any more, she cried out in ecstasy and the sound of her voice filled every corner of the house.

Dalí was prostrate on the sofa, motionless and exhausted by the physical exertion of his act. He opened his eyes slowly. When he caught sight of himself in the mirror, he smiled and hungrily licked the semen from his hands.

Click-clack…Click-clack…Click-clack…

Hearing Gala coming, Dalí wiped his mouth on his paint rag and adjusted his moustache. Seconds later, she appeared like Venus herself and sashayed across the floor toward him. She lay down on the couch beside him, allowing her silk kimono to slip away, revealing the breast Dalí had looked upon with such desire minutes earlier. He reached out his hand, trembling and still sticky with semen, and kissed Gala's nipple tenderly. "Gala," he murmured as he rested his head on her belly, "I think I'm going to die from an overdose of satisfaction."

Gala smiled enigmatically and twisted his hair absentmindedly between her fingers until her eyes closed and her breathing became shallower. Dalí could feel her breath caressing his cheek, and he watched them in the mirror until the tapering body of narcolepsy overwhelmed them both and they slept contentedly in each other's arms.

Letter to Valentino

Mitzi Szereto

RODOLFO ALFONSO RAFAELLO Pietro Filiberto Guglielmi di Valentina d'Antonguolla. A richly spiced mouthful of consonants and vowels that form your name. But I imagine *you* were a mouthful. A mouthful I'd never get to taste, except in my dreams.

Rudy, my Rudy, did you even know how I felt?

How I wished we could have danced together, your slim Sicilian hips swaying madly to the music, your hands encasing my more rounded counterparts. Pelvises joined in song—or as joined as they could possibly be under the circumstances. We would have danced the tango like you did in *The Four Horsemen of the Apocalypse*, our eyes boring into each other as we glided like a pair of seals in water along the dance floor, your hardness pressed to my softness, our breaths intermingling in mist and roses. How many times I dreamed of you taking me dancing at the Cocoanut Grove, me in a beaded gown, you in tails. You were such a good dancer. They say you used to be a gigolo at Maxim's before you came to Hollywood, a taxi dancer for lonely matrons. People say such cruel things.

Why did Jean leave you so soon after your wedding, I wonder? Foolish woman. I would never have left you, not even if those rumors were true. Your other wife, Natacha, was a witch, though. I read what they said about her in the papers. You deserved better. You deserved me.

They say you loved Ramon, then later, Paul. I don't believe any of it. How could I, when your black eyes burned into me as I sat in the front row of the movie house watching *The Sheik*? Eyes don't lie. Nor did the pulsing between my thighs as I watched you kissing Agnes Ayres. Sheik Ahmed Ben Hassan.

I wanted to be your Lady Diana Mayo.

And at night, in the lonely darkness of my bedroom, I *was*. Beneath the bedclothes my hands roamed the inexperienced contours of my body, taking inventory of my pleasure points. With you my entire body was a pleasure point. Cheeks, breasts, tummy, thighs—especially that secret place I was so afraid to touch. Afraid because I knew it would take me to a place I wasn't sure I wanted to go by myself. But then, you were with me, weren't you? "Sheik Ahmed!" I'd cry into the duvet, my face wet with tears. For a few minutes on the stage of my bed I got to be Lady Diana.

Then later, when you played both father and son in the sequel… What I'd have given to be Yasmin, the dancing girl. Did Vilma Banky know how lucky she was to be ravished by you? Such delicious cruelties she suffered! I'd have happily traded my soul for an eternity in Hell for the touch of your hands on my flesh. Your elegant fingers twined in my hair, twisting, pulling, then thrusting inside me, testing my wetness, my depth, for the thrusts to come. I'd be a river by then, flowing onto your palm, telling you I was ready for you to fill me. I probably left a pool on my seat at the picture show. Me and all the other women in the audience.

Sometimes I thought it might be nice to play the temptress for a change, Dona Sol corrupting your Juan Gallardo. You made such a handsome matador, with those brocaded toreador trousers hugging your backside and thighs and those delicious bits in front. Oh, I know I shouldn't say such things; it isn't ladylike to think of a man in that way. But when you're young and facing death it allows you to take *some* liberties, don't you think?

I could have lived with you at Falcon Lair. At night, after

dinner at Musso and Frank's, we'd go speeding up Benedict Canyon in your Avion Voisin, our hair flying in the warm California breeze as our thoughts turned from spaghetti to what would soon be happening in your bedroom. You'd spread me out on the yellow silk comforter, my body more exposed than that of the painted nude hanging above your bed. Beneath Señorita Gaditana's watchful green eyes, our cries of love would echo into the hills, alerting the coyotes to our passion. I would even have let you turn me around to take me the other way—*you* know, the way Ramon liked it. And Paul. Well, that's if those rumors were true. Which I'm sure they were not! But seriously, Rudy, I wouldn't have minded. Anything you would have wanted I'd have given you. Even my life. Had I known you were to die, I would've asked God to take me instead.

August 23, 1926. Thirty-one years old. You drew your last breath at 12:10 P.M. They say you died from peritonitis caused by a ruptured ulcer. I don't believe that. The Chicago press killed you with their accusations of effeminacy. *Pink Powder Puffs* was the name of the article. Two weeks later you were dead.

For nearly six days I waited outside Polyclinic Hospital, praying you would get better. There were others there too, but they didn't know you like I did. Their tears were not as real as mine. I remembered your smile, the way you held your cigarette. Most of all I remembered your eyes and how they pulled me in like magnets.

Did you know they rioted in New York City when you lay in state? Mourners tried to loot Frank E. Campbell's funeral home at Broadway and 66th Street, smashing windows, fighting with police, taking anything they could get their hands on: a flower, a scrap of wallpaper, a shard of glass. I wonder if they would have taken a piece of you, if they could have. Everyone adored you; even Mussolini sent you a wreath. The police let nine thousand viewers per hour file past you. This went on ten hours a day for three days. I was there too—did you see me? I made up my face like Pola Negri, fluttering my eyelashes at you as I passed. Your face was set like stone, though still handsome. I wanted to touch your cheek but was afraid I'd upset you.

Several women committed suicide. Or so people said. I thought about doing it myself but knew you wouldn't have wanted that. At St. Malachy's, Pola flung herself on your coffin, fainting over and over as photographers snapped her picture. Of course, Pola's an actress, isn't she? Rudy, I hope you won't mind my saying this, but I'm glad the talkies came in and no one wanted her anymore. You didn't really love her, did you? The thought of your tongues intertwined in a kiss, her painted lips wrapped around your cock, it thrusting deep inside her…it's more than I can bear!

I was also one of the thousands of mourners at the Hollywood Park Memorial Cemetery. I know you probably didn't see me that time because I was crushed by the heaving crowd as your casket was carried into the Cathedral Mausoleum. That was me standing by a palm tree, looking at the Hollywoodland sign up on the hill, thinking how much it must have meant to you when you first arrived. You surely heard the airplane flying overhead, showering us with rose petals. I thought it fitting that they should drop rose petals. Although I could barely breathe from the press of grieving bodies, I didn't faint. I remained still as a statue, feeling my blood run cold in my veins as I realized that my Rudy was gone. Forever.

In my widow's weeds I visited you every year on the day of your death, bringing you red roses and hiding my tears behind a heavy black veil. I wanted to thank you for coming to see me when I lay near death in a hospital bed, a fourteen-year-old girl with her whole life before her about to be cut short. You'd brought me a red rose, remember? The nurse wanted to put it in water, but I wouldn't let her. Instead I held it to my heart, breathing in its fragrance. Whenever I saw you up there on the movie screen, I smelled roses. I imagined that was how your skin must have smelled—like the dew-speckled petals of a rose on a spring morning. You told me I wouldn't die. And you made me promise that in case you died before me I should come stay by you so you wouldn't be alone. I've kept that promise. I kept it for nearly thirty years. I'm sorry I stopped coming to visit, but there were so many other women there that I felt my love for you had been tarnished. I hope you understand, Rudy.

They say a strong spirit never dies. Maybe that's why so many people have seen you since your death—at Falcon Lair, the Oxnard beach house, Paramount…. You like the costume department, don't you? Even the Santa Maria Inn. Room 210 it was. Guests say they feel you on the bed. Do you know I once stayed in that room? I kept hoping you might come to me. That you would lay your body down next to mine. We'd curl into each other like two cats, all slinky limbs and feline nips. I would purr as you stroked me, starting with my hair (I had it cut special at a fancy salon in Beverly Hills just for you), then down my neck, one ghostly finger tracing a line from chin to hollow. To my breasts—you'd tell me they were lovely and, no, not too small at all!—drawing circles around the nipples until they stood out so sharply they could have cut flesh. Then lower to the little indentation on my belly. You'd dip your tongue in there to tease me as your finger moved still lower, finding that special spot which made me squeal and shudder. Oh, Rudy, how did you know what I wanted as you bowed your head and loved me with your mouth?

Now I, too, am dead. Though, like you, I am not gone. I still wear my widow's black and have taken to visiting you again now that I am no longer of skin and sinew. The plaque behind which you sleep says *Rodolfo Guglielmi Valentino 1895–1926* in gold letters, and there's a little crucifix above your name. Crypt 1205: where, at last, I can share your bed.

By the people, for the people

Elisabeth Hunter

"ABE."

The president turned at the bellowing of his name to see his friend, Ward Hill Lamon, pursuing him down the hallway. The shuffle and clatter of the White House staff cleaning away the remains of the evening banquet echoed from the dining room behind him, the clink of silverware and china mixing with the sound of someone issuing quiet orders and the steady swift comings and goings of people hauling dishes to the kitchen.

The guests were finally gone, and none too soon in Abe's estimation. He was feeling whittled to the bone by all the socializing and politicking. The day had started out with the soft spring promise of May, everything abloom, the sun slanting across the White House lawn past the window of his office. But things had deteriorated rapidly and had hit an all-time low with this infernal evening reception. Since Confederate General Pierre Beauregard had ordered his artillery to fire on Fort Sumter last month and now civil war loomed, these soirées had become ever more tense, nothing but forums for political hashing and rehashing, for blustering old fools to call for immediate action against the Southern states. They acted as if recruiting and outfitting an army could happen instantaneously.

But still, on his wife, Mary's, orders, Abe had pasted a smile on his face when he'd entered the banquet and had kept it there throughout the long evening, despite the fact that New York Senator Ira Harris had attended the event, which made Abe more inclined to scowl than ever. Of all the politicians in Washington, D.C., Senator Harris was the most importuning and brazen in his attempts to corner the president. Abe and Mary sometimes joked that the man was so relentless they had to check beneath Abe's bed each night to see if Harris was lying in wait, ready to pounce. But when Abe had started to glower at the man this evening, there had been Mary squeezing his arm and standing on her toes to whisper, "Smile, husband. It would be unseemly for the president of the United States to pummel a senator in the White House."

He'd muttered back, "How about a duel on the lawn?"

Mary chuckled but she'd tightened her grip on his arm, her small hand warm even through his jacket and shirt. She brushed her lips across his cheek as he leaned down to hear her. "Smile and behave yourself," she'd murmured. And when he shook his head, she'd pinched him. "Abraham…"

Only Mary could have made him maintain that false calm, that seeming ease with the world, when all he really wanted was to go to his room, take off his boots, and close his eyes for a moment against the problems that were mounting all around him. Now his jaws ached and his lips felt numb from all that smiling, and his head hurt from the effort it had taken him not to rise to Harris's attempts to bait him.

There was some measure of comfort in the fact that Ward Hill Lamon looked equally exhausted and out of sorts. As Lincoln's former law partner and long-standing friend, the burly man whom Lincoln called "Hill" had appointed himself Abe's protector, supervising security at the White House. "Hill," Abe said, yawning. "Don't you ever sleep? What is it?"

Hill stepped close and spoke quietly. "I overheard some of the women talking tonight." He jerked his head back toward the massive dining room, obviously meaning that he'd listened to some of the guests speaking among themselves at the banquet. He sighed. "It's Mary again."

Abe pushed his long fingers through his hair, shoving it back from his forehead, exasperated. As if there weren't enough trouble in a nation on the brink of a civil war, why did people insist on targeting his wife with their gossip and judgment? Southerners said she was a traitor for supporting his antislavery views, while Northerners questioned her loyalty to the Union because she was born and bred in Kentucky and a number of her relatives would surely fight for the South. They said she spent too much money and was frivolous or shrewish, depending on whom you talked to. "Damn, Hill. Can't they leave the woman alone?"

Hill pursed his lips and shrugged his shoulders. "Abe, I like Mary, you know that, but maybe you should talk to her. Explain how it is. You're not a small-town lawyer anymore. She's got to know that everyone is watching her."

Abe glowered at his friend, spun on his heel, and marched down the hall. "Watching her?" he called over his shoulder. "Hill, the way they watch her, you'd think she was walking naked in a glass house. We're about to go to war, don't you think people could come up with something besides my wife to get their bloomers in a bunch over?"

Ward Hill Lamon pulled a flask from inside his jacket, took a long drink and considered the view of Mary Todd Lincoln naked in a glass house. Not a bad sight, he concluded as he watched the departing back of his friend. Yes, indeed, Mary naked must be something to see, with her dark hair loose around her shoulders. But since he himself was going to bed alone, this was not a wise train of thought to pursue. Nor was it prudent to consider the president's wife in any way other than as an entirely platonic friend. The Lincolns' marriage could hardly be called harmonious—Hill had skulked the halls of the White House enough to hear their late-night arguments—but there was something that ran deep between them, something that flashed and vibrated with a lingering passion and an abiding devotion.

Hill made his way along the hall, passing from one room to the next as he took one last precautionary stroll around the mansion, thinking that he should write a letter to his wife back in Illinois.

Unlike Mary Lincoln, his wife's loyalties did not extend to a tenure in Washington, D.C., with her husband. She had opted to remain in their home state, which might explain some of Hill's current irritation. He reached for the flask again as he opened a side door and stepped outside. He would speak to the guards he'd posted first. With the war beginning, Lincoln's safety was paramount.

Abe was still scowling when he reached his bedroom on the second floor, head bent, glaring just ahead of his long feet. All this nonsense about Mary was going too far, and he suspected it would only get worse as long as he was president. *Talk to her*, Hill had said. Abe grimaced. That was easier said than done, and Hill very well knew it. Reining in Mary was like trying to pull back a splendid high-spirited mare. And the real problem was that Abe liked to watch the mare run, mane and tail flying, prancing, spinning, cavorting. She'd lit his soul with her energy and charm for more than nineteen years, she still fired his senses. Mary's high-strung ways pulled him from the melancholy that plagued him. He didn't want to chastise her or make her fit into some prescribed notion of what a president's wife should be.

Without looking up, he pushed open the door, stormed into the room, and booted the door closed again, pulling his jacket off as he went. He flung it in the direction of a chair, noticing vaguely that one of the staff had built a fire in the small hearth to alleviate any lingering spring chill. It cast the room in flickering light and shadow, his enormous bed like a dark ship anchored beyond its feeble reach. He splashed water on his face from the bowl on the washstand. All right, it was true that Mary did spend too much money, but it was hardly the orgy of spending that the newspapers called it. And maybe her critics were right when they said it was unpatriotic in a time of looming war for her to host such extravagant parties, but God help her if she should curtail her entertaining, because then they would surely accuse her of skirting her social duties. It was an impossible situation. He sighed, and looked to the closed door that connected his room to Mary's, drying his beard on a towel. He would have to talk to her. What else could he do?

Abe took off his shirt and tossed it, too, toward the chair, standing in only his boots and trousers, the planes of his lean muscled torso sculpted by the firelight, the dark chest hair standing out in sharp contrast to his skin. He bent to light a lamp, carefully adjusting the wick and the glass globe, the flame rising up to further illuminate the room, making the bed loom up out of the shadows. The carved grapes and flying birds that graced the black-walnut headboard glowed in rich tones. As he straightened, a movement from the bed startled him. For one panicked moment, as the quilts rose in a burst of succulent colors and then began to fall away, he thought it was perhaps Senator Harris. But the person who was revealed when the blankets sagged back to the mattress was much more becoming. It was Mary.

The swell of relief he felt propelled him forward, a step, two steps, faltering as his wife pushed herself up onto her knees among the folds of the tangled sheet, and he was struck with what she was wearing. She had shed her formal gown and the infernal crinoline cage that went beneath it to hold out the skirts. Gone were her slip, drawers, chemise, and camisole. All that remained was a scarlet-red corset, a rich-hued wonder of a garment in embroidered silk brocade that tucked in her waist and lifted her breasts to him like offerings of fruit set on an ornate and delicate platter. It was like nothing he'd ever seen before, wholly beyond the utilitarian corsets he was familiar with, those white, heavily boned contraptions that ever seemed to defy his long fingers as he struggled to remove the damnable inconvenient things from his wife's body. This one, however, was a bit of perfection, the silver busk-clasps that hooked down the front twinkling like tiny stars against the vibrant red fabric. Where Mary's dark hair fell over her shoulders, catching against the ruby brocade at her breast, the shimmer of light from the lamp seemed to set the corset ablaze, the light fracturing, coalescing, sparking as she moved. Mary's skin was pearlescent in comparison, shimmering ivory tones as she rose still farther from the bed and began to shift across the blankets toward him, drawing his attention to her silk stockings and the garters that held them. They, too, were red! Mary was trussed up like a delightful confection.

Abe drew a breath, made himself release it, told himself to keep breathing, but he could not pull his attention from his wife's legs encased in those sheaths of red silk, her thighs deliciously bare above the stockings, pale, full, her haunches large and round, a perfect fit—he knew from experience—for his hands. He stood rooted to the spot as Mary began to crawl in a most provocative manner, with her hips high, her buttocks in full view. Her breasts spilled over the corset and swayed pendulously with every movement of her body. Her eyes on his shone with a compelling mischief, something both ardent and teasing.

When she reached the edge of the bed, she turned, a sinuous undulation that gave him an artful vision of her back in the corset, her flesh pushing over the upper edge at the shoulders, the skin along her spine pulled in and puckered between the lacings, her hips and buttocks jutting in all their glory from beneath the crimson. She offered him a coy glance over her shoulder. "I gather you like this latest style from France, Abraham? Is the new color not exquisite?"

"Mary…" Abe exhaled sharply, stepping forward, reaching for his wife, his cock burgeoning uncomfortably in his trousers.

But she was too fast, scuttling back to the center of the bed, laughing as she escaped him. "Open the curtains, Abe. Open the windows. I want to hear the sounds of the night."

Lincoln groaned. "Mary, we can't. Not here. I'm the president of the United States. The nation is falling to pieces. This isn't the time or place for…" he gestured to the windows with their heavy drapes "…for that. The windows overlook the South Lawn, for Christ sake."

Mary stretched upward, one small hand skimming the brocade of the corset, coming to rest on her full breast, her fingers toying with the areola and nipple, drawing them up, making them harden beneath her practiced touch. "I'm perfectly aware of the view from your bedroom windows, Abraham." Her other hand seemed to move of its own accord between her legs, and although Abe knew it was more calculated than that, that this move was engineered to undermine his resistance and common sense, he was entranced in spite of himself. He swallowed convulsively as the delicate fingers reached to pull aside her labia, questing between and, finding the clitoris she sought, pressing it between her fingertips, pinching it, seeking her own pleasure, applying more pressure until her mouth fell open and her breath came in increasingly ragged gasps. "At least admit that it arouses you," she panted. "You are as corrupt a devil as I, Mr. Lincoln." She gave a pointed look to the erection that was throbbing in the tight confines of his trousers.

At that moment, there was no denying his excitement. He tried to tamp down his traitorous yearning and, when that became a futile effort, to find some compromise, some small amount of logic to apply to the situation. But what raged between himself and Mary was, as it had been for nineteen years, a careening and wild thing, beyond either of them to control.

Mary saw his struggle, the great effort this internal battle cost him, and then, at the end, the very devil she had said he was. He reached for her and she came to him, shuffling across the bed again, letting him take her face in his hands, letting him capture her and batter her senses with a kiss that was meant to be punishing, that was intended to drive home to her the danger of what she wanted, what they both craved. The harsh kiss lingered and then ignited. Mary arched against him and Abe cupped her vulva in his hand, pressing and rubbing the swelling crest of her clitoris with the heal of his palm as his fingers sought between the folds of her labia, spreading them, opening her. She groaned and pushed hard against him.

"This is ludicrous," Abe ground out, his breath hot against her lips, heavy with a lingering musk of brandy and cigars. He tugged her bottom lip between his teeth and then pulled harder, sucking it into his mouth, releasing it, seeking the hollow at her temple. His beard rasped against her cheek. "It is mad, Mary, that we do this."

"Yes," she whispered, her hands on his chest, toying with his nipples in the most damnable fashion, "but it is intoxicating, this madness. Open the curtains, raise the windows."

"A compromise, then," he murmured. "We should strive for decorum, we should proceed cautiously."

But she just laughed at that, her head turned and thrown back so that the light from the lamp glowed along the line of her jaw and the tendons of her throat. "In all our years together, husband, there has never been room between us for conservative action. We can try for decorum in this, but I fear it will be a wasted effort. Stand with your back to the open windows if you must, and ensure that any passersby will never know what goes on below your belt, but I want the sounds of the night."

"You want the sounds of the people," he replied, but he was already hurrying to yank open the curtains and push up the windows, his movements abrupt, driven. "You want them to see us, you want them to hear us and to watch." If he had meant this harangue to come out a chastisement, he had failed. His voice had deepened, a rumbling baritone, leaden with his own desire of this very thing that he accused her of.

"Yes," Mary agreed. She breathed deeply of the night air, trembling noticeably as the sound of a passing coachman wafted from the street in the distance, the distinct jangle of harnesses and the man's voice calling out to his horses lilting through the window. Closer still were the voices of soldiers, members of the regiments that had begun already to gather in the capitol in preparation for the war, enlisted men out smoking and walking in the evening. "Any of the staff could be out there." Mary's voice was high, breathless. "Anyone really. One of the guests who lingered. Your secretaries. Strangers. Friends. Who is outside your window, Abraham? Who might see us?"

Abe had no doubt that somewhere on the grounds there were guards, silent watchmen posted by Hill, whose sole purpose was to keep the president and his family under their constant surveillance, who would even now be staring up at these very windows. Why that thought caused his heart to pound harder in his chest he had no idea. The surge of heated pleasure it gave him was not something he could reconcile with what he knew to be acceptable behavior, but he could not deny it all the same. He scanned the grounds in the moonlight, but there didn't appear to be anyone about. He turned to face the bed, his back to the South Lawn and whoever might be watching. A breeze slid around his naked stomach and skittered into the hearth, stirring the flames of the fire so that they flickered and danced, casting the room into a frenetic cotillion of interweaving shadow and light. "Men," he said. "Strangers will see you. The soldiers are out tonight. They are far from their homes, away from their wives. They're lonely. They walk the streets and the parks because they can't sleep with their frustration and wanting."

Mary was poised on the edge of the bed, sitting on her knees, her back straight and rigid in the corset, her breasts jutting forward. The dark hair at her pelvis cast shadows between her legs. "Yes," she sighed with relief, as if she had been holding her breath, and these words of her husband's had provided the oxygen that would save her. "The soldiers will follow the sounds of our lovemaking," she whispered. "They will come full of lust, to watch us." She leaned over the edge of the bed, putting first one hand onto the floor and then the other, her backside still high on the mattress like a harvest moon rising in the night sky, shining above the long downward curve of her spine. Her hair fell forward, sweeping the hooked bedside rug, laying bare her white shoulders.

Abe's cock jerked against his stomach. He was lost in the sight of his wife crawling from his bed on all fours, catlike, tail high, an angel-whore cloaked in alabaster and crimson. "The soldiers will bring prostitutes with them." He stumbled over the words as Mary stretched and slid her legs from the bed, moving across the floor toward him, her wide hips shifting maddeningly as she crawled. He wrenched an armchair forward and positioned it so that it sat in the gap between the curtains. "Here, you see? The soldiers will watch you ride me here in this chair while the prostitutes kneel between their legs to service them on the lawn. It will be in the newspapers tomorrow." He fumbled at the buttons of his pants.

Mary reached him and pushed his hands away from his fruitless labors, taking over the task of undoing the buttons herself. She let out a sigh of satisfaction as she released him from his trousers. "The newspapers?" she breathed.

Abe picked up a coil of her hair and wrapped it about his fingers, holding her head close to his crotch. "All of them. The soldiers will tell what they've seen. Tomorrow morning it will be in the local papers, and then the news will spread. By the end of the week, everyone will know."

"And will they know that my husband's cock is built much like the man himself, that it is long and lean?" She followed the vein on the underside of his erection with the tip of her tongue, from balls to head, trailing a simmering wet line. "If I were to suck your cock before this open window, would they know you by the shape of your penis?"

"No doubt," Abe stammered, drawing an unsteady breath as Mary's tongue flicked out again, probing at his urethra.

She took his testicles in her hand, lifting them as if she were examining their heft, her fingers playing over his scrotum, shifting and rolling his balls in their sac. "And they will tell the newspapers?"

The beseeching in her voice made Abe's cock twitch against

her lips, made him grasp more of her hair in his hand and feel for the back of her skull, where her head fit into the bowl of his palm, holding her to him as if she might otherwise slip away. "Yes, Mrs. Lincoln," he assured her, "the soldiers and the prostitutes watching you right now will tell the reporters you suck a man like a dockside whore. They are discussing it already. Listen."

The sound of distant male voices drifted to them. Not from the South Lawn, Abe knew, probably not even from the White House grounds, but from the streets beyond. "Do you hear it?" he asked. "They are out there on the lawn, craning their necks to see in the windows." He thrust his hips forward, pushing his cock barely between her parted lips.

She took the head into her mouth, slowly, lavishly tonguing it, following the ridge at its base, gripping Abe's hips so that he could push no deeper, so that he must hang there on the edge of this wet suckling hole. And then she withdrew. "It is probably your secretary, Mr. Nicolay," she murmured. "He will bring the reporters to see for themselves, and call the soldiers over to watch."

"Yes, you have been unkind to him, he doesn't like you," Abe agreed. "He would want everyone to know. For the people who are in the back of the crowd and cannot see you for themselves, he will describe in great detail all the things you do."

Mary gasped. "Have I been that cruel to him? What will Mr. Nicolay tell them?" Her hands slid up Abe's hips to tug his trousers down so that she could clasp his buttocks. "Will he say I am a strumpet?" she whispered, lifting her eyes for a moment to search his face, opening her mouth to him again.

Lincoln thrust between her lips and withdrew, pushed again, deeper this time, and pulled all the way out so that his cock head rested on Mary's glistening bottom lip. He stroked the arch of her eyebrow with his forefinger, and then the dipped bridge of her small nose. "Beautiful strumpet," he coaxed. "Even Mr. Nicolay will have to admit that, you know. They will all have to admit that you are a beautiful whore."

"Yes," she breathed, and recaptured him in her mouth.

In other circumstances, Abe might have encouraged her struggle to suck him, might have held back and made her strive harder for him, but the very real risk of someone coming onto the South Lawn was ever in the back of his mind, driving him, making him nervous, exciting him. He plunged full length into his wife's mouth, reveling in the sensation of her opening her throat to him, of her tongue cradling the base of his shaft while its thick head swelled in the heat beyond her tonsils. Abe groaned and forced himself to loosen his grip on her hair, to make his touch a caress instead of a demand, letting Mary have her way in this.

The night sounds of the city drifted through the open windows and seemed an aphrodisiac to Mary, firing her passion, driving her harder and faster as she worked Abe to a frenzy in clear view of the lawn. He couldn't keep track of how she did it. It seemed a diabolical thing to him. All he could manage was to cling to her and let himself be pulled along as her head pistoned back and forth on his cock, or alternately descended on him in luxurious strokes that rocked his very soul. She brought him again and again to the edge of orgasm, sucked him until he could not take one more touch of her tongue without exploding into her mouth, let him hang there like a man clinging to a cliff edge, then backed off to let the fire die to embers, only to begin again. It was an exquisite and endless torture.

Suddenly the sound of a door opening and closing below cut through the night, people's feet on the step and then the path, and a woman's voice, her soft laughter followed by the rumble of a man laughing with her. Mary started, but Abe held her to him. "It is a couple out walking in the night air, love," he whispered. "They are young lovers, members of the house staff. What will they think when they see you down on your knees?" Mary's moan pulsed over his penis and she went at her task like a woman obsessed, no longer trying to keep him at the edge of orgasm, but to drive him right over that precipice, her mouth demanding and supplicating.

Abe tried to concentrate on the approach of the couple outside. Was it really two young lovers? Really members of the staff? He had no idea. By the sound of things, they were moving along the south side of the mansion, their voices still indistinct but closer every moment. They were walking the path nearest the wall, it seemed, too close to the house to see more than the lamplight radiating from the president's room. As long as they stayed on the path, they could not see what the Lincolns were doing, but they could certainly hear them. Abe knew he should care, knew he should pull Mary away to the bed, close the windows, and draw the drapes. But he was lost to the volatile bliss that his wife was sucking from him, beyond caring about appearances or proprieties. As the climax crashed over him, he had just enough of his shredded common sense left to clamp his mouth shut. He drew a searing breath and held it, his eyes clenched, fingers tangled in Mary's hair. His body contracted, seized, convulsed, exploded. All silent.

Mary was caught up in her own craving, spiraling ever higher, working him as if she could draw every last tattered scrap of his soul through his urethra. Finally, when he could stand no more, when his legs were threatening to collapse beneath him, he took her head between his hands and extracted himself. He stumbled backward and nearly sank to the floor as he tried to catch his breath and calm the chaotic pounding of his heart. He smiled weakly down at his wife. She looked deliciously storm-tossed with her hair strewn about her and her breasts heaving. He leaned to cup her breasts in his hands.

A murmur of voices rose from directly beneath the windows. The couple walking outside had made it as far as the Lincolns' bedroom. Abe noted distractedly that their conversation seemed to have an odd cadence now, with long pauses between their indistinct words. And then a woman's moan lifted into the night. The man said something to her, there was another questionable pause, and the woman groaned again, a muffled whimper of a noise almost lost in the night. Although the man's words were unclear, there was no mistaking the lady's distress, the gorgeous purr of a woman about to be well pleasured.

Abe grinned at Mary. "It seems we have company, love," he whispered.

Mary almost laughed out loud, covering her mouth with her fingers, her face flushed with a bewitching delight in the happenings below the window. She crept across the room to gingerly lean out and squint down at the path nearest the mansion wall. Abe reveled in the stunning view of her ass, round and luscious, as her head disappeared over the windowsill. She popped back up almost immediately, her eyes wide and dancing, silent laughter shaking her as she hurried back to him and flung herself into his embrace, her arms around his neck. "Why, that man is tipping her velvet right there," she hissed. "Right below your window, Abe! He's got her pressed to the wall and her skirts up about her waist. He's face deep in her!"

Abe kissed his wife, her laughter bubbling into his mouth on the twining curve of her tongue. He wanted Mary out of the corset, he realized, wanted to see her waist and belly. "Step back," he whispered, gently pushing her away, leaving his flagging cock jutting out of his trousers. He used the moment to scan the lawn. It was dark, empty, and, with the exception of the couple on the path, still. "Stand with your back to the window, so everyone can see your fine ass," he murmured. He turned Mary, reaching around her hips to stroke her buttocks with both hands and to spread them as if he were displaying her to a crowd below, knowing the evening air would breeze along the crevice between her cheeks and lend a sense of exposure, another taboo, another bit of tinder to this thing that burned between them.

Mary held her breath, drawing in her stomach until he had undone the last busk clasp and the corset fell to the floor. Abe smiled as his wife drew an enormous breath of air, arched her spine, and thrust her hips back, wanton. God, the woman was perfect. The lamplight cast a honey glow to her skin. Abe pushed the silk stockings to her ankles and helped her to step from them. He ran his fingers along the stretch marks that mapped a path from her pubic hair to her belly button. After bearing him four sons, her waist was thicker than it had been when he'd first married her, her belly rounder, voluptuous, ripe, so beautiful.

Mary quivered at his touch and clutched at him. "Abe..."

"Shhh," he whispered. "It is out of your hands now, strumpet. You must be absolutely silent. Not one sound, do you understand?"

She nodded, a moment of panic in her dark eyes as her husband squatted before her. She reached to stroke his beard, to trace the rough-hewn bones of his cheeks and his long nose, to caress his lips.

Abe kissed her fingertips. "Spread your legs wider, put your hands on my shoulders. Good. The lawn is full of spectators, everyone is watching. Keep your hips up where they can all see." He leaned to inhale the musk of her, to feel the heat that emanated from her quim. He spread her with his fingers and touched his tongue to her swollen clitoris. She caught her breath and he felt her vagina clench and release, velvet soft in his mouth. Tipping her velvet, indeed, he thought, it was an apt description. He held her hips as he laved her, circled her clit, sucked it between his lips. Her fingernails bit into his shoulders. He slid his tongue along her labia and pushed inside her.

The man below the window must have been performing his task admirably as well, if the noises from the mysterious woman were any indication. She was whimpering now, a stuttering broken sound that vibrated through the night. Mary responded to those impassioned noises with an increased urgency, undulating on Abe's mouth, wound ever tighter by the rising groans of the woman on the path. Both his wife and the stranger below were lost in a spiral of need that could only lead to one end, and Abe intended them to get there together. He changed the rhythm of his mouth, forcing Mary to rock her hips in long strokes. She groaned quietly. Finding her clitoris swollen in the folds of her labia, he circled it with his thumb.

The whimpers from the woman beneath the window suddenly turned into full-fledged moans, apparently without regard for who might hear her. Her voice warbled. "Yes, there. Oh, God."

Abe pushed harder into Mary's cunt, his beard grinding against her. She pulsed around him, drawing him in, a rising shudder overwhelming her so that Abe had to grip her to keep her upright. Her whole body pressed down against his mouth. He recognized the signs of her impending orgasm. Her legs trembled, she undulated harder. He struggled to maintain the rhythm, driving her closer and closer to that sharp edge, reveling in the way her back arched and her voice rose in a breathy whimper. And just as she had tortured him—perhaps because she had done so—he held her there at that summit for as long as he could, tethered her at that line just before she would go howling into the moon. He felt as if he were performing a well-choreographed circus stunt, a high-wire performance with a pole and chair, and at any moment the wire would snap and Mary and the woman on the lawn would go careening into space. Even as he thought it, the woman below cried out, her climax a stunning thing in the night.

He felt the exact moment when Mary was hurled over the edge too. He felt her vagina open and unfurl, as if it would turn inside out. Her entire body convulsed and he feared that she would shriek, which would bring the household running and would likely have Hill breaking down the door, but the sound she made was strangled, as if the orgasm had overwhelmed her functions, had rendered her incapable of even drawing enough air to scream. The cries of the woman outside and the moan of his wife blended in his ears. Mary clutched his head to her crotch with both hands and rode out this tempest, sobbing his name again and again in a hoarse whisper until the climax peaked and then, at last, began to fade. Still he stayed with her, slowing the harmony of his hand and mouth, bringing her back, like a kite he reeled in gently, hand over hand, until the last of her orgasm had ebbed and she sagged into his strong hands.

Only then did he pull his mouth from her and stand, sliding up her body, holding her to him, kissing the curve of her skull as he turned with her in his arms and sat in the chair he'd placed there, cradling Mary in his lap. Her hair fell like yards of tangled silk over them. She settled against his chest, kissed his neck, and murmured, "Thank you, Mr. President. That was a fine bit of diplomacy."

Abe chuckled. "All in the line of duty, Mrs. Lincoln. Shall I send away the reporters, and the soldiers, and the other onlookers?"

"Mmm. I suppose you'd better." Mary smiled against his skin. "They're trampling the lawn, there are so many of them."

"Yes, we've drawn a crowd, as usual." Abe swiveled Mary in his lap. They both looked out at the empty lawn. Their laughter echoed into the night.

From below the window came a muted squeal of shock. "Oh, heavens," the woman gasped, "the president's bedroom window is open. What if he heard us?" There was a frantic rustling of bushes and fabric, and then a scurrying of feet as the couple ran back down the path. A door in the distance opened and slammed shut again.

"Shall I tell them?" Abe laughed harder. "Shall I tell them that my wife is a wanton exhibitionist and I her willing compatriot?"

Mary's breath was warm on his skin, her fingers trailing along his collarbone. "Mmm, that seems a politically unwise decision, but if you insist then you must also tell them that your wife is well pleasured and well sated, and has been for nineteen years. I won't have them thinking the president of the United States of America does anything in half measures."

Ward Hill Lamon leaned against the trunk of a tree, hidden in its shadow, and swigged the last drink of whiskey from his flask as he watched the president stand with his wife in his arms and cross to the bed. Abe bent to blow out the bedside lamp and the room was cast into near darkness, with only the dying glow from the hearth glimmering at one end. Hill swallowed the whiskey and exhaled through his teeth. He had been right. Mary Todd Lincoln naked in a glass house would be worth seeing. A man would pay hard-earned money to view such a thing. The display beneath the Lincolns' bedroom windows had been an added bonus, a ghost-like copulation of shadowy figures, the woman's skirts clutched up to her waist as the man knelt between her legs, his face well hidden in her spread quim. Between that woman's moans, and Mary Lincoln arching and writhing like a fallen angel, Hill's aching erection was throbbing against his leg.

He stalked across the lawn, already composing a letter to his wife in his mind. She would come to Washington, D.C., if he had to woo her, bribe her, or drag her here himself. With the goings-on in the Lincoln household, a man could not be expected to sleep alone.

Time, Movement, and Desire

Tom Bacchus

I AM IN THE RARE-BOOKS SECTION of the University of Pennsylvania Library, poring over books of photos by the famous photographer. Sequence after sequence details the infinite positions of men, women, children, and animals sitting, standing, walking.

Of course it is the nude images of men, alone and together, especially the muscular men, that interest me. Each shot shows a different angle and fraction of time, displaying the simple masculine charm of each man's body. Captured over a hundred years ago, they still create desire.

My curiosity led me to visit the Private Collections Section at the library, where my friend Alex has been so helpful over the years. Often he let me pore over famous playwrights' personal letters and documents. When I wanted to dig deeper into the love life of Walt Whitman, he produced boxes of documents and a seemingly endless bibliography.

Therefore, when I asked about the life of the famous photographer, his eyes lit up and he grinned.

"I have some very special items."

He led me to a large table and disappeared into the lengthy stacks. He returned, arms filled with a cardboard box. "Enjoy," he whispered as he left me with these treasures, which I have copiously rewritten for your enjoyment.

It seems the photographer had an assistant, a young handsome man who often posed for the series of action shots. The photographer never imagined the erotic potential of the images. They were strictly for academic purposes, weren't they?

A. J. Parker, a young artist of the era, who was also a rower, worked for a time as the photographer's assistant. He kept a diary of his activities during the period. Hidden away for nearly a century, it is faded around the edges and written longhand in pen and ink.

The young Parker took a job with the photographer out of scientific interest and with an interest in observing physical activity, as well as a search in rowing for what he termed "the perfect stroke."

But it turned out that other interests developed in addition to the filmed images. Parker wrote of a series of photographs that have yet to see the light of day. Now possibly destroyed, these images may have represented a beauty and magic that we can only imagine.

Nevertheless, we do have the diaries.

May 14, 1886 – Have begun a series of photographic works with Eadweard Muybridge. He has requested several brave young women and older gentlemen to participate in this scientific study of movement. Muybridge has worked in the courtyard of the Veterinary Hall and Hospital of the University of Pennsylvania. Who would have thought that such discoveries could have been made when a fellow professor made a bet to see if a horse's legs completely leave the ground while at a gallop?

After accomplishing the cumbersome task of bringing a rowing machine from the gymnasium to his outdoor photographic studio, and posing in uniform for him, I mentioned to E.M. my interest in the new science, and my enthusiasm in seeking employment. He hired me on the spot to assist his portrait work and the setting of equipment.

E.M.'s images have proved very interesting, however limited are those of the children, older men, and women. We use a large area behind his house, cordoned off by high fences and painted black with accurate white lines to represent meters. Eadweard has proposed that I make a point of hiring several strapping young men from the gymnasium. A few men are interested. Others put off. I worry about exposure of what I feel are my erotic longings for some of the fellows. Although some are highly affectionate toward each other, and rumors persist regarding a few of the more affable types, I find it difficult to bring up the muster to ask the more handsome fellows.

May 21 – After a session in the gymnasium, I inquired of a well-known boxer, Ben Bailey, his inclination toward posing. He did not seem put off by the idea, particularly when I stressed that these images were strictly for "academic purposes." Being a physical-culture athlete of renown, he seemed interested. We have made an appointment to have lunch tomorrow.

May 22 – Had lunch with Ben at a small restaurant. We were turned away at my preferred setting. Bailey is a mulatto, and although I had never considered it, he explained to me that he is sometimes the subject of ridicule for his half-Negro racial status. He spoke rather passionately about it, telling stories of being harassed in various places of employment. This had led him to pugilism, a sport in which he could strike back at opponents without legal repercussions. I listened, rapt, to his life story, but had difficulty maintaining calm. Spilled a glass of water. His every move inspired a flush of erotic longing. His hands are enormous. His head, shaved clean, brings to mind an enormous erect phallus. I find his demeanor utterly masculine, yet with an air of grace.

I feigned calmness enough to arrange our mutual appointment with E.M. As we shook hands before parting, I again felt a warm erotic tingling. I suspect I have sparked what could be an intense friendship with Ben.

June 20 – Ben arrived on time. E. was cordial, showed him around the documenting facility; Ben seemed impressed by the setup. E. showed him to the dressing quarters, a small room off to the side of his back porch entrance.

When Ben came out completely naked in the morning sun, my heart nearly ceased beating, then pulsed away like a wildfire. I'd seen him many times before in the dark changing rooms of the gymnasium, but here he seemed even more handsome, glowing in the sun. I fumbled with the equipment, preparing for the series, while Ben stood chatting with E., who showed him through the movements he wanted: first walking up a set of stairs, then performing a few boxing movements. With each movement, Ben's buttocks and back muscles flexed with a definition that E.M. found perfect for his studies. Ben's penis also had a habit of swinging to and fro with each movement.

Ben performed his duties quite well, and I prepared another series of exposures. E. offered a robe, but Ben preferred to sit naked on a bench. I was breaking out in a sweat under my clothing. E. noticed and suggested I remove my shirt. "A fine idea," I told him.

After Ben posed some more, E. decided to give him a rest and asked me to pose. I became flustered. Surely my visible excitement, which up to now had remained hidden, I could control if I concentrated. I did my best, disrobed, and E. and I agreed on doing another running jump. Ben decided to watch while I posed. He stood naked in the sun. I became distracted as he sat. E.M. didn't notice, but Ben became slightly erect while sitting. I made a mention of it. "Perfectly natural," said E., who smiled. Ben liked that and leaned back, exposing himself even more. His member pointed up to the sky. I became erect myself, and E. had to halt the exposures until I became more composed.

That night I abused myself twice, thinking of the images and the bodies of my gymnasium associates. I know my desires are wrong, but under E.'s watchful gaze and in the open sun of his property, all seems well. Perhaps if I limit my interests to this arena, scandal will not ensue.

June 21 – Ben poses nude again, this time wrestling with Peter Daley, another fellow from the club who is an acquaintance of Ben and myself. Daley is an acrobat. The two of them are quite athletic, being most jovial as they await our preparations. E. is calm, thinking it lovely that we have such fine specimens. "We can do some more athletic studies now," he proposes. Peter's skin is pale as milk in the sun, the patch of hair at his groin drawing my eyes like a magnet.

We ask Peter and Ben to wrestle. They think nothing wrong with that and promptly begin rolling about on the posing arena. E. admires it a bit, but then requests a more formal move be demonstrated. While Peter kneels over Ben, he rubs Ben's shoulders. Ben becomes erect. Peter thinks it's all in good fun and begins to play with Ben's member. The two are erect.

"Take a picture, Dad!" says Ben. The two men engage in oral copulation. E. and I watch, mesmerized. I become erect and decide to throw discretion to the wind. I strip and masturbate while watching, fighting off what I can only typify as jealousy toward Peter. E. watches too, enjoying it from a "scientific viewpoint." Peter and Ben become quite excited and ejaculate into each other's mouths. I ejaculate as well, nearly fainting with the excitement.

E. beams. "Good show, boys. Now may we get on with our work?"

It takes a great deal of discussion later for E.M to calm me down and propose his further ideas. I am hesitant, but only need a single push to fall into the stream.

June 23 – After discussing it with Peter, E. decides to photograph Peter naked, erect, masturbating and ejaculating. E. explains that there is very little film, so he must let us know when he is about to accomplish orgasm. Peter sits on a chair, pulling his member happily. Says he likes it when we watch. Peter asks me to come and "help him out a bit." I walk over and masturbate him. "Put your mouth on it," Peter says. I do so, quite nervous that he will finish in my mouth and ruin the experiment. Peter promises that he will be sure to pull my mouth away at the right time. It doesn't take long.

Overcome with the pleasure and sensation of another man's member inside my mouth, I notice a tremendous increase in my salivary function. My erection is almost uncomfortably hard, but as the photograph will be of Peter, I pay my own pleasures no mind and push hard while leaning over, bobbing my mouth and lips up and down slowly on Peter's engorged erection. He says very complimentary things about my novice technique, which is quite warming, considering this was my first witnessed act of inversion. Good old E., so sophisticated.

Peter taps me on the head and I pull away. Peter begins ejaculating, his sperm flying out in great arcs, well out of the range of the camera, I am sorry to report. Peter leaves his hands off and lets E. photograph his ejaculation without hand rubbing. Peter grins in the sunlight, happy to be of service to science.

E. has, of course, hit on a fantastic idea, to capture the moment of ejaculation on film. My skin crawls at the possibilities, the outrage of it all. I cannot remain calm in the photographic laboratory, worried that these precious images may become lost with a single slip of the chemicals. Every appearance of the nude compatriots draws me to another episode of onanistic frenzy. I remain utterly captivated by these images, to the detriment of my academic studies. Fortunately, time spent rowing relieves the condition somewhat.

I spend the next days in palpitations, fearing heart failure, but E. gives me a tonic and recommends a visit to the pharmacy for some relaxants.

The next days pass in a daze. All I can consider, as I take to drinking too much cognac in E.'s library, is the tremendous thrill of oral copulation. When will I be able to engage in such acts again? I go to bed and masturbate into a handkerchief.

I fear showing up at the gymnasium, even walking on the street. I feel the people looking at me, as if they had witnessed the moments of my pleasure with the men. I bathe daily now, changing clothes to remove the perspiration. I may go mad.

June 26 – E. M. introduces Morris Hacker, a baseball player, who will do some pictures with sticks and balls. Morris strips down quite congenially, and catches and throws ball. His haunches are quite well formed. His member is a bit small, but after a bit of chat about the fairer sex, it grows. E. notes how that is nothing to be ashamed of, "simply a masculine bodily function." He wants to see the sway of it. Morris blushes, but relaxes after a bit. He asks to relieve himself sexually, and E. complies, suggesting that I assist. I am more than happy to do so, having finally had a taste of such pleasures from Peter. Since this is my second time, I am more attuned to his needs, and almost smile at how enjoyable I know it will be. My perversion has become a comfortable sport.

Morris's member is smaller, but grows thicker, and he takes me by surprise when he ejaculates in my mouth. At first I am afraid, but then enjoy it. I finish myself off while kneeling between Morris's legs. E.M. seems unconcerned that the ejaculate was not captured on film.

Quite a day. I request to leave early, feeling quite exhilarated and exhausted. E.M. kindly complies. But secretly, I suspect he will want to engage the modeling services of Ben Bailey. We have begun to meet and talk, and I have taken several afternoons to observe Ben's practice sessions in the boxing ring. I have dismissed a few fellow students who question my association with a Negro. I have produced a collection of drawings of Ben from memory, and developed the photographs made by E.

When I presented one of the drawings to Ben, he blushed, and was quite flattered by it. He said he would be happy to pose for me at my home, if I were so inclined, "away from the old bearded scientist." Ben patted my back, leaving me stunned by the romantic possibilities. Alone with Ben, he lying nude on a chaise longue, or standing proud in a boxing pose, his bronze skin oiled and glowing in the afternoon light.

In preparation for it, I have encouraged my parents and servants to take a weekend holiday in the Pennsylvania vacation cottage we enjoyed in my youth. They have yet to confirm a date.

June 27 – E.M. says he wants to photograph an act of sodomy. He suggests I go and find a sturdy gentleman for such. I am shocked, but know just the fellow.

I am, however, overcome with fear at asking Ben. He is such a big fellow and could easily become violent if approached inappropriately. He is after all, a boxer. But I suspect that he has committed such acts and has a preference for men. I was told this by a fellow who committed such an act with the man himself. He said it was forceful but ultimately satisfying. He also commented on the great size of Ben's appendage, whose admirable qualities I have already witnessed. I take this into consideration, not only for my own curiosity, but for the quality of the image reproduction, of course.

I make a mental note to ask Ben tomorrow, at the club.

(Postscript: Ben will do it, he says, since he likes me very much.)

June 28 – We get set by first getting nude, then stretching a bit, then engaging in oral intercourse. Ben is a large man, like a pale gorilla, with muscles rippling all over his body, and an appendage that fits his large size. He has freshly shaven his head, which I find quite arousing to touch and caress.

We fondle each other in the sun, with E.'s black background making the setting all the warmer. We proceed to further oral copulation, which I find somewhat difficult, due to the enormity of his erect penis. I am shocked when the big man stands me up and kisses me on the mouth. Such intimacy affects my heart as well as my sexual organs.

Ben's member becomes quite erect, striated with a fascinating pattern of veins. E. asks me to position myself on a platform, my posterior extended. E. gives Ben some oil with which to lubricate his penis. Ben mounts me, and begins sodomizing me. It is incredibly painful, but the most passionate thing I have ever felt. Ben caresses my back and mutters pleasantries while slowly sliding his erection in and out of me. E.M. marvels at the "body mechanics" and shoots a few moments of film. Ben continues his insertions. With each thrust I find burning and tingling sensations unlike any I have ever felt. Ben had promised to be careful, but his excitement builds, and his thrusts become deeper and more vigorous, until his thrusting almost knocks me off the platform. E.M. is in a frenzy, shoving several new scrolls of film into the camera.

Ben ejaculates inside of me, making me wonder what the sperm will do to my bowels. Then Ben grabs me and sets me atop his lap, his still-erect penis planted firmly inside of me. Ben grips my erection firmly, and massages me to orgasm.

As I sit atop Ben, E. captures on film my ejaculation, which flies into the air and lands back upon me. Ben pulls out from under me and leans around to lick it up. My stomach quivers with shock. He then kisses me again! And this from a man from whom I had previously expected an assault. An assault, I suppose, but one of the passionate sort. Quite unexpected.

July 4 – Two days with the entire house to ourselves over the holiday, and my family and their servants safely miles away! Ben and I set up for me to make a drawing of him. He has stripped and oiled himself, and, to bring a fullness to the lighting, I have set a fire in the fireplace. I have also locked all the doors and closed the drapes, with the exception of upper areas for lighting.

Ben smiles and stands, and within a few minutes of my beginning hastily to sketch, Ben's penis begins to thicken, pointing forward, then at an upward, almost urgent angle. He says he can feel me "touching him" as I draw. I find myself too erotically charged to continue. I am torn between capturing his masculine perfection with my pencil and succumbing to capturing it with my hands and mouth.

We spend hours on the floor on a blanket, rutting with an animal passion I find so natural, yet I feel as if my world has been shed. Despite my hesitation, Ben offers to allow me to sodomize him. I find caressing his muscular buttocks incredibly arousing, and with some lubrication, I am shocked to find how pleasurable it is, and how much Ben enjoys it. His flexibility is such that he brings his hind end toward me with an enthusiasm that brings me to an intense climax, particularly at the moment when he cranes his face around for us to kiss while I lie atop his muscular back.

As the afternoon shifts to evening, we hear fireworks in the distance and along nearby avenues. Fresh from a bath, Ben offers to spark another session of fireworks as he flexes and masturbates for me. I hastily scrawl some drawings of his handsome form, but abandon them as Ben offers to spray his liquid fireworks on me.

All logic has abandoned my mind. I want nothing more than to be with Ben, to exercise with him, to caress him, to ingest his fluids, to be always close to the smell and taste of his body, the warm sight of his smile.

July 9 – Ben tells me at the gymnasium that he has much enjoyed our escapades with E., but prefers our private passion, and that he is looking to the possibility of our living together. I offer to find an apartment where we can live together, a lodging that does not prohibit Negroes. He takes me up on it, actually offering cash, as he makes a fair amount from his fights. He plans to move with me by the end of the month. We may have to find housing in a different part of the city, or even leave Philadelphia altogether. My family has threatened to disown me completely from its meager inheritance. I am blithely carefree.

July 12 – E.M. announces that he has decided to move to England. Ben and I seek employment elsewhere.

The Duckling and the Mermaid

Ann Dulaney

The handsome young prince fixed his coal-black eyes upon her so earnestly that she cast down her own, and then became aware that her fish's tail was gone, and that she had as pretty a pair of white legs and tiny feet as any little maiden could have; but she had no clothes, so she wrapped herself in her long, thick hair. The prince asked her who she was, and where she came from, and she looked at him mildly and sorrowfully with her deep blue eyes; but she could not speak.

—From *The Little Mermaid,*
by Hans Christian Andersen

THE PRINCE SIGHED—a lover's sigh—and turned away from the Mermaid to gaze romantically, wistfully, at the impenetrable black of the nearby window, in which the Mermaid's reflected silhouette, illumed by the single candle, was richly, gorgeously, framed. The

Mermaid stirred, refilled his teacup, and the warm wisps of her hair, like the steam from the tea, wafted over her bare shoulders to tickle away at the rounded tops of beautifully plump breasts. All evening he had longed to reach toward her, to stretch out nimble, quivering fingertips and touch that golden bosom, as an orphaned child left to fend in the cold might stretch its aching limbs toward the comfort of a grotto hearth. Her nearness, her luminous warmth, her beatified smile, and her halo of golden hair conspired to wrap him in an enduring spell of loveliness and grace. He began to compose the lyrics of his next soliloquy. He would ask, humbly yet firmly, for the Mermaid's hand in marriage.

She spoke, however, interrupting his visions with her cacophonic dialect.

"*Så Skat*, are we done with the polite conversation? I've other customers, you know. What d'ye say, love, shall we roll about?"

In that terrifying moment as he turned to her, eyelids aflutter, she crudely lifted her breasts out of her dress for him to get a good look. The tight bodice proffered her breasts most bewitchingly, and she squeezed them in her hands, as if to offer them as some sweetmeat with the tea—a serving of cream buns fresh from the oven, dark nipples like sultanas steeped in muscatel. On his tongue, he tasted roasted almond and cinnamon.

And just as quickly: the flood of embarrassment bursting upon his cheeks and throat; the delicious fire between his legs scorching him; unbearable cramps pinching the lengths of his arms and spine. He leapt to his feet—abruptly, awkwardly, like an overgrown duck, *honk! honk!*—bumping into the little table and spilling tea, which poured over his trousers and burned him quite at once. The cup and saucer clattered together.

"How dare you speak so, you vile, vile, saucy whore," he squawked. "To the devil with you!" And with that, he raced from the room, the Mermaid's robust laughter filling his ears as he fled.

Long before the Prince became the Prince, back when he lived as a peasant boy, neither more nor less—his father died, leaving him as the only male in a household of women, his mother and a coven of elder half-sisters, the products of his mother's former, illegitimate couplings. Johannes—for that was his given name, though he often went by "Johan" and sometimes "Hans"—found himself the unhappy little lord of a mean ramshackle house with but a single room for comfort, a pen with a single goat for milk, a yard with a single hen for eggs, and a hearth with a single pot in which to stew the parings of his misery.

The expectation that he begin work, the backbreaking long days of grown-up labor, weighed heavily enough upon his narrow, delicate shoulders. But what he dreamed of, what occupied his consciousness night and day, was the chance to sing. To sing and act upon a stage, to be garbed in glorious costumes, to entertain, and to be famous. Indeed, he was gifted with a most beautiful boy's soprano voice, which he exercised at every opportunity. Sadly, it was a gift wasted on the rough-hewn denizens of the countryside.

His mother worked principally as a laundress for the local highway stopover. Each day she carried out the unending task of expunging all trace of human sweat, blood, semen, and the other natural humors of a steady stream of strangers. She smoked a gnarled pipe and, being thoroughly versed in the region's superstitions and lore, often read palms and tea leaves for the occasional extra few *øre*. For the remaining *øre* that were required to round out the survival of the household, she clearly had some tertiary career that Johannes never knew of but certainly could guess at. The incessant smell about her, captured deep somewhere in the folds of her skirts, that unmistakable pheromone—it was the same odor he always found in his hands following his own innumerable private exorcisms. That odious odor, that scent of sin.

Johannes never returned home from the factory before nightfall—even in summer when the sun did not set until ten. At that late hour, his crone of a mother would still be crouched over the heavy barrel of wash, the astringent gray mist and the smoke from her pipe commingling in the rafters over her bonneted head. She looked older than her years, and in fact she was. Johannes would deposit a small package of filched tobacco into her apron pocket and fetch himself a bowl of broth. Then he would squat near her and finish his supper while his mother told him a story or two in the flickering firelight.

"Did'ye hear, there was a prince passed by here long ago, a real prince from afar, but blinded by a curse most wicked...."

He would go to bed with his mind full of these stories—tales of lost chances, of captive princesses, of ugly old witches, of cannibalism, of women with fish tails in place of legs, of women no bigger than thimbles, of ruinous greed, of unbreakable enchantment, of Seven Swans and Three Wishes. He began to write the stories down and craft stories of his own as well, and it wasn't long before a thick volume had accumulated. And when he was alone, the stories had a way of coming out: as he strolled the high path above the road on his way to the factory, he would act them out, playing each role in turn. Sometimes he invented tunes to accompany them. If anyone overheard young Johannes lifting his magnificent voice in song, they would shake their heads and laugh at his foolish ways, but Johannes took no notice. His voice and his stories were the only escapes from the tyrannies of rural poverty and his particular lot in life.

Then came a fateful day, a day when he quite forgot where he was. At the tobacco factory, he was caught singing unawares. As his carefree voice rose above the clamor of the other talk, he found himself grabbed a round the throat. Johannes's tongue flew past his lips and he found himself gasping for air.

"Gotcha, little warbler!"

"My, what a pretty songbird!"

The other workers ridiculed him then in that cruel, boastful way one teases orphans. "How pretty this one is, eh? Like a little girl. *Er du ikke en lille pige?*"

Their derision brought the sting of tears to his eyes, which in turn induced more of their mockery.

"Cry, little girl! Ahoo! Ahoo!"

He did look unfortunately feminine. In fact, he might have made quite a handsome girl if fate had only dealt him that hand—quite handsome indeed but for the long, drooping phallus of a nose. Skinny and with thick eyelashes and delicate pink lips, he stood upon awkward legs and was often prone to blushing uncontrollably. There was nothing he could do about it.

"Sing some more, little birdie-girl!"

"With that nose, he looks more like a skinny duck than a birdie. Eh? Are we a duck or a bird then? Is your shit green or white?"

"I want to see how many beaks it has. I'm betting there's only the one on its face."

A bawdy row began then, the kind that lurks beneath the

surface of any gathering of misbred and routinely besotted types with nothing but the rest of their miserable lives to look forward to. The boy soon found himself held tightly at the wrists and ankles, while other sets of hands worked to unfasten his trousers.

"What'll it be then?" called a crusty provincial who breathed the odors of cabbage and manure into the boy's nostrils. "Mayhaps she'll give us all a good ride!"

"Help!" Johannes cried to no avail. At once, he felt the stale factory air upon his legs and midsection, and he knew he was exposed to every pair of milky eyes.

"Hvad er det for noget?" one of the female workers cackled, an old hag with a puckered aubergine for a nose and cheeks flooded with bright red capillaries. She pulled at his tiny organ and waggled it playfully to and fro. "What do you call *that*?" The boy shrieked then, and finally managed to wrest himself free. He thrashed his way through the crowd and its laughter, his trousers still bagging at his ankles.

Years and years later, this memory of having been humiliated before the crowd as a boy would still filter through to him in his comfortable apartment at Nyhavn, and without fail he would grow uncomfortably hard at the recollection.

Young Johannes had struck out for Copenhagen the very next morning. His manuscripts under his arm and his tunes in his head, he left the rural slums of Odense far behind. He can still remember, days later, stalking the length of the Vestersøgade. To his left were the twinkling blues of the string of lakes that cradled the great city along its western border. It was noon and a nearby church tower was tolling the hour. It seemed to say: *"The ugly duckling is my name, but in Copenhagen I'll find my fame."*

It was a gorgeous autumn day, and the chestnut trees had sobered elegantly to bear their spiky, heavy, green orbs. He stooped to collect one that had fallen to the ground and broken open. The nugget inside was like polished oak, so smooth no woodcarver could have accomplished it. He stroked it in his palm lovingly, adoring the bells of the *klokkespil*, savoring the scent of roasting sausage from somewhere nearby, breathing the air of this glorious city that promised him the untold riches of a new life. At that moment a magpie rustled and gave a quick call from the tree. In that same moment a gorgeously weighty, ripe chestnut broke free from its parental moorings and plummeted toward its new life on the ground—smartly meeting the boy's forehead on the way down.

He found a place with the Kongelige Theater, where his fondest wishes soon unfolded. It mattered little to him that he was made to learn the roles of women and girls, for just being on stage brought infinite pleasure. It was still true that his bearings were quite feminine. So polished was his acting ability, when in costume he was often mistaken for a lass, and young Johannes endured more than one close scrape with an amorous theater patron. Still, his dreams were bright. At night, he would write in his journal, promising himself that one day the city would name its proudest boulevard after him, and he would not rest until that day arrived.

There were other things he told his diary—dark, carnal secrets. Hidden longings. His own Three Wishes. "Alas, I am still innocent," he wrote miserably. "There is a seamstress here named Ida-Marie, a runaway like me. Her hair is the color of honey, her lips are as blushing peonies touched with nectar. She is quiet, secretive. When I look at her, she turns from me but smiles. I dream she is a mermaid, and I have pluck'd her from the sea to be my one and only.

"Ida-Marie! I have only to think her name and my loins swell to fire. Even now I awoke from vivid dreaming of her—Alas! that the dream could not have continued, for it was heaven, heaven. Ida-Marie had pulled me beneath the waves and wrap't her mermaid's tail about my legs and I could not move, could not breathe. But then she set her lips upon me, and I breathed. But oh, oh! Her lips were not pressed to my own, no! Can I even reveal where her beautiful mouth was ardently fastened? For I was naked, and though the water was as chill as death, I myself was on fire, a fire as wicked and turbulent as the volcanoes of hell.

"Ida-Marie! I was in her mouth and she was taking my essence sweetly, excellently. As I write, the pain of it lingers still, lifting my nightshirt and filling me with a sense of power so intoxicating I'm certain I must die from its strength.

"There, I have discarded my night clothing and I study my body in the tall mirror as I write. My manhood stretches forth under the table, hiding in the shadows but longing, begging to be seen.

"Just now I took myself to the window and set the candle on the sill. There I spread my limbs wide apart, splaying myself for the fancy of the casual passerby. Would that sweet Ida should enter my room at this moment, at this very moment—ah! she would see immediately how fervently I desire her. She would see, and she would know—I would take her in my arms; her simple dress would soon bear the stains of my intense longing.

"Ida, Ida—! She would be powerless to deny the urgency of my seed."

The fame of the young poet, singer, dancer, actor, and storyteller spread such that before long he found himself welcomed in every house; and his stories came to be published, earning him renown among adults and children alike. Presently he even found himself in audience with the king himself. With all the goings-on, the pomp and his blossoming social life, Ida did not remain long in young Johannes's company. One day he observed in horror that her belly was rounding—and he had yet to speak his first word to her. Before the child was born she disappeared altogether. But Johannes's life was taking him in all manner of adventurous directions, and though he continued to lust for his mysterious Mermaid, the name "Ida-Marie" never entered his journals again.

One night, awakened as he often was from dreaming, Johannes raced to his journal and began to write feverishly, before the dream's details could subside. It had been about his Mermaid, who appeared to him this night in an altogether different incarnation: "She was here, she was here. She arrived at my doorstep in great distress, on the point of turning into a fantastic pink bird. Feathers emerged from behind her ears and in her hair. Her arms had turned to wings, the wings of an angel. Feathers peeped through the top of her gown, and she screamed at me to help her take it off.

"I did my best to comply, fearful all the while of hurting her unintentionally. I found, however, that the feathers had a way of coming off in my hands after a small amount of manipulation. I stroked her neck and back, and returned her skin bit by bit to its natural, smooth state. She seemed ever so grateful, yet still highly agitated. She sat herself upon my desktop, loath to soil my bed with what had become a blizzard of rose-colored feathers. I noticed that two feathers clung quite stubbornly to the nipple of each breast. I felt timid about touching these, but she begged me to. I worked them gently, but they did not come off.

" 'Oh! They pinch, they pinch!' she squealed, rosy lips pursing to my extreme delight. She held her bosom toward me, her tender nipples pursed to match her lips. 'And look: look here!' At this, she opened her legs for my inspection. A small graft of feathers, like a petite bouquet of blossoms, sprouted from the midst of her folds.

" 'What must I do?' I entreated her. I declare, I would have done anything to help her. It was at that moment that my own nudity was revealed to me. My member had burgeoned incredibly to twice its usual length and girth, but in the throes of my desire to placate her, I hardly paid it attention.

"She spread her legs as wide as they would go, grasping the nearby bedpost with one tiny foot. The toes of her other foot touched the corner of my dressing table. Her hands, no longer wings, but still dripping feathers, covered her eyes, and she could not see. 'Gently, gently!' she admonished me.

"I began to tug delicately at the little bundle between her legs. This caused her to squirm, but I do believe it delighted her as well. Keeping her eyes closed, she reached down and pulled her legs farther apart to aid me. I pulled and pulled at the feathers, toggled them gingerly back and forth. The dream was so real, I could feel moisture seeping from my temples. Her back was rounding such that her fragrant quim pointed toward the ceiling, and still I could not shake the feathers loose. She began to gasp and writhe.

"Before I knew what I was doing, the head of my outstretched member had penetrated her, a point like a lighted match. Her movements upon the desk made my member in due course sway and bob, as the tip was lying just within her entrance. Next she grasped her own feminine lips and stretched them wide, so that I could avail myself of the full view of this miracle—the feathers sprouting like a fountain from her, and my thick member lapping at its spray. I next found that if I rocked my hips a little—not too much, for the dear girl was still a virgin and I would never forgive myself for destroying that purity—but if I bucked my hips just so, that the head of my member licked softly like a tongue, the feathers became looser and looser, and I began to be able to pull them out one by one.

"Her screams and squeals were clearly those of pleasure as the feathers were gently plucked from her. The two at her breasts still clung to her, and I sought to pull at those as well. I found my attentions alternating between these three centers, until finally, with tremendous quivering and sighing, the maid was at last free from her terrible enchantment.

"She looked so happy. She was on the point of granting me my extraordinary reward when I awoke, and found myself smeared with sap."

One spring eve, Johannes wrote, "Tonight, Copenhagen is awash with mad desiring. The salt of the sea washes purely over the cobblestones, pouring in through my open window, and infecting my nostrils with that delightful urge to wander the streets and search for something to cater to my Enduring Need. I want to eat, drink, and breathe—and mate. God grant that the reign of my purity will soon end. God grant that this be the night."

He always chose carefully, a lady with honeyed hair and deep, silent eyes. He looked for a pair of lips that might firmly encircle him, a mouth that could pull him into the depths of his Charybdis and pinion him there until he spilled himself, emptying his own salt into the vast salt of her sea. But no matter how he searched, no matter whom he found, no matter how much he felt himself ready to give himself over to the Mermaid's compelling ebb and flow—once she spoke to him, with her coarse prostitute's lexicon—"Did'ye fancy a ride then, or no?"—the crystal facade would shatter into a thousand pieces. The epileptic cramping would wrack his narrow body, the phlegm would rise in his throat, and his own voice would be reduced to the honk of a gray swanling.

"How dare you—! How dare you—! You whore's daughter. You filthy, filthy slut. Take your fingers from my trousers. Let me *be!*"

And always: the furious dash from the room, the flight from the house, the cold comfort of the alley, the unchecked spasming—the spray of milk froth upon the cold, wet stones.

As his life wore on, he understood that he possessed two selves, both incomplete. His interior was a constant struggle, a continual dissatisfaction, a craving always for something that couldn't be found. His exterior, the side of him that faced the world day in and day out, that exterior that once brought unending humiliation for its gangliness and unhappy posture, had in the end become famous, not merely in his adopted hometown but abroad as well.

One fine summer evening, he stepped out of his apartment for a stroll. A small rosebush with bright yellow roses was in bloom on the sidewalk below. The blossoms had been set aglow by the dipping orange sun, and at once he found them so ethereally beautiful that tears soon soaked his cheeks. He picked one, just a small one, to take with him on his walk. Across the harbor, a lusty barroom brawl came spilling out of Den Havfrue. He stood opposite, on the safe side of the canal, and listened to the violent fisticuffs across the way. Between two fingers, he held tranquility.

He set out toward town and soon came to Kongens Nytorv, the magnificent oval-shaped plaza. He paused here and turned in a slow circle, gazing at each of the stately buildings looking down at him around the perimeter. The windows of many had turned gold in the setting sunlight. Horse-drawn carriages clattered by, but he was deaf to their noise. On the balcony of the sweeping Hotel d'Angleterre dinner parties had gathered. Fluttering parasols stood out over the balustrade like poppies on a windowsill. He watched couples chatting, lifting coffee cups and cordials to their lips, smiling, laughing. Upon the patio of the baroque opera house, more couples leaned into one another, contentedly arm in arm. He felt alone.

But all at once, he was recognized by a group of children. "Look! There's Herr A—!" They ran toward him, bouncing their ball along the ground until they clustered around him, chattering excitedly. This made him laugh his warm, pleasant laugh. He squatted on one knee to address them better. A little girl in a striped pinafore bestowed a sweet kiss upon his cheek and was surprised to find it still wet. "Oh, are you sad, Herr A—?"

"Not at all, little one," he replied. "I have never been happier."

He departed the plaza and wandered through the old town, sometimes pausing before windows that offered fine pens and writing papers or elegant books. He found himself standing beneath the Round Tower, a brown brick edifice constructed in the seventeenth century, and thought of wandering up its spiral slope to the top for a look at his city. He thought of Christian IV driving his coach and team of horses up that spiral to inaugurate the tower. The king had built the tower for his wife, who had desired a tall structure from which to better view the stars. It was a tower built for love.

But then Johannes smelled something delicious on the wind,

and remembered he was not far from Det Lille Apotek. He turned down Kannikestræde and found the tavern door wide open to admit the fresh summer air. He trod lightly down the few steps, ducking his head to avoid the low door frame, and was greeted immediately by Mettelise Hensen, who happened to be waiting at table nearby.

"Ah! Good to see you again, Herr! My, you're looking well this evening! Your usual table is vacant. Have you had your supper yet?"

Johannes smiled at her. He knew Mettelise very well. She had been bringing his meals to the little ebony table under the leaded window since she was twelve or thirteen. She now looked to be in her very early twenties, with eyes as gray as the sea and a blush on her cheek that never failed to set his heart aflutter. He knew Mettelise Hensen had no eyes for him; he was by then much more than twice her age, but he certainly didn't oppose her motherly coddling. She soon brought him a plate heaping with roasted pork and potatoes—it was always more than anyone could ever eat—and she set down a jug of rich brown ale besides.

"Mettelise," he beamed up at her, "you are a priceless pearl. Where would I be without you?" At this, he extended the rose he still carried and gave it to her. This brought on her inimitable bright smile and a fresh wave of blushing that he adored. To his immense gratification, she placed the blossom in the soft little valley of her bosom, where it could catch his eye as she attended to her other tables. Johannes tucked his napkin under his collar and attacked the steaming plate.

That night, he knew, would bring no unusual dreams. It would be the same dream he'd had all his life, his Mermaid come to visit him again. And her face would be Mettelise's, and somewhere upon her person would be the rose he had just given her. He sighed with resignation.

True enough, no sooner had he closed his eyes in sleep but the dream began. He stood upon a deep, empty stage, facing a vast sea of velvet seats. All at once, the candles at the lip of the stage, a good hundred at least, burst into flame, and he knew the play had begun. He turned upstage and saw that it had been set with decorations of the blue sea—great swaths of aquamarine silk swayed like surf. Sand lay swirled across the floor to simulate the ocean bottom.

And then she made her graceful, floating entrance. Mettelise, the Mermaid, was suspended from wires, he knew that of course, and yet the wires were so cunningly made they were practically invisible. He allowed himself to believe that she was truly swimming through the water.

Her costume was the most fantastic he had yet witnessed. A hazy shroud of pearlescent gauze was wrapped about her, dripping from her, revealing much soft, warm skin. She hovered near him, floating parallel to the floor, so that her face came close to his. Her golden hair streamed out in all directions, as if it had been spilled from a bottle. He reached up to grasp her garment and it immediately dissipated into a bath of foam and bubbled away. She held out her arms, and her breasts brushed his lips—O Beauty! he thought. Let me taste these simple fruits!

He suckled at her nipples, first one, then the other, and back again, losing his balance until he at last fell backward and was raised by the mysterious current. And so they floated together, above the stage, bathed in candlelight and the scent of brine. He buried his face in her bosom until she began to moan and sob, a delight sweeping over her he knew she could not resist.

She swam above him then, until his face came to be nestled between her legs. There he kissed her, tenderly for a while, and then so avidly his actions pushed them subtly about in the wavering air. She moved her arms and legs like a sea anemone, treading the air to steady herself, and steadily, steadily, her pleasure mounted. His cheeks were soon glistening with salt and honey, and he found he could not get enough. He wanted to enter her completely, headfirst. He wanted to dive in, give himself over to her, even if it meant his own death.

"Kill me!" he cried to her swollen lips. "I beg you! How can I be born again?"

At that moment, she lowered herself again until the two were face to face. She kissed his lips with such beauty and grace, he closed his eyes for a moment, savoring what he took to be the last moment before death.

"Look at me," came a voice just then.

He opened his eyes and found himself face to face with a being of his own likeness. His twin.

"Who are you?" he asked.

"I am yourself. It has always been thus."

But instead of giving over to dismay, the dreaming Johannes found his level of ecstasy did not diminish. He fell to ravaging the copy of his own body, attacking it like a lost love, kissing, probing. And the twin embraced him in return, just as hungrily, just as savagely. A floating Gemini of intoxicated rapture, deep beneath the surface, in full view of a vacant audience. A pair. One complete life.

And so it went. Before his virginal life reached its length of seventy years, Johannes had traveled the world and composed his own biography. In it, some events were truthfully rendered while others were...rather elegantly stylized. The conflicts of his interior self found their escapes under various harmless guises—in the twists and turns of his stories. The autobiography of the storyteller presented only his exterior self, the portions of him everyone knew or believed they knew—or, more accurately, the portions Johannes wanted known.

He titled it *My Life's Fairytale,* and to read it, one would imagine the narrator was a prince in bard's guise. A clumsy, ugly duckling grown into a regal swan. A flower among the chaff of humanity. A sweet melody blowing down the brown Danish plain, wending through the arms of remotely churning windmills, whistling down the lanes of rural Odense, and finally across the shifting seas, and beyond.

"Did'ye hear, there was a prince passed by here long ago, a real prince from afar, but blinded by a curse most wicked...."

Dietrich Wears Army Boots

Sacchi Green

THE RIDE THAT NIGHT through the forest near Pont-à-Mousson was the roughest since we had been sent into the heart of the Battle of the Bulge. In such chaos all details blur together, yet one or two, like a half-remembered face, may linger in the mind. The jeep lurched and jolted, speeding down a steep hill, swerving around a Red Cross ambulance in the narrow lane; and then came a screeching of brakes, a burst of light, and a thunderous tumult of sound.

"Crawl out," a sharp voice commanded. "Head for the shed."

And we did, on all fours in the mud, as the whistles and booms of shells echoed in the hills.

"The greater the danger, the greater the need," General Patton had told me. Not so much for the jokes, the music, even the flesh more revealed than covered by my costumes, but for release of tension of a different kind. If the troops saw that the old man was willing to send Marlene Dietrich to the front, they would reason that they couldn't be about to be destroyed.

Four shows a day we played, if we could keep our heads up long enough. Our stage was sometimes a truck bed, or tank, or even two crates turned upside down. We required little, only for the eternal rumble of guns to be muted enough for us to be heard, and for our jeep to somehow force a way through the mud or ice. But this time the cannons were much too close, the gathered men too uneasy, for us to provide anything but unwanted trouble.

"What idiot ordered you here?" a voice snapped, and muttered agreement came from the darkness where rows of helmets were barely visible. The occasional strike of a match reflected on upright rifles and glaring eyes and cast a brief glow over dirty, bearded faces. This was no time for costumes, or a comedian's patter. What could we do but sit in our muddy khakis, wait for a lull in the firing, and then leave?

But a few soft notes drifted from the accordion through the dusk—how had he carried it, crawling through such mud?—and just as softly, tentatively, I began to sing, a naughty song about listening to lovemaking in the next room. The shifting and muttering died away. Faces turned toward me, weary eyes met mine. I caressed them with my low voice, held them, drew them to me, even as the earth shuddered around us. Then, from the accordion, the lilting notes of "Lili Marlene" danced though the intimate darkness; and, as always, ghosts from that first Great War seemed to mingle among the weary soldiers of this one. Tears roughened my voice and stung my eyes as I sang, and who knows how many other eyes shared that ache? Ten minutes of blessed distraction, of reaching out to touch those tired, brave boys with my husky voice as I would have pressed my body against each and every one of them if I could; until there came an emerging awareness that the rumble of shells and cannons had retreated into the distance.

An arm reached toward me, offering a canteen. On the sleeve a band of white, with a contrasting red cross, gleamed as the beam from a flashlight arced across us. He must be the ambulance driver. Then more flashlights, and stamping, and shouts for us to scram, hurry, get out while we could.

I glanced at the face above the banded sleeve. Dark but smooth-shaven, high cheekbones, black eyes glinting below straight brows; there was something compellingly familiar about the sight of his cropped head. And so young! But I had grown as accustomed as one ever can to seeing near children sent to war. Had I met him when I visited a field hospital? No, the context was wrong, I was sure of it. If we had met, it had been in a world so different from this that we were scarcely the same people now.

Puzzlement must have showed on my face. He grinned, and winked at me, only heightening my sense of dislocation. There was no time for questions. He stood abruptly, pulling me to my feet; I saw that he was slim, and scarcely taller than I. Then he quickly passed me along the line of GIs hustling me to the jeep.

In other circumstances the many hands on my back, buttocks, thighs, would have been daring, rakish, grasping at a momentary thrill and a story to be told over peacetime drinks—if peacetime ever came. But now their touches, and mine on their arms and shoulders in return, spoke too of the grim comradeship we shared, as they hurried me away to a relative safety they would not share.

That night in my tent I shifted endlessly, the sloping ground hard but mercifully dry. Always in the distance there were guns, in one direction or another. The Calvados I had drunk for warmth lay uneasy in my stomach. If one must lie awake with visions circling through one's brain, better that they be of black glinting eyes above an oddly familiar grin than of destruction, dismemberment, death; I tried to open my mind to memory instead of fear.

Where had I known him? When? In Paris? No, the elusive image brought with it a sense of dust, and heat, and space. Casablanca? It seemed so long ago, that first show, two thousand soldiers in the red and gold Algiers Opera House, jittery with the wait to launch the invasion of Italy. A tough audience, at first, but Danny Thomas had handled them, tossed their heckling back at them, and we had played out our little drama.

First he announced that Marlene Dietrich was to have been there, but an American officer had pulled rank and claimed my… services. A wave of catcalls and boos. Then my voice, from the back, calling, "No, no, I'm here," and I myself, as the rank-pulling officer in my brand-new captain's uniform, ran up to the stage. There, in the sight of four thousand hungry eyes, I began to change from my uniform into my costume.

Down, down slid the tailored trousers; I bent to pull them

over my feet, flaunting my taut satin panties. The men shouted until the roof rattled. I would have held back nothing, but the army insisted on limits, so Danny pulled me behind a screen then, where I sat with my legs extending into public view as I rolled my nylon stockings languorously up over each smooth calf and thigh. When I emerged, my flesh-colored dress seemed made of nothing at all but scattered spangles molded to my body; the audience inhaled in unison and exhaled in an animal roar, until the piano struck the first commanding notes and I surged into "See What the Boys in the Back Room Will Have."

There was no doubt of what these boys would have, if they could, and I gave them all they could handle in a crowd. The memory gives my body warmth even now, huddled in a sleeping bag on the all-but-frozen ground, thinking of those performances, of the way it feels to present your body, your very self, to such a throng of men in acknowledgment of their bravery. To be goddess and flesh and illusion all in one, to seduce with voice, eyes, a thrust of breasts, a turn of hip and long, sleek legs—to project all your passion, and feel theirs in return, the roaring reverberations of their approval penetrating to your deepest center—this is something no single man, or woman, in one's bed can match. Although either would have been most welcome for warmth, and comfort, and distraction, on that cold, war-shaken winter night.

Which brought my thoughts back to the ambulance driver. What was it, beyond the teasing sense of recognition, that drew me so? A scent, perhaps? In war, at the front, all bodies accumulate the smells of sweat and tension. We performers were no different. But there had been some aura I should have recognized, I thought, in that brief moment when our bodies were close. And then there was his face, smooth, dark, exotic, beautiful in its way, not quite Gypsy, nor Arab; I would have known at once, I thought impatiently, in the proper context, but under fire in a forest in the Ardennes was scarcely that.

I twisted and turned, seeking a softer, warmer position. My layers of clothing twisted, too, and bunched. Ah, how my girlfriends of the infamous "Hollywood Sewing Circle" would have laughed to see Marlene bundled in army-issue woolens! But silk too is warm, and worn always next to my skin, even when I had to wash my lingerie (like my hair) in snow melted in an upturned army helmet.

What would Tallulah have thought of my frostbitten hands that no gloves could keep warm enough? Before we had met she had sent a note to me in a restaurant asking why I was wearing gloves. I, of course, had returned the note, along with the gloves themselves, on the waiter's tray. The story goes that she then returned a note saying that she would have sent me her panties, except that she wasn't wearing any—but only I know the truth of that.

Let them laugh. Nothing in my life has been worth as much as giving what comfort I could to the brave soldiers of my adopted country, who came so far from home to save Europe from, to my shame, the country of my birth. Perhaps that very fact gave my presence more meaning for them, that they could view the legs the Blue Angel would not show to Hitler, could see and hear the movie "star" (what nonsense!) who had turned down Goebbels's offer to be the "queen" of German films.

But one can be lonely even in the midst of tens of thousands of men. Perhaps especially there. I could have had my pick of them, from raw recruits to generals; when finally I dreamed, though, it was of touching a young, dark face, drawing my fingertips over cheekbones, firm lips, smooth jaw, down to the pulse in the hollow of his throat—where my hands slowed, became heavy, immovable, as happens sometimes in dreams, and try as I might I could explore no further. Such frustration! Still, when I awoke, my silk drawers were damp right through to my woolen leggings.

I glimpsed him now and then over the next few weeks, driving his ambulance as we passed the other way on a narrow lane, or unloading at a field hospital where I would be steeling myself to joke with an injured boy; or, at a GI's selfless request, speaking in German to comfort a frightened, wounded prisoner. And too often for chance I would see him far back at one of those performances in times of relative calm, when the men would put up a wooden arrow with "Dietrich Here Today" scrawled across it, or sometimes merely a drawing of crossed legs with garters. Once I had my driver stop so that I could draw army boots on "my" feet, and everyone laughed.

But he didn't come close again, or wink, or even smile, though I could sometimes feel the heat of his gaze. For some reason of his own he shunned recognition, I thought, while still being drawn, mothlike, to the flame I managed to ignite in performance, however much my teeth might chatter and my barely clothed body ache with the cold.

Then, in last-ditch desperation, Hitler's army broke through the American lines near the German border. We were sleeping in a shed, when suddenly hands were shaking us awake and voices were shouting "Clear out! Clear out!" So we went, bundling costumes and equipment with us, not realizing it was more than just another of so many such alerts.

We made it safely back to Rheims, but the young, green troops of the 77th Division did not. I wept for them, then wiped my eyes and pitched in wherever more hands were needed, winding bandages, filling soup bowls, writing letters for those who could not. In the pocket of my fatigues I felt always the weight of my pearl-handled revolver, nudging against my thigh like the touch of a deadly lover. General Patton had given it to me from his own matched set, knowing as well as I did what would be done with me if I became a prisoner. "Never believe anything I say on the radio," I had told him, "if I am captured." And so he had given me this final alternative to surrender.

Work was my alternative to despair, as weariness should have been the antidote to the longings of the flesh, but the body has its own counter-logic. I watched for the dark stranger, came to know every scrape and dent on his ambulance and the hours it was most likely to be on the road between the front lines and the hospital. When there was a brief lull in my round of self-imposed duties and I knew I must get away or crack, I would commandeer the jeep, promising our driver solemnly that I would have it back in an hour or two, and drive to a place I'd found outside the city where one could pull off onto a forest path and watch everything that passed on the road.

The first time I went, he saw me as he drove his ambulance past and raised a hand in greeting. The next time, I thought of sitting on the jeep's hood, leaning back with my chest thrust forward and my skirt pulled far above my crossed knees, "cheesecake" style, in spite of the cold. I had worn a skirt, a rare occasion these days, with just such a tableau in mind; but the crowd that performance would have attracted was not, this time, what I had an appetite for. In any case, when he went by he only nodded brusquely, his face grim and strained.

When I followed him back to the hospital it was clear why.

I went with the stretcher-bearers and did what I could, soothing, holding hands, doing my best to comfort or distract the wounded as they waited their turn for the doctors' attention. I wished I could stroke away the strain from "my" driver's face and body, but when I had a moment to look around I saw him in a corner, on his knees beside a stretcher, his expression strangely serene. I watched him tug at a narrow cord around his neck and draw a leather pouch from under his shirt, then extract some powdery materials and sprinkle them over and around the man lying before him. His lips moved in what might have been a prayer or blessing. I turned away then, feeling that my gaze intruded on something holy; and when I looked again, he was gone.

Later I had a chance to look at the soldier whose dying had been thus eased, and one mystery, at least, became clear. This face was at peace, but I had seen faces like it portrayed in war paint and eagle feathers, in paintings and in movies. And I knew, roughly, where I must have met my stranger; but still not how, or why some last block to my memory remained impenetrable.

The third time I approached the forest pull-off, the ambulance was there already. Waiting for me? I parked behind it and ran to the driver's side. The window was open.

He was slumped slightly askew behind the wheel, but there was a hint of laughter about his eyes and mouth. "Miss Frenchy," he said, "what kept you?" His voice was firm but light, more contralto than tenor, with a slight lilt to his western accent. All became suddenly clear to me. Calling me by my bad-girl-with-heart-of-gold name from *Destry Rides Again* only clinched it. There had been Indians among the stunt riders in another movie in production at the same location, and when a few of my hedonistic friends from the infamous Hollywood Sewing Circle had visited they had been enthralled by a pair of twins, brother and sister, with raven-black hair longer than the horses' manes. I knew suddenly beyond any doubt which twin now faced me.

I reached up to touch his dark cropped head. "A pity," I said, though a nostalgic tingle rippled through my body. A Canadian heiress with a similar crew cut had once offered to buy me an island in the Caribbean and build me a castle there. I stepped up onto the running board. "Do you have passengers? Is there a problem?" I knew, by now, the smell of blood, and whether it was fresh or old.

"Are you hurt?"

"Nothing much...just grazed, a stray bullet...but I'm not sure I can drive the rest of the way." Four stretchers were visible in the back, their occupants not too badly injured to be craning their necks to see me.

"I'll drive," I said, but he grabbed my elbow and leaned toward me, wincing. His injury seemed to be in his right hip.

"I just need a little help. I can't go to the doctor's, Miss Frenchy. You know I can't."

I did know it. "Wait a minute," I told him, "I'll see what I can do." I smiled at the men on stretchers and blew them each a kiss. Then I jumped down, ran to the edge of the road, and hiked up my skirt. My friend Claudette Colbert had done this famously in *It Happened One Night*—but I did it better, with longer legs. And no underpants.

The very first jeep stopped. And the next, and a general's staff car. In minutes I had arranged to send the wounded men and the jeep I'd come in back to the city without me, telling some tale about mechanical difficulties and a repair part on the way. Why I wished to wait with the driver in the ambulance I left to their imagination.

The forest path was just wide enough to move the ambulance out of sight of the main road, though with some crunching of shrubbery. Once it was safely concealed, the driver moved stiffly out of the cab.

"Drop your trousers, soldier," I said sternly, "and lean against the fender." Whether my captain's stripes gave me authority over a Red Cross driver was immaterial. "If I think it necessary, you'll be seen by a doctor, cute ass and all."

He obeyed without hesitation. His ass was more than cute; compact, muscular, but with just enough smooth flare to be unmistakably female.

"What should I call you?" I asked, working the bloody khaki undershorts slowly and carefully away from the wound. "I'm not sure we were ever formally introduced." My friend had not had any inclination to share her name, and in any case I had been much too busy with the film, and my leading man.

"Here I'm called Paul," he said. That it might once have been Paula, or some symbolic Indian name, was nothing to me, nor was there any need to rethink pronouns.

"And here I am Marlene," I said. It struck me at that moment that I was prouder of what my name had come to mean, in these last grim months, than of anything it had meant before. I knelt to untie his boots and ease them off so that his trousers could be removed, leaning my head briefly against his thigh and inhaling his pungent scent. How had I not known, that first night, that there was a woman's body under the uniform? But perhaps my own body had known well enough what my mind could not accept. It was certainly responding now.

A bone-handled knife hung in a sheath from his tooled leather belt. I handed his trousers to him, belt and all, and motioned him to the back of the truck, but he stood a moment, as beautifully natural with naked loins as his forebears, I imagined, would have been. "I would gladly have fought and killed, you know," he said, fingering the knife handle, "but there are—complications—to living among the men on the front lines."

"Yes," I agreed. "And I would guess that the army physical exam might be more rigorous than that for the Red Cross."

He concealed a wince as he swung his body up into the ambulance. I admired his smoothly muscled legs, longer even than mine. "Oh, I signed on as female," he said frankly, "but after a few transfers, who keeps track? And I had to be at the front, whatever it took, even after my brother was...was sent home."

I couldn't ask more, not yet. He lay on a pallet in the truck and I inspected his wound—and more of the surrounding flesh than was strictly necessary. The shot had, as he said, been a glancing one, cutting a shallow groove across the outer curve of his right buttock. Stitches might have been a good idea, but not required. He would always carry a scar—quite a striking conversation piece, in fact.

There were supplies racked along the sides of the canvas walls. I reached for disinfectant, and for a topic to distract him. "I saw you with that dying man," I said. "Are you some sort of chaplain, too?"

He held absolutely steady under the savage sting. "Some sort, I guess. In many tribal traditions someone like me would have been considered a shaman, or healer. I do what I can. There is no tradition I know of where the Spirit would be displeased at an offering of cornmeal and tobacco. And if a man believes his own spirit will travel in peace, then so it will."

I was kneeling with legs straddling his thigh. There was something else, I found, that I needed urgently to know. "To be such a shaman—surely it does not require—celibacy?"

He laughed, then drew in his breath sharply as I pulled the edges of the wound together and taped a bandage firmly in place. "No, it's just the other way around. What could give more healing power than the pleasures of the flesh?"

I lowered myself to rub my crotch along his thigh, and he gasped even more sharply. "I have seen you ride," I said, remembering streaming black hair mingling with a golden horse's mane as his lithe body clung to its back and then its side, seeming to defy gravity, "but today is my turn. You, as my patient, must lie absolutely still, for as long as you can bear it."

"I can still ride," he said, without enough conviction to convince me that he objected. I caressed the uninjured buttock, then pinched it soundly, and he jerked but did not pull away. I reached under his shirt to run my hands across his back, up to the nape of his neck, around very slowly to his chest, and he raised up enough to let me touch the hardening nipples on his small breasts. This told me all I needed to know. With no restraint I got his shirt all the way off, and unbuttoned my own, spreading the length of my body along his with just a slight shift so that my weight did not press on his wound. I wriggled against his warm skin, then braced myself so that I could stroke my own straining nipples across his back.

My thighs now straddled his left leg. I raised myself up higher and worked my demanding pussy along him, peering down between our bodies from time to time to enjoy the gleam of slick wetness along his thigh and up the curve of his buttock. I like to paint with my own essence on the bodies of my lovers.

And with their own essences, too. I rolled slightly to the side and drew my fingers along his inner thigh, each stroke coming closer to the source of dampness. "Tell me if I must stop," I murmured, but his only answer was a low groan and a slight lifting of his hips. I stroked deeper, probed gently, withdrew my fingers to draw glistening symbols across the curve of his buttock, then bent to lick at these shamanic designs while my fingers became more demanding.

The tempo of his groans increased in unison with my thrusts. My own need was sharp, but I quelled it in the interest of my art, and drove him onward until he forced out a tortured "Wait...let me see you..." and tried to twist around; but I leaned against him and thrust again and again, deep and hard, forcing this bravura performance to a crescendo that rocked the canvas walls around us and must have tossed the leaves on the sheltering trees.

Finally, when we had both regained some breath, I allowed him to turn over, carefully, and to fill his eyes and hands with whatever he wished of me; and, when my need could be denied no longer, to fill me with unrestrained joy as I rode his face and lips and thrusting tongue.

When we rested at last, pulling a rough army blanket over ourselves to ward off a chill we had not noticed until then, I felt blessed by the nameless spirit who had given each of us strength to do what we must in this time of crisis. Paul's work required hiding his sex, while I did what I could by flaunting mine; but still we were bound in sacred comradeship. How lucky, I thought, turning again to him, that this was a sanctity that did not forbid pleasure, but demanded it!

Back in Rheims, we labored on as we had, grasping comfort where we could. I performed privately for his enjoyment in all the illusory glamour of my costumes, as well as out of them; he, as he recovered, showed me traditional rites I doubt that any anthropologists have recorded.

The battle was close, but there was no surrender by the Allies. General McAuliffe arrived, with his famous "Nuts!" response (though what he actually said was far more colorful!) and eventually the Germans were driven back. Determined to be at the forefront when the Allies penetrated Germany, I went to General Omar Bradley at his command post in the Hürtgen Forest, and persuaded him at last to let me proceed, on condition of having two soldiers to be my bodyguards at all times.

"May I have my choice of driver, too?" I asked, and he agreed.

Fortunately, my choice was sufficiently healed by then to sit in the driver's seat. And there was never any doubt that he would guard my body, and I, in my own way, guard his, until war was only a memory, bitter but not without great sweetness.

Justine

LISETTE ASHTON

PARIS: 1789

"Sex sells!" Justine declared grandly.

Donatien squirmed in his seat. He was uncomfortable with the woman's strong language and wondered if he should leave her office. The temptation to go was so powerful it was almost overwhelming. But, because there was a slim chance she might help him realize his dream, he remained in the stiff wooden chair.

"Sex sells," she repeated, turning to face him. Her sumptuous smile gleamed hungrily as she added, "That's the direction you and I should take. We should do sex."

Aghast, he swallowed, and latently hoped the shock hadn't registered on his face and caused offense. The worry that she might be propositioning him made him feel giddy and he racked his brain for a way to politely decline.

"You're a very pretty woman," he began.

It was an understatement.

She was more than a pretty woman. She was strikingly attractive. Shards of sunlight caught the golden flecks in her sculpted coiffure and the glittering diamonds around her neck would have rivaled those same stones that had recently caused Marie Antoinette so much embarrassment and scandal. Justine dressed with the characteristic style of Parisian aristocracy. An abundance of cleavage threatened to spill from the neckline of her basque and the ripe swell of her bosom was shown off to glorious, plump splendor. The whalebone constraints of her corset had narrowed her waist to less than sixteen inches, and even for shy, reserved Donatien the temptation to trace his fingers against that svelte frame was almost irresistible. The voluptuous swags and hoops of her crinoline made her look as womanly as any of the society debutantes with whom he had ever yearned to dance. Yet Donatien kept reminding himself that she wasn't a woman: She was a literary agent.

Justine moved away from the window. Rather than resuming her seat across from him she glided to his side and perched herself on the edge of the desk. The fragrance of her perfume was rich and maddeningly exciting. He noticed her crinoline was fastened down the front, with an interlace of ribbon securing the swags of dusky silk. Because the hem of her skirt had lifted slightly, and because the crisscross of ribbon wasn't fastened as tightly as it could have been, he was afforded a glimpse of her stocking-clad ankles. Donatien blushed, crossed his legs, and glanced coyly up at her.

He kept his gaze fixed rigidly on her face and stammered, "It's very flattering of you to suggest that we should…"

She waved him silent, reached for a long-stemmed clay pipe from the table, and lit it quickly. Puffing plumes of acrid smoke into the stuffy office, she brayed caustic laughter in his face and shook her head.

"Sex sells *books*," she explained patiently. "*That's* the direction I think we should take," she continued. "I think we should get you writing dirty stories."

Donatien's relief was fleeting. He grinned bashfully, ready to apologize for the misunderstanding, then recoiled from the proposal of what she was really suggesting. Indignation and disgust fought for control of his reactions as he pulled himself out of the chair.

"I…I really don't think I could," he stuttered. "My works are an exposition of radical political theories. I'm trying to present a doctrine more revolutionary than the current vogue of equal rights. I wouldn't lower myself to…"

Justine placed a hand on his arm. Her caress was soft, as gentle as a lover's, and charged with an effervescent tingle that made the hairs on his flesh stand erect. When he glanced into her sapphire eyes her smile glimmered with a promise of sultry passion. The strength drained from his legs and, perplexed and confused, he dropped back into the chair. It crossed his mind that this shouldn't be happening to him. Women seldom noticed him, and never inspired anything like the wonderful arousal that Justine evoked. Yet she was effortlessly stirring all those unknown responses.

"Are you sure you couldn't lower yourself?" Her voice had fallen to a throaty giggle. She kept her hand on his and the feather-light contact was as arousing as her suggestive tone. "I could make you famous," she told him. "I could make you rich. Your name would be known throughout the land. Maybe around the world." With a knowing glint, she added, "You'd even see your work in print."

Donatien glared at her, despising the way she had easily managed to tempt him with his most heartfelt desire. He reasoned that it probably wasn't such a well-kept secret—he had appeared at a literary agent's office carrying a copy of his treasured manuscript—but he still wished she had allowed him the dignity of retaining a little mystery.

Putting the nuisance of his bruised ego aside, he studied her guardedly. "You could really get my work into print?"

She drew on her pipe and spat plumes of smoke with her reply. "If you can write smut, then I can get it published," she assured him confidently. Turning to the manuscript he had left on her desk, she sniffed derisively and said, "Political *merde* like this is already saturating the marketplace. Desmoulins's *La France Libre*, and Paine's *Rights of Man…*" Shocking him with another bout of unladylike behavior, she turned her face and spat onto the polished wooden floor. "They'll publish the bloody *Book of Grievances* next and then serialize it in that rag *L'Ami du Peuple*." Snorting angrily, she pointed at Donatien's manuscript and said, "There'd be another revolution if I put an unedited version of your *Les Malheurs de la vertu* on the shelves."

Embarrassed, Donatien studied his lap.

Justine placed her fingers beneath his jaw and lifted his chin. Her touch was electrifying and made fine beads of sweat pepper his brow. "But," she continued, "spice it up with a couple of naughty nuns..."

Donatien placed a hand over his mouth.

"Throw in a subplot of sex and violence," she went on. "Beef it up with a handful of gratuitous orgies, some scourging, and maybe a buggering monk or two, and I think we'll have next year's bestseller on our hands."

For an instant he forgot to breathe. To hear such horrific crudeness coming from the mouth of a woman, and an allegedly professional woman at that, was so unexpected it left him feeling ill. He knew he had to retrieve *Les Malheurs de la vertu* from her desk and flee her office as fast he was able.

But Justine's hand remained on his arm, and the contact was so blissfully arousing that he didn't dare spoil the moment. An alarm sounded at the back of his mind and it spoke with the clarity of obvious truth. If he left Justine's office now he would never see his work in print and, more important, he might never know the pleasure of the promise that glinted in her smile.

"Can you do it for me?" she asked. "Can you lower yourself?"

She pressed herself closer; the enticing swell of her bosom hovered inches from his nose. The scent of her perfume was overwhelming and made him light-headed with the temptation she presented. Peeping above the neckline of her basque he could see the dusky half-moon of an areola. The semicircle of flesh was only slightly darker than her porcelain breast but its rouge deepened with each passing second and he couldn't drag his gaze from its mesmerizing allure.

"Well?" Justine pressed. "Can you do it for me?" Waving an absent hand in the direction of his manuscript, she said, "You've proved to me that you can write. I just need to know you can write good sex. Prove that, and we're in business."

"How can I prove that I'll be able to write good sex?"

The triumph that illuminated her eyes was unsettling. "Oh! Donny," she breathed theatrically. She dropped her pipe on his manuscript, clutched his head in her hands and said, "You're a writer, aren't you? Isn't the first rule of writing that you should write what you know?"

Donatien shrugged. He had thought the first rule of writing was to have ink, sharp quills, and a good supply of quality parchment, but he conceded that, with Justine being a literary agent, she might know more about the subject. "I guess it might be," he allowed.

"Then prove to me that you know the subject," she demanded. "Prove to me that you'll be able to write good sex."

He shook his head free of her hands, sure their conversation was going around in a circle. "But how?" he asked meekly. He felt certain he had asked the question before but her ambiguity made him sure that it needed asking again. "How do I prove I can write *that sort of thing?*"

"You can start by kissing me."

Her words remained between them like a thrown gauntlet.

Courage had never been one of his greatest attributes, but Donatien knew he needed to show some spirit if he wanted to achieve his dream. Behind her, still waiting on the desk, he could see his manuscript, and it was the sight of that nearly realized ambition that made him stand up. The desire to kiss her was not forced: She was intimidatingly attractive and darkly exciting, and her nearness aroused him. And, although he had never before dared to place his lips against a woman's, Donatien pushed his face close to hers and clumsily brushed his mouth against the crimson luster of her smile.

Justine placed a hand against his cheek. Gently, but with inarguable authority, she pushed him away.

Donatien didn't bother to hide his confusion as he studied her. "You told me to kiss you," he reminded her. "I thought..."

"I told you to kiss me," she agreed. "But I never said you should start on my lips. Placing her hand on his shoulder, encouraging him to kneel on the floor, she pulled the hem of her crinoline aside and presented a polished leather ankle boot. "You can start by kissing my feet," she decided. "We'll call it an apprenticeship that allows you to work your way up."

He quashed the urge to rebel—fought the impulse that insisted he should climb from the floor, retrieve his manuscript, and then leave—and rationally considered his options. He could go and retain his precious virginity and dignity; he could go and never see *Les Malheurs de la vertu* published; he could go and never know exactly what she wanted from him, or what she was prepared to give him in exchange. But, while those potential consequences tumbled through his thoughts, it was the growing arousal within his breeches that made the decision for him. Slowly, savoring the moment, he lowered his face to her boot and kissed the toe.

Justine shivered and retrieved her pipe from the table.

He was aware of her striking another match and he could smell the acidic smoke as she exhaled. But stronger than those observations was the knowledge that she was watching him. Without needing to look up, he knew her gaze was boring into the back of his head and he felt certain she was relishing her domination as much as he was enjoying his first experiences of sexual excitement and servility.

"Kiss both my feet," she prompted. "Worship me properly, Donny."

The instruction was needless. He had already encircled her other ankle and was testing the tactile pleasure of stroking her stocking-clad flesh as he kissed again. Her responding tremors inflamed his arousal, and the bulge pressed uncomfortably within his tight pants.

"Kiss them again," Justine insisted. He could hear the breathlessness in her voice and was elated to think he had caused that response. "Kiss them again," she repeated. "And then kiss a little higher."

Obediently, he placed his lips on the tip of each boot before nuzzling her ankles. The flimsy sheath of silk stockings that concealed her flesh was an infuriating barrier and he drew a sharp gasp of frustration. The sound was lost as Justine cried out with her own mounting passion.

He dared to glance up and was amazed to see she was reaching down toward him. For an instant he dared to hope she was going to encourage him from his knees and tell him he could have her as an equal. She would encourage him to undress, they would wallow in their shared nudity, and then they would join bodies in that divine coupling he had always longed to know. The idea was quickly banished when he saw her reach for the ribbon that secured her crinoline. Justine released the tie with a flourish and the swags of silk puddled on the floor. The skeletal hoops of the crinoline followed, leaving her naked from the waist down.

Donatien stared at her and swallowed.

Noise from the bustling streets of Paris continued to flow in through the open window—and the danger of Justine's secretary bursting in on them was never far from his thoughts—but in that moment Donatien was oblivious to every other distraction. In that moment his attention was fixed firmly on the glory of her near nudity.

The stockings stopped just above her knees. They were held in place by lacy garters bound tightly enough to make her thighs dimple. Her legs were the color of the finest alabaster, a pale expanse that he yearned to touch, leading up to the haven of her bare sex.

His eyes widened as he took in his first glimpse of a near-naked woman. She was endowed with a trim triangle of golden curls, darker than the hair on her head, and slick with dewy wetness at the crotch. Behind the smoke from her pipe he could detect a subtle musk that radiated from her cleft; the scent was intoxicating. The hope that she might let him pay proper homage to her body was enough to make him shiver with anticipation. He held his breath as he gaped reverentially.

"You were kissing my ankles," Justine reminded him.

Greedily, he fell on her. The tips of his fingers traced her stockings as he delivered kiss after kiss. Barely aware that he was doing it, Donatien's hands perpetually crept higher as he brought his lips in contact with her lingerie. When his fingers reached the silky delight of her bare skin he knew it would be mere moments before he was able to press his mouth onto the blessing of her bare flesh. And, once he had properly worshipped her thighs, he would be allowed to bury his nose against the golden curls that covered her womanhood.

"Do you think you can write about this sort of thing?"

She spoke in a husky whisper, and Donatien knew she was trying to appear unmoved by his attention. Accepting the unspoken challenge that her tone presented, he tried fervently to excite her so that she couldn't conceal her response. His fingertips inched higher, sliding smoothly up the glossy backs of her thighs, while his lips finally moved past the lacy garters.

They sighed in unison.

Raising his hands, enjoying the sensation of touching her buttocks as he moved his face closer to her cleft, Donatien inhaled her delicious fragrance once again. This was the closest he had ever been to a woman, closer than he had believed fate would ever allow, and the experience was more exhilarating than his most lurid fantasies.

"Well?" she asked. "Do you think you can write about this sort of thing?"

Her speech was slurred with passion and, again, he knew she didn't expect him to reply. Sensing that her eagerness matched his own, he felt sure she didn't want him to waste his lips on anything as prosaic as words.

With his fingertips teasing against the swell of her buttocks, he cupped a cheek in each hand. When her sigh turned into a groan, he knew his massaging was the balm she needed, and he continued to caress her flesh as he alternated kisses against each thigh. His nose brushed the slick hairs over her sex, and they both shivered in response to that small pleasure. But it was in that moment of shared delight that Donatien finally found the strength to pull away.

He remained on his knees, hands holding her buttocks and the promise of her sex only inches from his mouth. He wanted to continue, he longed to taste the sweet musk that fired his passion so ardently, but the need to appraise her pulled more strongly. Gazing up at her, determined to savor the image of her naked beauty forever, he was not surprised to see that she was indulgently pleasuring herself.

Justine's arms were folded across her chest—the pipe had been discarded, its smoldering coals burning pockmarks in the title page of *Les Malheurs de la vertu*—and she had released her breasts from the basque. Cupping an orb in each hand, stroking her thumbs back and forth over the erect nubs of her nipples, she didn't bother to glance down at Donatien as he studied her with genuine reverence.

Savoring the image, he squeezed her rear, allowed his fingertips to slip into the crease between her cheeks, and then buried his face against her sex. The folds of flesh were slick with excited wetness as his tongue eagerly explored her juicy depths. Drinking the flavor of her desire, tracing his tongue against the slippery bliss of her labia, he marveled that his life had been spent bereft of this simple, incredible joy. He was tempted to think that he and Justine might become regular lovers, but her attitude left him in no doubt that this would be a unique liaison. And, because she was the only woman who had ever shown any sexual interest in him, he feared this would be his life's single experience of physical intimacy.

"That's it, Donny!" she gasped. "That's just right!"

Her exclamation snatched him from his reverie, and he smiled grudgingly. He had been able to tell he was doing it right from the tremors that bristled against his tongue and the fresh flood of wetness that lathered his cheeks and mouth. The pulsing nub at the center of her sex throbbed urgently as it declared the onrush of her orgasm, and Justine's encouragement warmed him.

"That's exactly what I need from you."

Her speech had been slurred before, but now each syllable came as scarcely a grunt. Judging by the convulsions that racked her body, it was clear she was in the throes of an extreme response, and he struggled to kiss her more forcefully and make her ecstasy complete.

At the height of their passion, with his tongue writhing mercilessly in the deepest confines of her sex and Justine squirming wantonly against his face, he tasted her orgasm. She came with a shriek that echoed around the dusty bookshelves and probably startled some of the passing peasants as they bustled along the busy streets.

He clutched her buttocks tight as the climax rushed through her. At the same time, he kept his mouth pressed hard against her wetness. She tried to move away, the tremors of her arousal fighting for dominance, but, because he was determined to please her, Donatien remained in absolute control. He teased the thrust of her clitoris with gentle flicks of his tongue, and was rewarded by her heartfelt screams of gratitude. He only stopped when she whispered that she was spent and told him he no longer needed to remain on his knees.

Donatien climbed from the floor, not sure what to expect. His heart pounded with the fervent dream that she might take him in her arms. He studied her with undisguised hope.

"You never answered my question," she reminded him.

He graced her with a sad smile, knowing she had no intention of dealing with his arousal, and not really minding that injustice. The pleasure of satisfying her, the unconscionable joy of doing her bidding, had been sufficient reward in itself. He was pleased it had been good for both of them because he now knew it was something he would never experience again. Admittedly, she had made him want more—he had yearned to feel his own flesh pressed within hers, and know the sweet joy of true physical intimacy—but the small taste she had allowed him was enough to sate a lifetime's appetite, and he could imagine himself writing a thousand variations on this memory that would more than match the pleasure of a repeat experience.

"You never told me whether you think you'll be able to write good sex."

"You were the judge," he said coolly. "Do you think I'll be able to do it?"

She looked set to respond, then hesitated, as if reluctant to give praise. "We can set you an assignment," she decided, "and see how you succeed." Shuddering with the last vestiges of her climax, taking a deep breath, and once again donning her cloak of professionalism, she said, "But I think we'll need to build you an image." She shifted away from the desk and quickly went about adjusting her clothes.

Donatien watched her slip her ample breasts back into the corset, then quickly don the hoops and silk of her crinoline before refastening the lace. Her haste was so proficient it was almost unseemly and he realized it took less than a minute for her to disguise all traces of the sublime intimacy that they had just shared. If he had been cynical he might have put it down as another skill that could be attributed to all literary agents, but he would never let himself think of her in such a callous way.

As soon as she was properly dressed, Justine began to circle him. Her gaze flitted from his face to his frock coat and then his breeches. Donatien tried not to be unnerved by the lascivious lilt of her smile. "Now that newspapers are becoming more popular," she began, "I believe that image is everything."

"Image?" he repeated doubtfully.

"Maybe we can give you an infamous little history," she continued. "We can say you've spent time in mental hospitals, maybe even say you escaped the Bastille before it was stormed—

that would add color." She was obviously excited, possibly as filled with passion as she had been when she reached her climax, and she spoke with inelegant haste as she bombarded him with her ideas. "Perhaps we can publish something really vile and outrageous, and say it's a lost manuscript that you penned before escaping a death penalty. How does that sound?"

Donatien's doubts began to resurface, but he could see a way around that small problem. It would be a shame not to enjoy the fame she was suggesting, but he was loathe to bring notoriety to the simple folk of his home village. "I'll want a pseudonym," he said quickly.

Justine nodded. "You'll *need* a pseudonym," she told him. "Donatien is a weak name. Your full name, Donatien Alphonse Francois, makes you sound like a trio of suspect coiffeurs. Readers will think you're a *pédale.*" She clapped her hands together as a smile illuminated her face. "We'll give you a title," she declared. "The peasants just love to be offended by the excesses of the aristocracy at the moment. It's all you can read in the damned papers, and I don't think they'll ever grow tired of printing the same old *merde*. We can give you a title and use that as your springboard to notoriety."

"A title?" Donatien said warily.

"How about the *Comte?*" Justine grinned. She raised her eyebrows and then winked. "How does that sound?"

He thought about her suggestion for a full minute before replying. Her idea was sound, but the name needed something else. And, if she was going to sell his books on her image of notoriety, then he thought the name ought to be stronger and more distinctive. "How about the *Marquis?*" he returned. "If you're going to give me a pseudonym, why don't you call me the *Marquis?*"

Seeing the glint of approval in her smile, Donatien dared to add a final detail. He didn't want his intended infamy to reflect on the people of his village, but he didn't think it would hurt to add the color of that borough's name. It would certainly make his *nom de plume* sound more commanding. Returning her grin, he said, "Why don't you call me the *Marquis de Sade?*"

Olympia Bears Fruit

Jane Graham

IT IS WIDELY HELD that the Slavic languages are by their very nature vulgar, while the Latin tongues contain the lyricism of love and its pursuit. In France they pour forth sonnet after sonnet proclaiming Paris as the city of romance; I maintain that Paris is a hive of dissolute decadence, the riverbanks of the sluggish and polluted Seine caked with its filth, and its mother tongue the natural voice of the lascivious.

I remember very little of my life before I arrived in Paris, but while I have not since known any other place to call "home," I have never felt entirely at ease in this great, bustling urban mass. My parents came here, penniless and bewildered, from our native Poland, along with myself and my two elder sisters; another sister was born shortly after our arrival. We were peasants, of Gypsy descent, wholly unaccustomed to city living and ill equipped for the perverse foibles of metropolitan France.

Masha, the eldest sister, wasted no time once she came of an age able to exploit her naturally ample assets, and posthaste got down to the business of finding herself a man capable of pandering to her tastes, which increased at a rapid pace with every promenade she made. She was an inveterate window-shopper, often to be found stalking along the Champs Élysées, marveling at the horse-drawn carriages and gazing with covetous eyes into the displays of the new department stores, in which are contained surely the real wonders of this novel and sparkling time, making mental note of all she wished to have. It seemed her single desire was to lose every trace of that farm girl she had once been. She was, however, shrewd enough to retain a little of her heritage, in the form of various herbal brews strong enough to undo those indiscretions which, if left unchecked, would have halted her dubious career some nine months later.

I, on the other hand, gravitated toward a more clandestine Paris, finding myself in smoky basements and rowdy cabarets where revolutions were plotted and anarchist tracts peddled. I longed to be an artist but knew I would never gain admittance to the exclusive Académie des Beaux Arts. I hung around Montmartre and its cafés, *ateliers*, and squares, hoping to gain some kind of entrance into their world. Its door remained firmly shut to me, however, until a chance meeting one day altered my fate forever. It began with a dispute in a bar whose clientele trod the fine line between artistic genius and pure psychosis, where I rescued a strange, shrunken man from a violent beating. Thanking me profusely, the man inquired as to the name of his knight in shining armor. "Stefan Malinowski, at your service," I replied, and placed my hand firmly in his own peculiarly shaped palm, whereupon he introduced himself simply as "the Count." Under the tutelage of this stunted, horribly deformed yet hopelessly charming aristocrat I fell deeper and deeper into the decadent underworld of Montmartre, his domain one of prostitutes and pimps, aesthetes and anarchists, flower girls and *flâneurs*.

The Count was what you might call a "hobbyist" of the Pigalle area, not tied to its clubs economically yet following the twists and turns of the inhabitants' sordid lives avidly, as one devours penny novels picked up at any newsstand. Despite his obvious health problems he was possessed of an immense energy, and I do not recall ever hearing him suggest taking himself "off to bed," though the thought of jumping into another's fine linen sheets seemed often on his mind. When I once asked him if he felt vulnerable in some of the more shifty neighborhoods he frequented, especially with his recurrent ill health and diminutive stature, he told me he preferred them to others because they were always so busy and well lit, no matter what time of night. He found this of all the worlds he inhabited to be the one where he could feel most at ease, where his affliction was not constantly gazed upon in shock, horror, or distaste, and the constant hustle and bustle, far from unnerving him, wrapped itself around him like a well-worn blanket and made him feel safe. He told me his closest and most genuine friends were to be found there.

I understood vaguely, though he mentioned little of them, that the Count had quite a considerable independent income from a wealthy, landowning family in the south. At the time, though he sketched and painted obsessively, he had not yet received anything like the recognition he was to find later in life.

"Stefan, I hope you have nothing planned for this afternoon. I have something a little out of the ordinary in mind."

In that esoteric way he had of forming statements, the Count announced to me one afternoon as we were taking coffee in our usual meeting spot that he had been so forward as to have made an arrangement for the both of us. The Count loved secret assignations, and I invariably played along obediently. Perhaps, I thought, like Baudelaire's *flâneurs*, we might take a trip through Les Halles in order to promenade up and down in front of the dolled-up windows of Liberty's department store, shocking the shoppers with our extravagant manners. Or maybe a tour of his favorite whorehouses, where we were treated more as family than paying customers. But no, the Count uttered in a low voice as he took care of the bill. He had someone he would like to introduce me to.

We left the café and I followed him, as he limped and waddled down alleys and narrow streets, into such a maze of walkways that even I, an habitué of Paris, had trouble following our direction. I am unusually tall, and what a sight we must have made, the penguin and the stork, padding our way through Montmartre on a cold and wet February afternoon. Finally he led me up a dark staircase in a narrow building with a vile, ill-mannered concierge, rotten banisters, and the aroma of overripe oranges, to the top floor of a building in the Rue de Douai. He knocked on a dingy door.

Slow footsteps moved toward the two of us on the other side of the panel. A stooped, wrinkled, and almost bald woman peered at us through the crack before opening the door just wide enough to allow us entrance.

"My dear Victoria," cried the Count with overdone theatricality, opening his arms wide in an embrace. He fumbled in his pocket for a package which, upon locating, he handed over to her with a flourish.

"Henri! Chocolates!" said the woman, for it was a woman, under her mask of age, and a twinkle in the eye emerged when she heard the familiar voice of my colleague.

The Count introduced me to his special friend, who led me into her apartment and enjoined me to sit. I had to bend my head; the sloping roof was so low there was no room for me to stand at full height. There was a small table over by the window with three spindly chairs, one of which I gingerly lowered myself into. A makeshift line of much washed, graying laundry hung morosely across a narrow, unmade bed.

While our host found some cups in the flotsam of dirty dishes stranded next to the sink, the Count whispered in my ear.

"That—" he pointed at the feeble old lady stooped over the trough, "—is Victorine Meurend, the model for Manet's *Olympia*."

I could not quite believe it. So this was the Count's game, to show me the end which all youth must inevitably reach! My hostess's wrinkled hands, the skin toughened to rawhide, shook perceptibly as she rinsed out the rough beakers. I was in the presence of infamy. Victorine Meurend, whose disrobed form and direct gaze had so shocked the art world years before, shuffled her way back to us, placed the beakers on the table, and sat down. The Count brought out a small bottle from his inside coat pocket and filled the cups with the green elixir that was to be his downfall, absinthe.

Mademoiselle Meurend guzzled her drink greedily, pulling her head back and sighing. "Ah," she murmured. "That hits the spot."

I got the impression the little old lady had emptied more bottles than this in her time.

"You must tell me, my dear boy," she implored me, bending her body forward. "I am unable to get out as much as I would like, but Henri has told me of this new erection—" she enunciated this word with particular care, as if its utterance in the presence of young men gave her a perverse pleasure "—built for the Great Exhibition by a Monsieur Eiffel. Have you seen it, or walked up to its top? I understand you can see the whole of Paris from there, laid out such as only the gods have before viewed it."

I nodded. "It is true, though I have never attempted the climb myself. Surely, a miracle of modern engineering, one which shall be marveled at for many years to come."

"We have a little deal, Vicki and I," explained the Count, changing the subject impatiently, as if bored with the constructive follies of the Monsieur Eiffels. "She tells us her stories if we tell her ours. Please, Stefan, go first. And make it something juicy. Dear Victoria here can't walk down the stairs too easily, as she just pointed out, and it's years since she had a man, or set eyes on any kind of erection."

The Count was a devil for finding puns, the baser the better. The old woman cackled lewdly.

As the absinthe relaxed my nerves, I began. I recalled the outrageous behavior of last year's ball at the Académie des Beaux Arts. It had been held at the Moulin Rouge, and, while I had always looked enviously through the gates of the school where, through parentage, I was denied access, I was delighted to gain admittance to this exclusive party thanks to my association with the Count. It was a costumed ball with the theme being the fall of Rome; I pandered to the Count's wishes by dressing as an armored general and he as my slave. We were masked, and the anonymity let my normally shy nature grow in confidence and excitement. Finally I could free myself from the shackles of my impoverished upbringing.

As always, the climax was the presentation of the artists' models, carried in by a long procession of art students who offered them up onto the stage almost naked. By the end, the ball had disintegrated into intoxicated riotousness. Young women were being stripped and molested by gangs of precocious students. The police were called, arrests were made, and many needed hospital treatment.

"And you?" asked the impatient Mademoiselle Meurend, listening avidly.

"I failed to notice the law's entrance, I'm afraid," I conceded. "I admit that, awestruck as I was to be allowed into such circles, I was quite appalled by the depths to which my betters had descended. Fearing arrest even before the uniformed lads arrived, I hid myself under the stage. It had grown very dark when I realized there was someone else pinned to my side; soft hair brushed against my naked arm and a perfume of the kind used by a female made my nostrils flare. In the dimness I saw her ringlets of auburn hair, her barest excuse for a dress almost torn completely off, her porcelain skin radiating its whiteness, and the very devil took hold of me.

"Perhaps she mistook me for someone else; perhaps she didn't care. I am a little ashamed at my lack of manners, or the haste to which I got to it; I believe it was the sense of danger that drove me, or the thrill of my masked identity. I felt as if the whole order to which my life had been set were collapsing, and in that split second a hot-breathed, almost hysterical little redhead, her body bared to mine, appeared in my arms, malleable and giving.

"I was crouched in a small corner, my legs slightly pulled up toward my chest and my sandaled feet pinned against the side wall. This budding nymphet reached beneath my Roman skirt, searching for my foot soldier, who, upon his summons stood immediately to attention, responding promptly to her tender yet direct touch. Impetuously, Redhead took hold of my brave recruit with both of her tiny hands, the pair of them scarcely containing him, and guided the bold fellow, who moved toward his fate fearlessly, into her sweetest, most terrible place.

"This doll-like creature was so light that I could perch her atop my thrusting form in my cupped palms, swiveling her buttocks upon my swollen staff while she curled her gymnastic legs around my neck. Her body gave forth an animal scent I remember from our Polish farmyard, of adrenalin and fear, and yet as my lips located her quivering bosom, I found she tasted as if she had been dipped in the fruit punch (as well she might have). What's more, the triangle of hair which adorned her entrance was as soft and downy as gosling feathers.

"A violent, yellow ray of light, almost certainly from a police lantern, shone suddenly on the region where union was being reached, illuminating it in a probing globe. I saw everything in stark clarity; suffice it to say, my miss was not a true redhead. She seemed scarcely aware of the probe to which her most intimate areas had been subjected; her thick hair tumbled over her features, and she was lost completely to the pursuit of pleasure. The policeman passed us, and we dissolved into the shadows again. With her hands grasping my shoulders, I felt her grip tighten around my manhood with a burning desperation I had only before dreamed of, and as finally I released the seed of my unholy desires within her, she throbbed uncontrollably as if it were not just the Academy which had descended into chaos and perversion, but the very pattern of the universe that had been disrupted. Elsewhere in the room were the awful sounds of the riotous mob—a terrible drone, as of humanity ceasing to act as individuals—and yet my divine redhead simply whimpered softly. When the area had been cleared, she was already gone, and though I am certain that if I could only smell her hair again I would know it, I admit ashamedly I couldn't recognize her face for all the tea in China."

"Ha-hah!" chuckled the Count, who had already heard this story several times before. "Your initiation was the complete success I knew it would be! It was probably that tight little pussy that saved you from arrest."

The woman clapped her hands in delight. "What a glorious account! And how wonderful of you not to hold back when speaking to me, as so many do when in the company of ladies!"

I blushed and looked at her tiny feet, only just peering out from a mass of long skirts and petticoats. Here she was, Olympia, clothed so not even the merest inch of leg was visible. I had not meant to speak so candidly; the absinthe had made me reckless.

Then it was the Count's turn. With aristocratic elegance, he told us both of his latest foray into the brothels. He recounted every aspect, every scrap of chipped paint, every laddered stocking and every wilted lily, with a loving tenderness and an obsession for detail. With eyes half-open as if lost in the recollection, he began with the corpulent, greasepainted madam and the way her heeled feet clanked on the marble-tiled hallway, the way her obscenely loose buttocks sagged through her almost transparent negligee. He had no wish to indulge in intercourse with these women, he confessed; to become so close was to make it almost impossible to admire fully their shapes, their gestures, their peculiarities. Their lush, pink fruits set off by the tilt of their chins, or gently opening labia, glistening so as to hint at the treasures within, framed by a gloriously arched back. Rifling through his many disordered pockets, the Count showed us his sketches, drawn in haste on anything—napkins, menus, receipts for drinks bought, torn-off portions of tablecloth—fascinated as he was by the ladies of the night. So used to him by now were the ladies that he had become one of their own, petted like a favorite dog. Though they acted in a staged, prescribed manner while with their clients, they disregarded such protocol around their dear diminutive Count, and so he gained access to their private domain, witnessing a far freer view. He took a particular delight in watching their naked forms as they dressed and undressed, discarding the choreography of the stage and instead finding the shape necessary for the task at hand, twisting themselves into wholly private, introverted poses.

"On this particular night, I believe a little too much drink found me tucked up in a vacant bedroom," the Count elaborated, giggling like a schoolboy. "I roused myself upon hearing the cooing of females in the company of their kind, and at once became inquisitive. The two rooms adjoined, and were separated only by a flimsy screen; through its narrow slats I witnessed an ingenuous pair of young tarts, between customers and washing themselves. It touched me to see how they assisted one another, the one soaping the other as she, in turn, made sure her colleague would emerge clean as a whistle. You can imagine how such a display of female collaboration fascinated me! Out came the spout, firm as bronze and bold as brass, as the fair-haired of the couple got stuck into rinsing the soapy bubbles from her raven-locked girlfriend. She pulled her legs far apart so the job could be done proficiently, allowing me a vista of divine proportions, fresh, and tender, and slowly growing rosier as her girlfriend's attentions caused the blood to pump stronger into the region....

"...And I stroked and I blessed that great spout of mine, and as the last of the soap bubbles were wiped away, I let it pour...."

The Count's deep, bellowing laugh was simply Bacchanalian as it resounded around the small room. "...But oh, how I smudged my sketch.... See where it's stuck together," he admitted, flaunting his vice like a triumphant adolescent.

Vicki, as the Count youthfully called her, began last. As the Count's eyes began to glaze over contentedly I could see that it was always like this—every time saving her story until the end and every time the same, akin to a lullaby for the great artist himself.

With leathery yet still slender fingers she plucked a moist, dark chocolate from the opened box in front of her and placed it in her mouth, beginning to speak while her orifice was still full, though the cocoa beans seemed to enrich her speech rather than impede it. Engrossed as she was, as the chocolate smeared around her lips I soon forgot her grotesque caricature, her obscenely hairless head. I closed my eyes and listened, not to the coarse, crackly voice of a septuagenarian but to one thrown back into her youth, eager and lilting, filled with vigor.

" 'Why do you sit in so demure a manner?' Manet would ask me, goad me, as I modeled for his great work, *Olympia*. 'Is that how you were sitting in the window, looking out with the wish to ensnare a gentleman, that night I first noticed you? Let's shock Paris! Don't lower those beautiful eyes of yours, but eat me with them. As if you are saying, you can have me, but you can never keep me.'

" ...It was all talk, of course. He dallied, my dear Édouard, but never committed. He never knew which way to turn—toward bohemia or the Establishment. Finally, he chose the Establishment. I was the sacrifice.

"The studio was always filthy, because Manet never stopped work long enough for it to be cleaned. The floors, the walls, all were caked with paint, and in the corner a cracked sink was so full of saucers, rainbowed in oil, one could barely locate the taps. Dear Édouard, he flirted constantly with libertarian values, but he was at heart a conservative, unable to shake the rigid rules of his upbringing. He had been married some years before and would run out on his family from time to time, get drunk with Baudelaire, complain bitterly about the restraints of conformity, then retreat again with his tail between his legs, full of remorse and embarrassment.

"We had had something of a conspiracy going with the paintings he produced of me, a little standing joke at the rigid rules of the art world. There I was, as naked as the day God made me, enjoying a picnic in the park. That raised a few eyebrows at its unveiling, let me tell you! Yet in all that time we had never become physically close. I knew, of course, he wanted me. I had seen the way his eyes lingered over certain parts of my body as the sable hairs of his brush caressed the canvas, how, with a sigh of frustration, he would thrust violent hues of oil into my image; and how he would walk over to where I lay, immobile, and hold his brush maybe half an inch away from my unclothed body in an attempt to better understand an angle or to confirm a measurement. Artists, as you both know, talk a lot about negative space, the area around the objects represented which can only be described by its lack; there is always so much going on inside that negative space. For the two of us, Édouard and I, there was a tornado of yearning and desire building up, something which could not be given expression by any number of lines traced onto paper or canvas.

"Édouard waited until *Olympia* was almost completed to make a move. I was ready and waiting.

"I arrived for work that morning as usual and undressed behind the screen. When I walked out, naked as the day I was born, I saw that Édouard, rather than being clothed in his painter's smock and filthy, oil-spattered moccasins, was dressed from head to toe as the perfect gentleman, right down to the hat and the black polished boots! Laughing, I asked him what in heaven was going on.

"'My dear Victorine, we are going on an outing,' he answered.

"'But I have nothing to wear!' I complained.

"Édouard had brought me an outfit which belonged to his wife, and begged me to put it on as quick as I could, for there was no time to waste. So there we were, traveling in style, in a hansom cab pulled by two young colts, to the Bois de Boulogne, the painter and his studio rat—that's what they used to call us models back then—dressed the very picture of gentlefolk. I even swung my parasol, as in a painting by Seurat!

"It was the weekend. Out in the park, nannies strolled by with infants in baby carriages, young boys flew kites, ladies riding sidesaddle cantered past with their colts and fillies, flanks glistening, and courting couples floated arm in arm as if on air. The boating lake was filled with giggling lovers letting their oars rest for a moment or two to grab a stolen embrace. We sat down on a blanket beneath a grand old beech tree, its branches forming a cradle above us. We had strawberries, just ripened so the juice drips onto your fingers when you pick them from the basket. A faint breeze was stirring. It was a fine afternoon.

"My borrowed outfit consisted of many petticoats layered

underneath the lace-trimmed dress, maybe five in total. Édouard said he had mislaid a strawberry and wouldn't be satiated until he had found it. I asked him if another one would do, they were all perfectly delicious, but he said that he must have this one.

"Suddenly he dived under my skirts, presumably after the missing fruit. I felt a tickling between my legs and the urge to open them out a little more. His whiskers, then his tongue, were upon me. All around were the faces of genteel society, slowly fading out of my consciousness as I felt only pleasure, hot and damp between my thighs. The giggling of children and the cooing of babes merged into one note of urgent lust. The sun's rays sheering through the old beech's branches seemed to be radiating from the triangle beneath my petticoats. He used his tongue as he did his paintbrush, with assured dexterity and firmness, first flicking the tool lightly over the whole canvas and then working harder and more intensely on the focal point of the piece, which he painted a throbbing and impassioned scarlet.

"...It was almost as if my body were split into two separate entities—above the waistline of my many skirts, I still projected the facade of a gentlewoman lunching in the park, while below, oh, below, it seemed as if Bastille Day were being celebrated, fireworks were going off so....

"As I peaked, a little boy's balloon, escaping from his grasp into the sky, burst on the branches of our tree."

The old woman paused for a moment to catch her breath, repositioning herself on the chair and taking a sip of her drink. She gave another small sigh of pleasure before continuing. I tried to hide the obvious bulge in the crotch of my trousers, a little disturbed by the feelings such an elderly lady was capable of awakening in me.

"Emerging from under my skirts, Édouard's face had taken on a terrible demeanor, his temples bulging with reddening resolve," the speaker took up her tale again. "He grasped my arm with a ferocity I had never before witnessed in him, pulling us both to our feet. The basket of strawberries tumbled, unheeded, over the grass. We went in search of wilder, more secluded regions.

"As you are both aware, there is a part of the Bois which is less tended, more overgrown, where couples do more than stroll arm in arm and nannies dare not take their little charges. Édouard and I gathered up my skirts and walked with a singular purpose toward the enclosed privacy of the copse, and, dispensing of all formalities, I laid myself upon the woodland floor, the leaves attaching themselves to my by-now disordered hair, as Manet unfastened the required tool. Swollen impatiently as it was, there was no doubt in my mind of its intent. We lifted the many skirts, wrestled with the silk of my stockings, until finally the jewel could be prized from its setting....

"Already primed, I felt as agony the brief moment of time spent unfilled. As my entire being tensed with impatience, he thrust himself into me. Oh! At once I felt rooted to the spot by a great surge, like an electric shock. He filled me with a white heat which penetrated my very core. We heaved together like animals, oblivious to all but the force which was pulsing between us. I pushed my hips up toward him, lifting my padded rump from off the grassy ground, reaching up like a magnet—I was insatiable, unable to get enough of him pounding and pounding into me until I gasped for air and the sweat began to drip down the side of my face. I looked upward at Manet for signs of recognition, and yet this was no conservative gentleman pinning me to the ground, but a purely primeval being....

"...Convulsing terribly, Édouard emitted an impassioned cry which seemed to come from deep within. I felt the release, and then it was all over. His face was once more calm, his grip competent, his hands no longer shaking. I sat up, noticing that the sun was sinking toward the horizon and the park emptying as dusk began to fall. We had been here longer than I had thought. Manet, my Manet again, the one who observed me with a critical eye as he sketched my outline, replaced a wayward pin into the captive bonnet of my hair.

"So you see," the speaker reflected, "despite all we went through, I never did look upon my dear Édouard naked. After our picnic in the park he finished the painting in a matter of days, as if by unleashing that desire he had slotted the last puzzle piece into the portrait. He finally turned the easel around to me where I lay, and that gaze he had caught, with all its cocky confidence, took my breath away. It held me captive, an unwilling double, so that I had no choice but to stare into the eyes of that unrepentant mirror image.

" 'Now, you see, you will be young forever, *ma chère*,' he said to me, smiling. 'This is the one that will make you immortal.' That day in the Bois he had told me I was the most narcissistic person he had ever met.

"I left Paris soon after, unable to cope with the outrage generated by *Olympia*. Manet had his wife, of course, and retreated into respectability once the scandal had peaked. As an artist he was great, as a lover he was breathtaking, but as a man he was weak: I couldn't lean on him for support."

I opened my eyes from the reverie engendered by my own vision of *Olympia*, so different from the one sitting in front of me, chocolate and absinthe dusting her aging lips, and took a sip from my drink. The storyteller's dress had pulled up ever so slightly and I caught a glimpse of fawn stockings crinkled over septuagenarian ankles. The Count, like a lecherous satyr, was running a fat paw over that bulging crotch of his.

"Ah, Vicki," he murmured, "you still have the ability to gaze directly into my very soul."

"And you return that gaze better than most," the elderly lady replied, "even to a discarded old studio rat like myself."

He took three cigarettes from a slim silver case and, lighting them, handed one to each of us, as if in homage to the celebrated act. "But this rat must not forget," Henri de Toulouse-Lautrec reminded Victorine Meurend, "my generous purchase of *Olympia* for the Louvre. The piece is an education in itself. Manet was right, *ma chère*. You will be young forever."

The Rival

NEAL STORRS

MY MOMENT OF TRIUMPH AT LAST DRAWS NEAR. Tonight will mark the first occasion on which my beloved and I have been together in much too long a time, and the first time ever that I have been with her *chez elle*.

If I make it there alive and in one piece, that is. The innkeeper assured me that the distance from La Châtre to Nohant is scarcely more than five kilometers, but walking a country road at three o'clock in the morning is not a genre of activity to which I'm accustomed. Fortunately the night was warm for early May. Warm, but blacker than sin. I was feeling, not seeing, my way. I'd be lucky not to take a tumble and wind up in a ditch, my head cracked open against some rock. Like her father. Finding an escort at the inn would have been simple enough for a person of my qualities, but the business I was on was not of a nature that called for the presence of two.

Was she even expecting me? I was no longer sure. Her last

letter made it sound as though she couldn't wait to hold me in her arms again. She would smother me with kisses, she wrote, suck me dry (like the vampire people accuse her of being, and there's more truth to *that* than anyone will ever know), twist her long black locks around my neck and choke me to a divine death. It was like reading a page from one of her novels. Better, actually, because while reading her words I was able to reconstruct—in exquisitely delicious detail—the things we had done to each other the last time we were together.

It was at the Comédie, following a performance of *Figaro*. She waited until the theater was empty before coming backstage to my dressing room. I had removed most of my costume and was beginning to wipe the rouge from my cheeks when I saw her reflection in my makeup mirror, slipping silently through the door.

I pretended not to notice. I preferred the illusion of reacting with surprise to her touch.

When it came, it was with an intensity that betrayed her need as being, if possible, even stronger than my own.

She wrapped her arms around me, pinning me to the back of the chair, then sank her mouth into my hair, her tiny teeth pressing into my scalp with such force that I could not but emit a cry that was an equal mixture of pleasure and pain. She yanked my head backward, covering my face with a succession of violent kisses. My chair tilted precariously as my lips groped hungrily for a space of exposed flesh upon which to reciprocate. The moment in which they found their sweet reward was the same one in which I lost my balance and fell to the floor.

Laughing, she threw herself on top of me, her backside buried rudely in my face. As I was already half undressed, her mouth had little trouble completing a speedy journey to its destination between my legs, which were spread wide apart in anxious anticipation. So expert were the ministrations of her lips and tongue upon my sex, and so tantalizing the feeling of her bosom crushed against my belly, that my body soon tingled with waves of intense pleasure. Although she was relentless in her attack, I am not inclined to long endure such a posture of submission. Also, I wished to delay my gratification so that my release, when it came, might be all the more satisfying.

Summoning every ounce of strength in my possession, I

threw her off me. Then, taking advantage of my superior weight, I pinned her body to the floor. Hastily disposing of several layers of clothing, I set about arousing in her the same condition she had lately brought about in me. After licking my way up her satiny inner thighs, I fell upon each of her breasts, nuzzling and biting each in turn until her areolas had darkened to a deep crimson, and her nipples jutted outward to their maximum length. Satisfied with my accomplishment, I flipped her onto her belly, thrust my hand between her legs, and lifted. As I plunged my face into her luscious crevice, I was pleased to note that she had had the foresight to apply perfume to *every* portion of her anatomy.

And so it went, the two of us rolling across the floor like schoolchildren engaged in a game of wrestling, oblivious of the fact that at any moment another person might have entered my dressing room.

Fortunately, we were left undisturbed.

But for memories like that to light my way, I'm not sure I'd have the courage to continue on through the blackness of this infernal night.

Surely her love for me cannot have weakened, not after writing such a letter as that one. How the Parisian shopgirls who drool over her books would love to get their hands upon it. And to think people accuse her of being frigid! I only wonder why her letters stopped so suddenly two months ago. Should I worry that I've been replaced—again? I must admit that taking a new lover so quickly would not be outside the realm of her customary mode of operation. She changes men faster than some people I know change their underclothes. Why should I expect her to behave any differently toward me? Although I must say the fiasco with Musset in Venice might have been expected to cleanse her of the promiscuous side of her nature, if anything can.

What's that up ahead? Trees? Hard to say. Blacker than the sky. I remember she told me it was next to one in a row of poplars where her father's horse hit something in the road and stumbled. Which one was it…the thirteenth? That was the only part of the whole sad story I suspected she might have made up in her novelist's mind, the unlucky number thirteen. Definitely nothing of the rest of it. You could see that it hurt too much not to be true. Hurt her to say it, and even me, a little, to hear it.

She described the whole lamentable incident the very first night we spent together.

Why is it so often the case that sex and death go hand in hand?

It was at one of those gatherings of literary luminaries she liked to host in her apartment on the Quai Malaquais. Balzac and Sainte-Beuve were among her guests that night. Dumas, too, now that I think of it. I remember experiencing an overwhelming urge to hasten his departure with a shoe planted up his fat behind, as he launched into yet another of his interminable scatological anecdotes.

It was after midnight when the last of them was gone, leaving me alone with this woman of the dark eyes, melancholy smile, and legendary sexual escapades. A woman I had desired from the first time I laid eyes upon her.

I hoped I was not wrong in sensing that she had awaited that moment as fervently as I.

She was seated upon an ottoman next to her piano, her fingers absentmindedly searching for some melody or other, a tune from one of the operas of Rossini, if memory serves.

I had already mapped out my opening move, as the narcissistic ramblings of her fellow writers had afforded me ample time to plan my strategy. Feigning drowsiness from the wine and the late hour, I reclined upon the carpet next to her feet. I planned to allow my hand, as if by accident, to fall against her leg. I would pretend to have drifted asleep, and to be awakened by the intimacy of our contact.

It scarcely ranked among the more brilliant of my romantic ploys, but I trusted that events would work themselves out in my favor, as they usually do.

As events unfolded, my scheme was unnecessary. No sooner had I stretched out upon the floor and begun thinking of the proper words to use for the occasion, or whether I should speak at all, then *she* took command.

I was transfixed with delight and surprise as my darling reached down and began to slowly lift up the hem of her skirt.

The view that emerged, inch by tantalizing inch, left me dizzy with desire.

What was revealed to me were the most elegant and finely turned ankles a man could ever wish to see. Followed by calves of an exquisitely perfect shape. Next, a pair of slender thighs whose creamy whiteness was all the more unexpected for its marked contrast to her Mediterranean complexion. Best of all, their meeting point was in a place which, if my eyes did not deceive me, my beloved had chosen upon the occasion to leave uncovered.

I of course deemed it expedient to undertake an immediate exploration of this newly discovered region. But just as I was on the verge of entering that world of forbidden pleasure, she let her skirt drop back to the floor, stood up, and disappeared without a word into her bedroom.

I scrambled to my feet and hastened to follow her. As I entered the room, she turned to face me and, still without saying a word, began removing her clothes.

Naked, she presented a more alluring sight than I had conceived in even my wildest imaginings. She had the high, firm breasts of an adolescent. Her legs were as perfectly sculpted as Greek columns. Her light-brown skin, glistening under a sheen of sweat, seemed to glow.

It was a body made for love. I found it hard to credit that she'd recently passed the age of thirty.

While in the act of removing my own clothes, I circled behind her to inspect the view from the other side. Which I found to be, if anything, even more enticing than the initial apparition. The temptation was irresistible to seize and squeeze each of those adorable buttocks, and I would surely have done so had she not then whirled around and, with a capricious gleam in her eye, pushed me roughly onto her bed.

Apparently, she was equally as pleased with my body as I was with hers.

She mounted me in one swift movement, like the expert horsewoman she is, and immediately covered my face, neck, and chest with an onslaught of violent kisses, followed by bites sharply enough administered, I feared, to leave a mark in the morning.

Next came the attack of her long fingernails, plunged into my shoulders and raked downward across my breast like tiny daggers. This was followed by a second assault of her lips, this time, I noted gratefully, conducted with a greater degree of tenderness, as though to atone for and heal the wounds inflicted in her opening sally.

When I reached up to pull her face down to mine, desirous of playing a more active role in the proceedings, she intercepted my hand and guided it into her open mouth.

Clearly I was dealing with a woman who, when it came to satisfying her amorous cravings, had far less patience than I.

After sucking and licking my fingers to the desired state of moistness, she guided them between her legs. With eyes half closed, her tongue darting back and forth across her lips, she assisted me through the sequence of thrust and stroke which, for her, resulted in the ultimate measure of sensual gratification. That I was able to perform the task adequately was attested by the deep moans that soon began arising from deep within her.

It struck me as odd that I, of all people, was being given a primer on the proper technique of pleasuring a woman's body.

When I heard her moans change to a series of short, high-pitched squeals, and felt the warm discharge of moisture inside her, I decided it would be wise to begin seeing to the satisfaction of my own needs, a practice at which, I need scarcely say, I am more than passingly adept.

It was shortly after we had achieved an almost simultaneous peak of ecstasy, and lay contentedly in each other's arms, that she recounted to me the story of her father's death. I'd have preferred she wait for a less intimate moment. It was a little annoying, not being sure whether her rapturous cries had come from the pleasure I was giving her or from something that happened almost thirty years ago.

I don't fear being compared to living rivals. It's hard to compete with a dead man.

If she has admitted a new lover to her bed since our tryst in the theater, I'm confident that either she or one of my spies in the city would have told me about it. She tells me everything. At least I believe she does. And if she believes I keep nothing from her, well, good. She's close to being right. There is one secret I'll never tell her, one suspicion I think it best never to share, and it's this: I'm convinced that every man she takes (a dozen and counting, to hear Paris talk, and the rumors probably aren't far from the truth) is just another attempt to resurrect her dead father. To what purpose, I wonder? Is she making love to him, or killing him all over again for leaving her? I wish I knew. Maybe I will, some day.

I flatter myself to think that I alone, of all of them, am unique. I take some pleasure, if not quite the sense of absolute security I might wish for, in my rank of distinction. There is a thing…a service…I can give her which none of my rivals can boast of possessing.

Of course, there is also something they can give her that I cannot. But one finds ways to accommodate.

As far as I know, there is but one dark cloud looming upon the horizon at the moment—one rival worthy of entering the field against me. Chopin. I fear he may have an advantage over the others, and it gives me pause. She's far too susceptible to the seductive powers of his music. Who isn't? But she, even more than most women, is subject to coming under the spell of those divine harmonies. I know there have been periods in her life when, oppressed by sorrow and suffering, music was her only consolation. What better music to be consoled by than that of Chopin? I'm confident she hasn't made him her lover—yet. But I fear that consummation may not be far away. Unless I have something to say about it. I know all too well how incapable she is of resisting the imperious need that takes possession of her senses whenever spring is in the air. She's worse than one of her peasants' field animals.

I only hope it's not already too late.

Above all, I hope the reason she stopped writing me has nothing to do with young Frédéric.

Expecting me or not, she's sure to be awake, even if it is… what time could it be? Four o'clock? Five? Night for her is day. She really is a vampire, in a way. Whatever secluded corner of her house she does her writing in, that's where I'm sure to find her. Scribbling away, filling page after page with those tight black lines of hers. Making mistake after mistake, like changing the color of her hero's hair from one chapter to the next. I wonder if anybody but me caught that one? Not that she cares, so long as she meets her editor's monthly quota of words. She knows she can trust one of her numerous lovers and would-be lovers who watch after her affairs in the capital to clean up the grossest of her errors.

She never trusted me with proofreading, or anything else like that. I don't blame her.

I wonder if any of them know the real reason she writes at such an inhuman pace. I do. It has nothing to do with fame, or wealth, which is what the rest of them crave. When you get to the bottom of it, all those books of hers are nothing but a way of keeping her head filled with someone else's story, *any* story, as long as it isn't her own. I'd probably be doing the same thing if I had suffered through a childhood like hers.

If my eyes are to be trusted, I'd say those two yellow lights in the distance might well be torches fastened upon either side of her main door. Will there be servants awake at this hour to let me in? Or better yet, she herself? If I were taller and stronger, it might have been amusing to try the same secret route of ingress used by simpering little Sandeau that night he hoisted himself into her bedroom through a ground-floor window. They went at it for hours, she told me, tearing into each other like hyenas in heat, while all the time her idiot husband snored away in a drunken stupor.

How delicious it would be to surprise her, to approach her from behind, silently, like a cat, close my hand over the one in which she holds her pen, stop for a while that endless pathetic stream of words. To finally feel again her soft breasts cradled in my palms, as I crush her nipples between my fingers until they rise to attention and beg for the touch of my lips. I'll caress her body in all the places where I know she enjoys it the most, with just the degree of pressure that never fails to bring her to the proper point of arousal. I'll be sure not to neglect my favorite part, where the curve of her neck meets her beautiful white shoulder. Heine wasn't that far wrong when he said her shoulders are her best feature. The *best,* of course, are her eyes. No other woman in the world has eyes like hers.

Stop. It isn't wise to indulge in such reveries until I'm safely out of the darkness of this night, and inside her home.

Inside her bed.

Inside her.

In any case, for me to perform such a feat of athleticism as entering through one of her windows I'd need to have followed her example—her *scandalous* example—and left the inn dressed in trousers. As I have done on occasion in Paris, mostly because I knew it would please her. In general I prefer a more conventional mode of dress, such as I'm wearing now.

So many shadows in her courtyard. Probably carriages. Is she entertaining a houseful? It's not unlikely. When her husband was around she needed people as a distraction from him; now she needs them as a distraction from herself. God forbid she finally managed to talk Chopin into coming down for a visit. A visit that might well turn into a *séjour* of God knows how long. Poor boy. Once she got her teeth into him, it wouldn't be easy for him to get away. I know her. She wouldn't release him until *she* decided to. The worry is that she's such a fool for his music.... No, what am I thinking? He could be a reincarnation of Mozart himself and she'd still tire of him in her own good time. Besides, he's as wrong for her as she is for him. Love his music, don't love *him*.

I'll tell her that, perhaps. Have to be careful not to be too obvious.

Could there be something going on at the rear of the house? Seems to be more light there. I'll go around and see. Perhaps a surreptitious entrance through terrace doors....

Who in heaven's name is *that*? Hair as long and beautiful as hers, but golden as a king's chalice. Same slender shape, but more elegance in her bearing. Is she nobility, or is she just putting on airs? Who is she? And why in God's name, at such an hour as this, is she pacing back and forth upon my darling's terrace, looking for all the world like a lost soul of the Elysian Fields? Whoever she is, she's not for disturbing. Not now. Best to hear her story later, from my George's own lips.

After I've kissed and chewed them to a state of bloody tenderness.

Must not have been a servant, the man who opened the door for me, though from the look of him he doesn't come from George's higher class of acquaintances. Not one of her lovers, I'm certain of that. His eyes would have given him away. But he knew me by name, even if I didn't know him. That says something for him. Looked me up and down with a lecher's leer. Probably remembers seeing me before and can't remember where.

It would have been on stage, no doubt.

I wonder if George really is feeling under the weather, as he said she is. Feigning illness always was one of her favorite ruses when she wanted to avoid unpleasant situations. So what might the problem be?

As long as it has nothing to do with Chopin.

I almost hope she is suffering from some malady. I'll bring her back to life the way she used to bring *me* back to life. After killing me with the wild abandon of her savage embraces.

What an extravagant fantasy it is, that idea of hers that she might actually cause her lovers to expire in the throes of passion. No doubt it's a mark of the intensity of passion she herself feels. If she were afraid of killing Sandeau with love, how would she feel if she ever got Chopin between her sheets, with his body of a teenage girl?

That was when I loved her most, when she called me her adorable invalid, and vowed to nurse me back to health. I'd pretend to be sick even when I wasn't, which of course for me was an easy thing to do, with my acting skills. Just to have the pleasure of being made well again.

If she could arrange it, she'd have the whole world fall ill.

As to her home, I've seen better and I've seen worse. All I'd say is that it's *her*. The moment I stepped inside I remembered all the hideous details of her childhood. After the death of her father, the mother and grandmother fighting over her as if she were a piece of meat. She couldn't help but lose, no matter who wound up with her. I still can't decide whether I think it's better that it was her grandmother who was given custody. The old lady was a semi-aristocrat, while her mother came from the street, so the mother's case was hopeless from the start. And she was a former actress to boot, the mother was, with everything *that* implies. Still, as they say, blood is thicker than water. Losing her mother so soon after her father.... You have to wonder what that must have done to her.

I like this spiral staircase. Nice touch. And I've the feeling that even at this ungodly hour there's more than just the man who let me in, and George—and the mystery woman on the terrace—who are presently up and about in Nohant. What time could it be? How close to daybreak? I hope we'll have at least an hour before dawn. I'll need that much time to do what I have in mind to do.

This must be her door. How should I make my entrance? Shall I be silent, and speak only with my eyes? I know she'll be overjoyed to see me. I think she will be. At least she'll be relieved for the excuse to put aside her writing for a while. Will she be surprised? Has she forgotten that I promised her I would come?

The lamp upon her night table is lighted, so I take in everything at once. It's not the tableau I expected. She's in her bed. Her eyes are closed. The body I know so well is covered by sheets, and the sheets are covered with dozens of sheets of paper. Even from here I can see that every one of them is filled with that familiar cramped handwriting.

Her face, neck, and shoulders are exposed. Her hand hangs over the side of the bed, its fingers still clutching the pen.

She must have fallen asleep in the middle of a line.

It requires an immense effort to stifle my desire to race across the room and throw myself upon her, but I make myself cross the floor slowly, softly, so as not to awaken her.

When I am next to the bed, I see below me, through the window, a corner of the terrace. Is the beautiful mystery woman still floating to and fro over its red flagstones, I wonder?

Slowly, cautiously, I begin sliding the pen from between her fingers. But before I am able to completely extract the instrument and place it upon the night table her hand grasps my arm, halfway between my elbow and wrist. With such fierce intensity does it squeeze my flesh, it is as if I were in the grip of a dying man. My instinct is to pry the fingers loose, but that would mean bringing an end to the contact I have desired for so long, and I would sooner give up not only my arm but my life and my soul.

Finally, of their own volition, the fingers release their hold.

I lean over her. Her hand reaches up and strokes first my right cheek, then my left, then slips through my cloak and inside the material of my blouse. It caresses my breasts, kindling in them a flame that I feel all the way down to the tips of my toes.

Her fingers wrap themselves around my neck, pulling me downward until my lips are almost touching hers.

I am not sure whether she has yet even seen me, if she even knows who I am. Though her breathing has quickened, her eyes are still closed.

I pull back the covers and slip down beside her. Exulting, my eyes feast upon every inch of the beautiful body that for so long has filled my dreams. Now that I am so close to attaining the goal of my quest, I am determined not to hurry. I intend to take my pleasure slowly.

I begin by nibbling gently upon her left breast, savoring the sweet salty taste like a man who has been rescued from the brink of starvation. The throbbing between my legs is almost painfully intense. It cries out to me that I must have her *now*—*all* of her—but

I know my ultimate pleasure will be made even greater if I have the strength to delay it.

A familiar musky aroma tells me that *she,* at least, has not been able to wait. Awake or not, she has responded to my passion with an even greater passion of her own, more intense than anything she has ever given me.

Lower and lower, my lips continue their journey. They can almost taste the prize that awaits them. Shunning the ferocity with which we have been wont to attack each other in the past, my fingers and tongue exert the softest of pressure as they move downward from her breasts, down to the point where the triangle of her woman's hair begins.

At those moments when her eyes flutter open, I can't tell if the look she gives me is one of recognition, or merely an acknowledgement of the supreme pleasure we are giving to each other.

In that sacred place at which my lips have now arrived, she is all moisture, sweetness, and warmth.

Every nerve in my body is on fire with the flames of paradise.

Paradisiacal, too, the music that I hear playing in rhythm to our passion.

I have not imagined it. It really *is* music—piano music—as beautiful as any I've ever heard. Entering through the open window, it provides a delirious accompaniment to our lovemaking.

Then he *is* here! She has summoned him from Paris. Damn him!

Yet it's not one of his compositions. I'd know if it were something Chopin had written. That style is unmistakable.

But he can play anything.

If only it would go on forever, and yet it has to stop—it has to stop now! It drives me mad to see George respond as much to the music as to my tongue stabbing deeper and deeper inside her.

It's a piece I know. Where have I heard it before? If only I could place it? Of course—how could I not have recognized it from the very first note. If ever a song expressed the ecstasy I'm feeling at this moment, it would be "Liebesträume."

No wonder I sense that her body is responding as much to *it* as to me.

It is, I must admit, a worthy rival.

But then—too soon—the melody dies away, replaced by an insistently repeated, horridly macabre theme. This, too, is music I know, and this time I place it instantly. "The Erlkönig." With such inhuman power are the keys struck (who would have thought such force resided in the frail fingers of a sop like Chopin?) it is as if our bodies are being nailed together.

Suddenly her body tenses. She turns away from me. Her hands thrash wildly across the bed until they seize upon one of the loose sheets of paper. She twists to the side and holds it under the light.

What can it be that she reads with a look of such fearful agitation? Surely nothing as mundane as a chapter of one of her own romantic potboilers. No words which she herself has written could act upon her in this way. I lean over her and read the same lines that she is reading.

> *My dear Marie,*
>
> *Divine in nature, love is capricious in its choice of those with whom one is fated to become enamored. All too often, the object of our desire is not the person one would have chosen had the selection been made by the faculty of conscious reason. It happens, as you of all people know, that one may fall in love with a person who is already pledged to another. Whether or not Franz thinks it appropriate to ask your forgiveness is a matter which it is for him to decide. He has not yet become my lover, although I am sure you believe he has. Our relationship is rather one in which our two spirits have become inextricably fused in a union of perfect harmony….*

There was much more to it—when writing, George can be so dreadfully long-winded—but I'd read enough.

So this was what she was scribbling when she fell asleep. Not the chapter of her latest novel, but rather a letter confessing that she has become the lover—no, not the lover, not *yet* the lover, but rather the soulmate—of the inestimable Franz Liszt. Then it must be he, not Chopin, who is the genius responsible for our amorous accompaniment. And the letter is addressed to his current lover. Her rival. Who must be the beautiful woman strolling ever so disconsolately up and down the length of George's terrace. Who must, then, be none other than that social-climbing bitch, Marie d'Agoult.

I could have wished for nothing better.

Tenderly, I remove the paper from her hand and gently push her head back onto the pillow. I watch as her body trembles, tossing from side to side, her hips arching up and down in an instinctive expression of timeless human need. From somewhere deep within her there emerges that low, animalistic moan I know so well.

I stand and begin to take off my clothes. At the sight of my breasts, so much rounder and heavier than her own, she emits a soft whimper of contentment. I bend down, allowing her to take one of my nipples inside her mouth. She sucks with the desperate hunger of a nursing infant.

Finally, I can relax. My journey has reached its destination, its holy grail, its divinely glorious climax. I shed the last of my garments and stand naked before her.

If this is death, may I die a thousand times.

It is now a matter of supreme indifference whether she sees in me a fantasy substitute for her father, Musset, Liszt, Chopin, or any of the others. I have won out over all of my rivals.

I climb onto the bed and straddle her, positioning my flower of Aphrodite inches above her face. As I move slowly lower, I savor the sight of her beautiful black eyes which, for once, are filled with tears. So George Sand can cry! Those celebrated eyes, so rich, so dark—the shape and color of Arabian almonds, as someone once wrote—it is I who have caused them to fill with tears. Those eyes that have enflamed the heart of every man in Paris, now, for this night at least, they belong to me.

Forgotten are the long weeks of doubt and anxiety—wondering if she would ever again be mine—obliterated by the single sweet sensation of her lips pressing against my *dôme d'amour*. She is now wholly under my control, and I shall be without mercy.

With her head trapped inside the vise of my legs, I grind down upon her, harder and harder. When I raise myself a bare inch or two, it is only to reach down and open myself completely, to feed her tongue inside me, to that place that craves to feel its touch.

Finally I am at peace. My victory has made me whole. As indescribably intense waves of pleasure wash over the walls of Venus's cavern, vibrating upward through my body, up into my very soul, I sense my poor angel struggling to twist away.

Is my beloved suffering? Am I suffocating her?

I care not. I am determined to make of this moment an eternity of bliss.

If I am to die this night, let us die together.

At last, in that moment when I experience the supreme release for which I have waited so long, I mark how pleadingly her eyes gaze upward into mine. I wonder how they'll look when, in the next minute—or hour—they learn of a dalliance I permitted myself to entertain not so long ago with a certain Hungarian piano virtuoso. Of course I'll need to adjust the chronology. I don't want her to think I had leapt from her bed just so I could run to his.

Although that did happen, more than once.

As for you, my dear little Frédéric, all things in their place. There will be time enough to dispose of you in the brightness of a new day.

The Good Doctor's Night Off

August MacGregor

VOICES SWIRLED INSIDE SIGMUND FREUD'S SKULL like a blinding snowstorm. Only moments ago, barbed voices and barely muffled chuckles from around the conversation circle had flown at Freud like spears. Mercifully, the Vienna State Opera House had disgorged him from its lobby into the night. Yet, the rough attacks from the Neanderthals haunted him.

Wrinkled matron: "So if I dream about being young again, that is...my deepest, darkest wish?"

Gentleman with a silver monocle: "Come now, Herr Doktor. Dreams are silly little things."

Plump lady with an alpine bosom: "Often I dream that my dear husband is suffocating under his pillow."

Monocled gentleman: "And your new book? I hear it tells us that little boys have sexual feelings for their mother."

Wrinkled matron: "My goodness!"

Monocled gentleman: "And they wish daddy dead. For, after

all, he is competition for mommy's heart."

Finally, the great scientist: "There's more to it than that! The Oedipus Complex is quite complicated, so much so that I had to devote a book to its effects."

Alpine bosom (with arched eyebrow): "I'm sure it is complicated. And fascinating. Dreams and boys lusting after mommy? Quite fascinating, indeed. And what do you base these theories on, Herr Doktor?"

The great scientist (after a laborious sigh): "Well, I *am* a professor of neurology, after all. My research involved psychoanalysis of a great many patients. Most were poor women suffering from hysteria. I was able to help them by unlocking the mysteries of their minds." (A satisfied click of the heels.)

Alpine bosom: "Fascinating that most of your patients are women. Tell us, Herr Doktor, since you know women's minds so well, how *is* the weaker sex going to change Austria now that we can vote?"

Clearly, this woman envies the penis, Sigmund thought.

Sigmund tried to banish the doubting voices. Several gulps of the warm late-summer-evening air were medicinal.

Curse those cattle. They know nothing. Herr Monocle could use a good thumping with my cane. And Frau Bosom? Ach, if I could have her on my couch. She'd spill her dreams and wishes. I'd show her. And her too-tight corset would pop loose, and her mountains would spill forth in an avalanche of flesh.

Let them be ignorant. Someday I'll be recognized. Someday I'll illuminate their crude minds just as electricity did for those who needed candles and whale blubber to see in the dark.

Frau Alps, I would show you in the dark how right I am. Strip you of your fancy gown and expensive jewelry and set you on your hands and knees on the floor like an animal, with your mountains hanging down. I would show you with my stiff cane between my legs. You would grunt and you would cry out and you would forget all your precious morals so you could finally see the truth.

Gott in Himmel.

Nein, nein. No God. Only science.

Martha was right. I am *working too hard. My wife knows my mind better than I do. But does she realize how exciting this feels, this rush of knowing you are exploring something new, something vast and barely known, diving into the brain's labyrinth to find the unconscious hiding like a little spoiled child wanting all the pleasure in the world with an urge so powerful it is...*

Scary.

Enough! Enough with these thoughts. I need to walk. Yes, a walk and a smoke will refresh my mind.

Sigmund lit a cigar, then began his leisurely stroll, clicking his cane on the sidewalk among the shadows from flickering streetlamps. Horses pulling carriages clomped on the cobblestones. Couples holding hands passed him. One couple sat deeper in the shadows, the gentleman nuzzling his lady's neck. Laughter and loud conversation burst from coffeehouses and wine taverns, lifting his spirits. He floated on the giddiness, letting it clear his mind and whisk him around like a leaf fallen from a tree that had already succumbed to autumn's touch.

Eventually, his feet stopped in front of a house that appeared just like the others on the block. *Why am I here? What engine directed my legs toward here? I still need to discover many rooms in my mind's maze. And what could I learn here?* Of course he had heard of such places, but he had never been to one.

His feet climbed the stairs; his hand tapped on the door. It creaked open to reveal a lady with graying hair, elegant dress and poise, exceedingly polite in her greetings.

"Madame," Sigmund said, "I...um...was just strolling by and...well, I thought I...well..."

"Please," she replied, calm and reassuring. "Please, sir, do come in."

The parlor was an exotic, sumptuous world far different from the one he left. Deep-burgundy walls were adorned with gold-framed paintings of nude women. Dark-green velvet drapes. Red Oriental rugs. A woman at a piano played "The Blue Danube" while two couples of women slowly waltzed. Other delectable females played cards around a small table. All looked up at his entrance.

Sigmund coughed into his fist.

Madame smiled. "Please, good sir, make yourself comfortable and meet my exquisite ladies. Let your eyes taste each one. Take all the time you need. Choosing among such delicacies is not an easy decision."

The dancing duos parted. The piano player rose from the

bench. The card players stood. All wore sweet smiles with their silk finery. They reminded Sigmund of the Swiss chocolates wrapped in bright paper that he gave the children on special occasions.

His head stopped roaming. The brunette's downward-cast eyes demurely rose to meet his. Her smile spread further. *Is there a hint of something behind that pretense of modesty? Mischief? Naughty delight?* Either way, she was a fetching creature. Large bosom, small rump.

Madame's face beamed and her hands clasped together. "Ah, sir. A superb choice. I congratulate you." She turned toward Sigmund's object of attention. "Please join us, my dear." As the young woman approached, the labyrinth design on the borders of her red dress became clearer. "Gentle sir, I would very much like you to meet Keirsten."

The woman offered Sigmund her hand sheathed in a white satin glove.

"The pleasure is all mine," he said, and bowed to kiss her hand.

His eyes lingered on the tops of her breasts as they rose and fell with her breathing. The lone emerald at the end of her sparkling necklace pointed to cleavage as deep as a valley.

She clearly noticed the attention, yet not a touch of scarlet flushed on her cheeks. "This is just the beginning of your pleasure. You have a long journey before you." She drew a breath and slightly pushed her chest out.

"Madame, I do believe I have found a guide." Sigmund's eyes refused to move as his voice addressed someone besides the owner of the two hypnotic crescent moons.

Madame nodded, a smile gracing the corners of her lips.

Keirsten slipped to Sigmund's side, resting a hand on his shoulder. He was awakened by her movement and the scent of her perfume. She gently turned her pliable client toward a staircase.

"Shall we?"

Her breath, hot on his ear and neck, sent vibrations all the way to his feet, spurring them into motion. Up the stairs, down a dimly lit hallway, they entered a boudoir that was decorated in the same colors as the parlor and contained a bed and couch.

Keirsten closed the door behind them. "You have a strong, fine mustache." Her smooth gloved hand caressed his bearded cheek.

His hands flew toward her bodice and she expertly stepped into their grasp, filling them with her bosom. His face melted. His body sagged. If not for his strong grip, she feared he would faint.

She stepped backward and teasingly held up a length of lace. His shaking fingers took it and clumsily unlaced her bodice, level by level, until the sides parted like stage curtains and her breasts flopped into view. Sigmund, wide-eyed, gasped. His hands leaped to squeeze the soft globes.

"Mmm," Keirsten said. "Your hands are big...and strong."

As his hands massaged, they left her nipples exposed in the arch of thumb and forefinger. His lips clamped on a nipple and sucked, slowly at first, then speeding up in excitement, moving from one to the other, tongue flicking across the hardening nipples, lips sucking each lovely areola.

Moans poured from her throat.

After a while, she said, "Oh, good sir, your lips tease me. But I wish for you to enjoy my other...charms."

"Sorry, sorry. I got carried away there. Yes, quite. Let's...um, proceed."

She gently eased off of him, those magnificent breasts gliding away. She undid buttons and her skirt fell with a whisper. She slid onto the bed, like an undersea creature, moving with such grace and fluidity.

He fumbled with his jacket, tie, vest, shirt, shoes, socks, trousers. He seemed to have forgotten how each was affixed. But eventually managed until he, too, was naked. And hard as his cane.

"Mmm," Keirsten purred. "Your manhood is wondrous. Large. Powerful."

His heart pounding, blood echoing in ears and cock, a little embarrassed at his nudity, he forced himself to be patient. *Control yourself.* He climbed aboard her and laid tiny kisses upon her neck.

"Your mustache tickles," she giggled.

Her hand slid between them, found his cock, and guided it toward her sex. This unfamiliar touch froze his body, causing his mind to reel. Martha had been the only woman in twenty years to touch him like this. Scores of women had lounged on his couch and shared their private, dirty thoughts as he sat mere inches away, his concentration sometimes drifting into sinful territory. This new, intimate touch felt wrong, wicked, exhilarating.

"Are you all right?" she asked.

"Oh, yes."

He thrust into her so hard that she gasped. His hips bucked frantically. His groans were closer to grunts. Reflexively, she arched her back and held onto his upper arms for fear of him losing balance. No telling if he would fall, with his body shaking like the frenzied loins of some wild animal.

Her worry didn't last long, as he froze again. Eyes popped out. Mouth hung wide open. Then he fell to her side, his chest heaving.

It was all so quick and anxious that she wondered if she were seeing things. She thought, *What just happened? Did he climax?* She blinked the thoughts away, needing to remain the consummate professional.

Turning to him, she caressed his chest hair and whispered in a deep and sultry voice, "You were wonderful. A wonderful lover. So strong and handsome and skilled."

Panting was his response.

After his frantic chest calmed, Keirsten gently left the bed, and then dressed in a robe of translucent deep purple. "Would you care for something to drink?" she whispered.

"Water," he croaked.

When she returned, Sigmund was sitting on the couch and puffing away on a cigar. "Sorry I was rude," he said. "It just...I surprised myself. I'm not usually like that."

"No need to apologize. It was wonderful."

She handed him a glass of water and set down a bottle of champagne with two glasses. He took several gulps of water, all the while watching her cross the room toward the windows. When she opened one, a slight breeze ruffled her robe, creating glimpses of bare breasts, more skin than was allowed by the teasing of the translucent material with misty purple views of her plump charms while her nipples poked against the fabric. Sigmund tried hard not to stare, imagining the nipples fighting and finally tearing the robe to free the globes and allow them to fully sway with her movements.

"Would you like to go downstairs and join the girls in the parlor?" she asked.

"No, thank you," he said, snapping out of his hypnosis with a shake of his head. He placed his cigar on an ashtray, then shuffled to his pile of clothes and rummaged through them, digging into the vest pockets and producing a small round silver canister, which looked like the back of a pocket watch.

"Are you late for an appointment?" she asked.

"No, my dear. Not at all." After unscrewing the top, he separated the halves to reveal white powder in the bottom half. His fingers dropped a few pinches of the powder into his water glass, then stirred it with his forefinger, licking it once finished.

"Coca," he said, then took a swig. "Long ago, people in South America chewed the leaves for stamina and stimulation. They considered it an aphrodisiac. I've thoroughly studied it." He extended the glass to her. "Try some?"

She hesitated, but tried a sip. A moment passed before she said, "I have heard of cocaine, but never tried it. Strange. My lips feel...numb."

"That will pass. Don't worry. Tell me how you feel. Sit. Please." He gestured to the couch, and she placed the glass on the end table, then sat down. Her hands folded on her lap. A proper lady.

"I feel slower," she said. "Lightheaded."

Sigmund popped the cork on the champagne bottle, filled the two glasses, and handed one to Keirsten. He retrieved his cigar and studied her. Standing fully naked, cigar in one hand and champagne glass in the other, he felt his shyness melt, replaced by a bravado reminiscent of the star of last evening's opera. *Was this how Don Giovanni felt in seduction?*

"Now I feel...giddy?" She giggled.

"Ah. Exhilarating, no? A toast, then. To you and me. To our journey of pleasure."

They clinked glasses and drank. Keirsten sipped; Sigmund downed all of it.

"Oh, this tingles. It tingles my toes, my fingers, my…"

"Yes? Yes?" He sat on the couch beside her, plunked the cigar back on the ashtray.

"My nipples. Oh, sir. My strong lover. This is marvelous."

"Indeed, it is, my darling. Indeed." He slipped his head onto her lap, gazing up at her breasts, and stretched out his body on the couch. "Please, could you call me Sigi?"

She suppressed a tiny giggle before it grew into laughter. "Excuse me. The champagne. Then...what is to be my name?"

"Amali. I will call you Amali."

She nodded and sipped the bubbly nectar.

"Let's play a game, Amali. Tell me one of your dreams and I will tell you one of mine."

"My dreams? Why?"

"The ancient Greeks thought dreams were messages from their gods. Dreams help me unravel the mysteries of the mind. I will be famous for this. Now. Describe a dream that was especially vivid. Sweet Amali, close your eyes and relax and tell me of your dream."

"All right, um...Sigi. I had a strange dream the other night. I was in a garden. Beautiful flowers everywhere. I am warm. Happy. The grass feels good and the flowers dance in the wind." She absentmindedly smoothed his hair. "Bright yellow blossoms, reds, blues. Long purple flowers. It all feels wonderful. I touch my mouth. But something is wrong. Dreadfully wrong. My teeth feel odd. They're falling out. I touch a tooth and it wiggles and falls out. I touch another tooth. Same thing happens. I look around, but see no one. I am alone with the beautiful flowers and my teeth falling out. See? Strange. But my teeth are still there. So what is the mystery of this dream?"

A long pause. Finally, Sigmund said, "I'm not sure. Let me ponder it. But first, let me tell you my dream. I've never told anyone this dream. It frightens me. I am climbing a tall mountain. Maybe in the Alps. The mountain is covered in snow. It's freezing. I climb inch by inch. My hands are red and chapped and shaking with cold and they grab rocks so I can pull myself up. Sleet pours down and hits my head and my hands. But I am determined to climb all the way to the peak. Then I hear laughter. Up, way up above me, I see a naked man on a precipice. His hands are on his hips, and he throws back his head with long black hair and he laughs. A cruel, powerful laugh. Like a roar. And he has an enormous...um, phallus. Did you know that a bull's penis is two feet long when erect? Never mind. This man's penis shakes when he laughs. Still, my hands reach for the next rock to climb up. What does it mean?"

It was her turn to be silent.

Sigmund quickly sat up and framed her cheeks with his hands and planted a kiss on her lips. "But enough of this. I shall not solve all mysteries tonight." He leaped to his feet and relit his cigar. "Now *that* is refreshing. Darling, would you be so kind as to fetch mother girl?"

As if the talk of dreams weren't puzzling enough. She said, "Excuse me? Mother girl?"

"Sorry. A slip. Meaningless. I meant to say *another* girl."

Keirsten frowned. "To replace me?"

"My goodness, no. Not at all. You are too good a therapist. Another girl to join us."

"Ah, three of us then." She tried not to show excitement over what promised to be a big payoff. "Any requests? Another well-endowed lady?"

His hand waved. "No, no. But wait. She should have long, silky, black hair. She should be tanned, if possible. Cheery. Full of vigor."

The second woman turned out to be close enough. One doesn't receive perfect copies of an early love, even in memory. Every now and then a face in a crowd stood out and he drew a sharp, quick breath as wild thoughts sprang forth: *Could that be she? After all these years?* But a second glance proved otherwise. This woman was far from a doppelgänger, but tonight she would do. And do well.

After introductions and her polite curtsy (which seemed very much out of place), Sigmund said, "I would like to call you Gisela. Is that all right?"

"Yes."

Amali had probably warned her about this. But surely they had received more bizarre requests. *And I will not tell you the whys, my dears. Is it really a good idea to tell your whores you want to call them after your mother and your childhood love?*

Instead of offering this explanation, Sigmund suggested that Amali undress Gisela. Watching the younger lady being stripped was quite arousing. A thin line of smoke rose from the cigar resting limply between his lips, seemingly forgotten. Gisela obviously enjoyed not only Amali's fingers unbuttoning and untying, but Sigmund's gaze, which dared not miss the uncovering of skin as each garment was loosened and fell to the floor. Not even Amali's fluttering robe distracted him.

Until Gisela was naked. Then Amali's eyes locked with Sigmund's and held them captive while she slipped the robe from her shoulders and her ripe breasts again held the spotlight. Once his eyes freed themselves of Amali's chest, they studied the details of the light that flickered across the skin of both women.

Then Gisela reached out and delicately took the cigar from Sigmund's lips. She brought it to her own lips, inhaled, then puffed a little smoke at him. A bold move, one that made his erect phallus eagerly twitch. He blinked away the smoke and aimed his cock, a wooden lecture pointer, at her to communicate that it was her turn.

"Gisela, please lay on the couch."

She laid his cigar on the ashtray, then did his bidding. Sigmund awkwardly balanced over her, thrusting shakily into her tight sex.

The frustration ended with his grunting, "This won't do."

So they tried another position. He sat on the couch, and, facing him, she lowered herself to his lap, teasingly moving in fractions of inches, mind-numbing in slowness, until finally her warm flesh gripped his cock in a snug embrace. Bouncing seemed to suit Gisela better. Holding onto Sigmund's shoulders, she worked her thighs as energetic pistons, crying out every time her cute bottom slapped against his lap.

But Sigmund grew impatient. Halted her anxious thighs. Instructed a change in positions—he on top of Amali this time. Yet this didn't last long either. He felt like an opera director, commanding his players to this position or that, then inserting his cock into one of them until he grew bored, then retreating so all three had a chance to rest while drinking champagne and cocaine water until he thought of yet another formation, and so the start-and-stop action continued. It was a disjointed performance where neither actors nor director had any inkling of a script.

"Enough!" Sigmund said finally, plopping on the couch with a heavy sigh. A sip of the cocaine water slipped under his top lip, beaded with sweat. "Gisela, kneel before me. Play for me, my dear. My sweet, sweet dear. Play on my magic flute."

Gisela pushed a carpet next to the couch and started with her fingers. Taking her time, she walked her fingers up the underside of his shaft, still slick with their juices. Then, she massaged his testicles.

Riveted to her work, Sigmund whispered, "Amali, sit next to me."

Reading his mind, she kneeled next to him so that her heavy

breasts waited within easy reach. His mouth pounced on a nipple; his hands rushed to grab wondrously large, soft, cushiony, motherly flesh. He sucked as if desperate to unlock the fluid inside.

Gisela kissed the knob of his cock as if puffing on a cigar. Her tongue rolled in a circle around it.

Mein Gott. Finally. Finally, a luscious little whore to worship my spear.

Sigmund's lips tore away from Amali's plump globes, smearing his cheek with drool. "Fräulein...your tongue...is an eel. Did you know...they...oh, Gott...they are born with...with sex organs of females? But then develop male organs. Shocking, no?"

Gisela's lips hugged the purple knob for many pounding heartbeats. Sigmund lashed back to Amali's nipples, lustily slurping.

Then Gisela's head descended, surrounding his cock in a hot wet cave, her tongue the moist floor. All of him disappeared within her. Thrills lashed through him; he shuddered like a patient in electroshock therapy. As her head bobbed on the top half of his cock, her delicate fist around his shaft slid in rhythm along the bottom half.

Time and logic flew out the window. Back he was in the childhood summer when he and Gisela pranced in the woods near Freiburg with the supposed mission of hunting wild mushrooms, longing to eat their tender caps. A few years older than he, the teenage girl giggled as she ran to hide behind a tree, her head bouncing, long black hair flowing, yellow dress flapping. Enchanted by her beauty and carefree spirit, little Sigi doggedly followed with an empty basket, desperately wanting to embrace her. Giggling, she peeked around the tree, but it was Mama's face on Gisela's body. Sigi reached for her, but she slipped away and flitted to another hiding spot.

The fantasy dissipated like smoke from fading cigar embers as Sigmund sucked faster, harder, devouring Amali's nipples, and Gisela devoured his cock with white-hot lips and tongue, eating him as no woman had ever done to him, this man no longer the desperate boy or bespectacled scientist or Don Giovanni the seducer, but now a god, now Zeus himself, pleasing himself with these glorious mammaries offered to him as gifts while Gisela prayed to him on her knees.

With this fleshy worshiping from these two lovely followers, who cared about the doubting, small-minded people back at the State Opera House?

Those ridiculing morons were forgotten as his libido demons waltzed around a raging bonfire. Forgotten within saliva and sweat, within Sigmund's grunts and Amali's groans and Gisela's "mmms," within every tiny bump of Amali's areolas and the tiny shafts of her nipples and the smooth skin of her breasts, every tiny bump of Gisela's tongue sliding against the ruffles of his mighty spear's corona and the smooth skin of its cap, within her palm sliding against his shaft and fingers massaging his scrotum, even within his toes, feeling Gisela's ankles folded under her thighs. Forgotten within his delirium, the intensity spreading like a feverish chemical introduced on a microscope slide, its fuzzy tentacles stretching and expanding into full blossom, until...

His cigar exploded.

On the Eighth Day

Vanesa Baggott

THERE WAS ONCE an all-powerful super being called God. He spent his time wandering around the universe creating life and imposing order. One day he happened across a planet he had created a few million years earlier. He sat astride its pockmarked moon, gazed down at the blue surface, and wondered how it had survived without him. As his head breached the outer atmosphere, he was astounded by what he saw; the oceans were teeming with life. He flew down for a closer look. In the southern ocean he caught up with a wandering albatross that told him a flame-haired woman was responsible for creating everything in the sea. God headed north and found a vast rainforest crawling with life. He lay down in the canopy and breathed in great lungfuls of the sweet damp air. He meticulously examined all the flora and fauna. He interrogated the wriggling insects and the fabulously colored birds, the scaly crocodiles and the leaping monkeys. Everything he spoke to gave him the same answer. He learned that the flame-haired woman was called Mother Nature and that she had a twin sister called Mother Earth.

The more God heard, the angrier he got. Who were these females that dared to challenge his authority? Why had they presumed to usurp his power over his creation? He circled the globe looking for them. He caught sight of a dark-haired woman climbing into a crater, so he flew after her. Down and down he fell, deep into the heart of the planet. But all he saw were molten iron and bubbling magma. He followed a lava tube back to the surface and came out in a crack at the bottom of the ocean. He searched the seven seas and the five continents and still he couldn't find them. It was nearing the end of the day. Tired from his travels, God bathed in a thunderstorm. He whipped up a tornado to dry off and noticed two figures, their bare arms outstretched to the wind. One was tall but round-bellied with auburn hair that flew around her head like a circle of flames. The other had purple-black skin and a body like an athlete. She wore gold chains about her waist; emeralds, rubies, and diamonds twinkled on her fingers and toes. God gazed at the sisters and started to burn. His mouth drooped open and his breath quickened. His very core throbbed with a heat that overwhelmed him. He took a deep breath in and the swirling winds grew quiet. He was revealed in all his glory. The sisters stared at him. They seemed neither surprised nor afraid. A little unsettled by their level gaze, God said, "I am God, the creator." The women smiled. "My lord," they said and bowed low before him. His chest swelled with contentment.

The women showed him the bounty of the planet, and God saw that it was good. Mother Nature reached up and peeled off a strip of blue sky. Smiling, she wrapped it lovingly around his shoulders. She smelled of lilacs carried on a summer breeze. Her eyes were as green as a freshly opened leaf and her skin was as golden as a field of ripe corn. Mother Earth's features were as hard as a chiseled rock face, but her lips were full and smooth like pebbles. Her skin shone like polished stone. God felt the gaze of her glittering black eyes probing his body. The three super beings spent the day frolicking like children, chasing the sunrise and playing hide and seek with the moon.

At sunset the sisters led God to a grove of fruit trees. There they lay him down laughing and fed him peaches, plums, and apricots. Mother Nature squashed oranges into his chest and sucked off the flesh, clamping his chest hairs between her teeth. Mother Earth pushed berries into his mouth and then scooped them out with her tongue. Then to God's delight they squirmed down to his belly and flicked their sticky tongues between his legs. They gathered armfuls of mangoes and squeezed them into a pulp. They smoothed the pulp all over his engorged flesh and slowly licked it off. When the sisters had swallowed the last mouthful and felt God's giant frame shudder beneath them, they sat astride God's face and rubbed against him until his skin shone and his beard dripped. He gulped down their juices. They tasted sweeter than nectar and hotter than lava. All through the night the sisters made love to him. They rubbed his whole body with their scent. His beard grew sticky and his face glowed. They smothered his mouth and his sex at the same time laughing and sucking on each other's breasts. When he entered one sister she fed off the other. When he entered the second sister she lapped up the first. Then they plucked a smooth moonbeam from the sky and pleasured him together. As the rosy-fingered dawn clung to the horizon the three lovers lay down on the shore with their feet resting on a coral reef and let the brightly colored fishes play between their toes.

Later that day, God awoke and sat up. The beach was empty. Marram grass sprouted where Mother Nature had lain. God walked along the shore calling them but there was no answer. He sat down heavily on a sand dune, feeling weighed down as if there were a stone lodged in his huge heart. He flew across the ocean and asked a basking shark if it had seen them. The shark told God the sisters were on the farthest shore giving birth to two sets of twins.

When God arrived Mother Nature was still in the throes of childbirth. He stood around feeling awkward. Two baby girls plopped into the waves. Where the birth fluid touched the water it was transformed into a thousand golden elvers. Soon a glistening shoal wriggled at Mother Nature's feet. Her sister leaned against a dune nursing two infant boys. God surveyed his new family and seethed. He had not meant for this to happen. He felt used. He suspected the sisters of somehow luring him to the planet to satisfy their own ends. He vowed not to fall into their tender trap again. It was the end of the second day.

The third day dawned. The Father was missing. The sisters

nursed their children and looked up at the sky uneasily. God was venting his fury on the solar system. He whisked the clouds of Jupiter into a frenzy, creating a giant red spot the color of his anger. He threw asteroids at Saturn's icy moons and shoved Uranus off its orbit, leaving it tilted on its side. He sucked the atmosphere from Mercury and spat it at Venus. His energies spent, God returned to Earth resolved to confront the sisters. Mother Nature waved to him from the top of a snowy mountain range. Snow tumbled from the hem of her gown and a frozen mist hung around her head like a halo. She was flanked by two young women; Eve had pale creamy skin and flaxen hair, while Lilith's skin was white like snow but her hair was as black as night. Eve shyly averted her gaze. Lilith stared at her father and smiled coquettishly. God acknowledged his daughters with a nod and drew his cloak around himself to hide his engorged flesh. He took Mother Nature by the hand and led her to a continent in the southern ocean.

There he paced up and down a beach, roaring like a wounded lion. How dare she usurp him, how dare she seduce him and bring new life onto this, his planet, he complained. Mother Nature stood in the shallows listening, and at her feet a million silver fishes played. She went to him and stroked his long blond hair. She told him that her sister was to blame and reassured him that she would never do anything against his wishes. She laid his head on her shoulder and plaited white flowers into his beard. She kindled a fire, roasted a wild beast, and fed him its succulent flesh. Then they raised a toast with sparkling wine and strolled along the sands. Crimson flowers sprouted at Mother Nature's every footfall. Her beauty bewitched God. She whispered in his ear but the roar of desire so filled his head he heard only the suck and fizz of the sea across the sand. Two chocolate-colored nipples as big as his fists rubbed their hardness against his chest, and as the sun set they clung to each other, their bodies steaming in the cooling air. Mother Nature's belly was rounded like the bend in a river. God rubbed his beard over its curves and slid down to the warm nigrescence at the top of her thighs. She wrapped her legs around his head and the sand beneath them boiled and turned to glass. A great blast of steam rose into the air as they tumbled into the sea.

Cradled by the water, the lovers coupled. Their rhythmic movements created a tsunami that swept across the southern ocean and generated a hot current that circled the planet. They swam as one throughout the seven seas, a trail of phytoplankton and zooplankton blossoming in their wake. Twisted together they plunged to the seafloor and lit up the pale creatures swimming there. As the third day ended they floated in the shallows of a warm sea. Mother Nature swam under God's legs and pushed herself against him. Silver fishes nipped her breasts as they dipped in and out of the water. As God reached his climax he pulled himself free. Mother Nature cupped him and lapped up his seed but some dripped from her lips and fell into the sea. A host of strange animals sprang from the waves. Scorpions and poisonous snakes, huge hairy spiders and luminous frogs hopped and wriggled over the sand and disappeared into the bush. A shuddering jellyfish with long tentacles floated out to sea and a shoal of fish with sharp pointed teeth migrated up a river estuary.

On the fourth day, God awoke to find himself deep in the belly of the earth. Close by, Mother Earth stirred a bubbling lava lake with a spear of lightning. She dipped a golden goblet into the lake and beckoned to him, but God was wary and did not budge.

Two handsome young men appeared from a cave. God recognized his grown-up sons; Adam had dark hair and looked identical to his father, whereas Lucifer had olive-colored skin and hair like strands of gold. A light shone from Lucifer's skin and, dressed as he was in pure white, to God he looked like an angel. The boys dipped two goblets into the lake and drank the bubbling lava. Instantly they appeared invigorated. Adam offered a cup to his father, this time God took it, and the three men shot out of the volcano and high into the sky.

God, anxious to impress, took his sons on a tour of the solar system. Together they did a slingshot of the sun. Lucifer flew into the center of the star and came out trailing clouds of light. Adam stayed by his father's side. They explored Mercury's craters and the extinct volcanoes on Venus. Adam remained silent, in awe of all he saw, but Lucifer scoffed. He lifted a fistful of Mars's red dust and laughed. "This is nothing but a barren wilderness," he said. God's face reddened, but he said nothing. On Jupiter their father stirred the atmosphere until it spun like a tornado. Laughing, Adam flew straight through the gas giant. Lucifer yawned. God plucked a ring from Saturn and gave it to Adam, who threw it spinning into the

Milky Way. Adam explored Uranus on its strange tilted orbit while God rolled ice, gas, and rock together to create moons. Lucifer took a run at the planet and kicked it hard. They all watched as it reversed its spin. God was furious. He seized a passing comet and flung it at his son. Lucifer dodged out of the way, and the comet careered off into space. Adam was bringing a bundle of bright blue methane from Neptune to show his brother. The comet struck, the methane exploded, and Adam's body was petrified inside a ball of ice and rock. God fell to his knees. The aura of white light surrounding Lucifer faded and turned green. He spat at his father and fled. God gently lifted the new moon and set it in orbit around Pluto. It was the end of the fourth day.

The next day, Mother Earth found God curled around a sand dune; he reminded her of an immense fetus. His tears had created a trail of salt that meandered down to the sea like a stream of crystallized moonlight. She dipped her fingers into a flaming goblet and coaxed him to taste. Tentatively, he licked her finger. The lava sizzled on his tongue. Beneath the burning was a delicious tang. God licked his lips. He snatched the goblet and drained its contents. As the lava flowed into his belly it rekindled the fire inside him. An insane longing surged through his body. Mother Earth's eyes flickered with a green light and she began to laugh. She loosened her golden bodice, allowing her breasts to peep out. Her skirts billowed apart, and God fell on his hands and knees, panting like a dog. She seized his beard and dragged him after her. The vast white wastelands of Antarctica stretched below them as Mother Nature hauled God into a cave dug into the side of a mountain. She filled her mouth with crushed ice, dribbled it over his thighs and swallowed him up. She took a draft of lava and licked his buttocks until they sizzled. Her mouth probed his perineum, then settled into a strong rhythmic suck. God shuddered. His hot breath formed a shimmering layer of melting ice over the walls of the cave. Mother Earth poured more lava down his throat and continued to suck. She broke off an icicle, fashioned it into a smooth nub, and pleasured him with it. God reached a crescendo but lost none of his vigor. He lifted Mother Earth's thighs and pushed his face between them. She wriggled and twisted as he drank deeply. The juices made his blood roar for more. He flipped her over and slowly, deliberately, pushed himself inside. Mother Nature reached between her legs and cupped him with her hand. The heat from their bodies melted all the ice around them. They slid out through the mouth of the cave and down to the sea. Penguins and seals swam past, brushing themselves against the couple, infected by the warm currents that swelled around them. At the bottom of the ocean Mother Nature sat astride God while he sucked on her breasts. Attracted by the heat, great clouds of plankton swirled around them. As he reached his climax, he withdrew and pleasured her with a smooth piece of whalebone. His seed touched the water and instantly the swirling plankton was transformed into bacteria, viruses, and microscopic parasites.

The noxious clouds bubbled up to the surface and out into the cold, clear air. The trade winds sucked them up and distributed them across the planet. Mother Earth was furious. She roared, and the noise was like a million tons of rock falling down a mountain. She opened a crack in the ocean floor and dived in. It was the end of the fifth day.

The sixth day dawned. God lay on a bed of snowy owl feathers looking out at blue glaciers. He felt elated. His plan not to father any more children had worked. Instead he would clone himself; create another Adam. So he split himself in half and clothed his new self in robes of silver and gold. Together God and his son flew across the oceans to find the sisters. Mother Nature sat on the floor of the now-silent rainforest, rocking back and forth. She was holding the flaccid body of a dead jaguar. God sat down beside her and asked her what had happened. She could not answer. Mother Earth appeared and raised her arm to strike God. Adam blocked the blow, and she glared at him with undisguised malice. "Help us!" cried Mother Nature. "Only you have the power to save them." God shrugged and shook his head. "Every creature on this planet is *your* creation," he said. "I can do nothing." Mother Earth spat in his face and dragged her weeping sister away.

God introduced Adam to Eve. Adam was humbled before her beauty. Their father promised they would be immune to the diseases sweeping the Earth. They would have dominion over the fowl of the air and over all the earth and every creeping thing upon it. But they had to worship him alone. "Forasmuch as it pleases me being an almighty God of great mercy," he said, "you may go forth and multiply in the sure and certain knowledge that you will be saved from all the ills and misfortunes of this world." Adam and Eve kissed their father's hand and bowed low before him. God fashioned them an arbor and surrounded it with a lush garden filled with fruit trees and freshwater springs. So ended the sixth day.

On the seventh day, Mother Earth raised a storm. Thunder pounded through the skies and lightning smote the earth, slicing the tops off trees and mountains alike. God chided Mother Nature for allowing her sister to destroy the world. But she wept and turned away. Lilith and Lucifer stood on a mountaintop and taunted God. Could his power match a tempest raised by Mother Earth? "Show us your strength," they said. "If you are truly a God as you profess to be, then calm the storm and populate this planet with *your* creations," cried Lucifer.

"Save us from that unhappy occasion, brother." Lilith smiled. "If puny Adam is evidence of his creative power I would rather have another lifeless desert." Lucifer roared with laughter. God drew himself up to his full height and he towered above the highest mountain. "Get thee hence, Lucifer!" he shouted, and struck him a mighty blow that sent him falling headlong, flaming from the ethereal sky. With a hideous screech, Lilith flew at her father. God silenced her with a sweep of his hand and she too fell.

The floodwaters rose higher and higher. Adam and Eve cried out in terror.

God built a wooden ark and installed his children safely inside. Then he blessed them and repeated his promise to make them rulers over all the creatures of the earth. Perched on the ark's roof was Lilith in the form of a great black bird. When God disappeared over the watery horizon she tore at the roof with her talons. Adam and Eve tried to beat her off, but she burst into flames. Fires erupted all over the ark, then all went out with a hiss. A huge red serpent rose from the ashes and slipped into the ocean. It was the end of the seventh day.

The eighth day dawned to a blue washed sky. Mother Earth lay asleep. Mother Nature swam with herds of sea creatures: whales, dolphins, sharks, and swordfish swimming alongside tuna, cod, and salmon. Jellyfish, octopuses, and squid curled around her fingers and toes. A string of eels slithered in her wake. She sang whale-song and dreamed of all the new things she could create.

The ark settled on a mountain. Adam flew out to find shelter. Eve fell asleep. She dreamed of Adam in a cave. He had lit a fire and spread animal skins around it. She could feel the softness of the fur and the heat from the fire. Adam offered her a cup, and she drank. The liquid was hot and burned her throat. She screamed in pain, and a fire kindled deep inside her. Adam watched. He took her by the hand, and together they dived to the bottom of the sea to a bed of hydrothermal vents. Giant tubeworms wriggled in the heat and blind white crabs scrabbled for food. Adam removed his robes. Eve was mesmerized by the sleek curve of his thighs and the broad sweep of his shoulders. He stepped into the pillar of hot water and beckoned to Eve. She stood beside him, feeling the heat from without and the heat from within, rising, rising. Adam kissed her gently and she fell upon him. Her ardor took him by surprise—she opened like a flower and pushed him inside. She slid to her knees and swallowed him up. She pushed her fingers inside him tight and hot. Together they bucked and writhed in the hot current that lifted them finally to the surface. Adam took them to a desert. He whispered to a snake and a lizard that flicked their forked tongues between her thighs while he plucked the spines from a cactus. He licked the succulent and pleasured her with it. A she-wolf trotted up and nuzzled Eve's face. The animal's female parts were human. Eve licked till her tongue bled.

She awoke. The sun was rising above the dunes. Her thighs throbbed and her mouth felt sticky. She lay on a beach, as if she had been washed up by the sea. Adam stood over her. Eve examined his face, searching for answers to the riddle, but Adam shied away from her gaze. He walked off down the beach, kicking sand.

Adam too had dreamed. He had found a cave and lit a fire but had fallen asleep beside it. He dreamed of Eve. She was stirring a cooking pot and offered him a taste of broth. The liquid was hot and burned his throat. He cried out in pain and felt a fire kindle deep inside him. Eve watched him. She took his hand and together they flew over the sea to a great forest of birch, oak, and beech. Moss and fern carpeted the forest floor. Eve unfastened her robe. Her skin was as white as apple blossom. She kissed Adam gently and he fell upon her. He sank to his knees and devoured her. They coupled against the smooth bark of a birch tree, then in the soft, dank leaf mold, and again amid the reeds and the bulrushes on the shore of a freshwater lake. He woke up in a forest clearing, naked and shivering.

Adam and Eve never spoke of their dreams. They lost their ability to fly, and when Eve fell ill it became clear that they were no longer immune to God's accursed diseases. The dreams had robbed them of more than their virginity. Lucifer and Lilith rolled about the heavens laughing. At the end of the eighth day Adam and Eve sat in the cave and prayed for God's swift return.

And they're waiting still.

About the Authors

ANONYMOUS has made her reputation writing satire and transgressive stories. In college (The Cooper Union) she was called, by a professor, "a gadfly." At the time, she had to look up the meaning. She will be having a third book of stories published by The Fiction Collective (whose motto is "Making fiction, making trouble") in the spring of 2005. She lives in New York City.

Under the pseudonym LISETTE ASHTON, Ashley Lister has had more than two dozen novels published through the erotic imprints Nexus and Chimera. As well as writing countless short stories for various magazines and anthologies, Ashley also produces regular columns for the Erotica Readers and Writers Association website and book reviews for *The International Journal of Erotica*. Ashley lives in Blackpool, England, with too many cats, far too many dogs, and a supportive partner and son.

TOM BACCHUS's two collections, *Bone* and *Rahm*, were published by Bad Boy. *Rahm* is available in Spanish from Boys Press as *Sueños de Hombre* and in German from Bruno Gmunder, 2005. Bacchus's short stories can be found in the fiction anthologies *Happily Ever After: Erotic Fairy Tales for Men; Best Gay Erotica 1998; Stallions and Other Studs; Obsessed: A Flesh and the Word Collection of Gay Erotic Memoirs; The Best of the Best Meat Erotica;* and *Kink: Tales of the Sexual Adventurer*. Bacchus's visual art, MetaPorn, has been exhibited in New York, Los Angeles, Milan, San Francisco, and occasionally on eBay.

VANESA BAGGOTT lives in the Pennines in the real Royston Vasey, which is apparently just as bizarre as its fictional counterpart. Over ten years ago she was initiated as a witch by a small village coven in South Yorkshire. She no longer practices but retains her lifelong interest in witchcraft. Vanesa plans to train as an Iyengar yoga teacher next year. She is currently studying poetry at the postgraduate level. To date she has written a film from an adapted short story and is halfway through her first novel, neither of which she has attempted to publish, yet. The idea for "On the Eighth Day " came from a conversation she had with a close friend who is the daughter of a gay Church of England vicar.

TULSA BROWN is an award-winning Canadian novelist who slipped into the erotica lane in 2003. Since then, her short fiction has appeared in thirteen anthologies, including *Best Women's Erotica 2004, Best S/M Erotica II,* and Black Lace's *Wicked Words 9* and *Sex in the Office*. In 2004 she took first place in erotica writing competitions at both CleanSheets.com and Desdmona.com. Her zgay romance novel, *Achilles' Other Heel,* will be released by Torquere Press in 2005. When librarians ask her what she is doing these days, she just smiles.

ANN DULANEY's work has appeared in *Erotic Travel Tales, Best Lesbian Erotica 2002, Best Women's Erotica 2003,* CleanSheets.com, and MindCaviar.com. While Danish storyteller Hans Christian Andersen celebrates his 200th birthday in 2005, Ann Dulaney is learning how to Z-transform discretized low-frequency sinusoidal signals at the IT University of Copenhagen. She notes that there is always room in the brain for new ideas, and always time to pen new happy endings.

Novelist, short story writer, and essayist JANICE EIDUS has twice won the O. Henry Award, as well as Redbook and Pushcart Prizes for her short stories. Her books include *The Celibacy Club, Vito Loves Geraldine, Urban Bliss,* and *Faithful Rebecca*. She's co-editor of *It's Only Rock and Roll: An Anthology of Rock and Roll Short Stories.* Her work appears in many leading literary journals, such as *Arts & Letters, Epoch,* and *Fourth Genre,* as well as in such erotic-flavored anthologies as *Fetish, Stirring up a Storm, Eros Ex*

Machina, and *The Unmade Bed*. She lives in New York City with her husband and daughter.

Decadent, devilish, and *delightful* are just three words that have been used to describe the work of K. L. GILLESPIE. Born in 1971, she was seven when she wrote her first story about a child-eating nun. Since then, she has worked as a music journalist for Britain's Channel 4, curated for an international art gallery, and written several screenplays, including *Not Every Fish Wants to Fly* for Flamingo Films in Berlin, and *12 Ice Cream Vans and a Wedding* for the BBC. She has also had some of her offbeat short stories published, most recently in *TANK* Magazine. At the moment, she is holed up in an attic somewhere in London, working night and day on her eagerly anticipated first novel.

Yorkshire lass JANE GRAHAM spent many years traveling Europe as a striptease dancer as well as performing with her satirical alter ego, Minx Grill, before hanging up her garter belt to raise a family in Copenhagen, where she also works for an expat newspaper. Previous works include *Floozy* (published in 1997 by Slab-O-Concrete), an often funny, sometimes nerve-racking peek at the more grubby haunts of the North of England; "Kitchen Sink," which appeared in the anthology *Brit Pulp!* in 1999; "Expectanz," in the *Naked City* collection in November 2004; and the self-published zine *Shag Stamp,* produced throughout the '90s. She's also a regular contributor to the underground periodical *Headpress* with a series of articles on nightclub hostessing.

SACCHI GREEN writes in western Massachusetts and the mountains of New Hampshire. Her work has appeared in five volumes of *Best Lesbian Erotica,* four volumes of *Best Women's Erotica, The Mammoth Book of Best New Erotica 3, Penthouse, Best S/M Erotica, Best Transgender Erotica,* and a knee-high stack of other anthologies with inspirational covers. Her first coeditorial venture, *Rode Hard, Put Away Wet: Lesbian Cowboy Erotica,* is scheduled for release in June 2005.

When ELISABETH HUNTER told her mother she was going to have an erotic story published, Mama gave her the same look she'd cast on Elisabeth when she moved to a commune, got a tattoo, and had body parts pierced that should apparently never be skewered. Some things, Mama said, are just more than a mother should have to endure, and Abraham Lincoln getting a blow job is one of them. Which explains why Elisabeth Hunter is a pseudonym for an author whose work has appeared in *Prairie Schooner, Mississippi Review, South Dakota Review, Iron Horse Literary Review,* and *Writers' Forum.* She is the recipient of an Individual Artist's Award sponsored by the National Endowment for the Arts, and a Silver Rose Award for Excellence in the Art of the Short Story. She received her MFA from Vermont College and lives in the Pacific Northwest with her husband and three children.

MAXIM JAKUBOWSKI is a writer and editor of erotica, with seven novels and too many anthologies to his credit. He lives in London but was educated in Paris, where F. Scott Fitzgerald was for him both a passion and a subject he studied in obsessive depth. His next novel will be called *I Was Waiting for You.*

MARK KAPLAN earned his Bachelor of Arts in English at the University of Michigan and his Master of Fine Arts from the American Film Institute. One of the films he scripted, *Red Lover* (aka *A Time to Remember*), won the prestigious Golden Rooster award in China. He currently lives in Pasadena, California, with his wife and daughter. Kaplan writes screenplays, plays, and novels and has published book, music, and restaurant reviews. His work has been produced or published in New York, Beijing, Los Angeles, and Seattle.

AUGUST MACGREGOR is the pseudonym of a writer and freelance graphic designer who believes that a cigar is rarely just a cigar. The sensual world of erotica not only offers him steamy (yet refreshing) breaks from designing book covers and page layout, it opens his life to rich, colorful fantasies and characters. His stories have appeared in the anthologies *Naked Erotica* and *Ride 'Em Cowboy,* as well as on Desdmona.com. He lives in Maryland with his wife and two daughters.

GARY EARL ROSS is a writing professor at the University at Buffalo Educational Opportunity Center. His books include *The Wheel of Desire and Other Intimate Hauntings* (which the *Buffalo News* called "an African-American cross between *The Twilight Zone* and *The Red Shoe Diaries*), *Shimmerville: Tales Macabre and Curious* (hailed by the *Boox Review* as "a shimmering engagement of a book"), and the children's tale *Dots*. Named Erie County's 2003 Artist of the Year, Ross also won the 2003 New York State Broadcasters Award for on-air editorial comment for his public-radio essay "If Strom Thurmond Had Been Elected President." His short story "Lucky She's Mine" appears in the Penguin anthology *Intimacy: Erotic Tales of Love, Lust, and Marriage by Black Men*. Ross is also a playwright. *Sleepwalker: The Cabinet of Dr. Caligari* had its world premiere in 2002, and the courtroom thriller *A Matter of Intent* was staged in 2005 by Buffalo's Ujima Theater Company.

LYNDA SCHOR has published two books of short fiction, *Appetites* and *True Love & Real Romance*. Her stories and articles have appeared in many magazines and anthologies. She is the recipient of numerous awards and prizes, including two Maryland State Arts Council Grants for Fiction, The Ann Tyler Award for Fiction, and an O. Henry Award nomination. She teaches fiction writing at the New School University, and lives in Manhattan. A new book of short stories, *The Body Parts Shop*, is forthcoming in February 2005 from The Fiction Collective Two (FC2).

NEAL STORRS has been editing the literary magazine *Oasis* since 1992. A Ph.D. in French, he has taught that and other foreign languages in several institutions of higher learning along Florida's central gulf coast. In addition to a scholarly study of the French novelist Claude Simon, he has published stories, poems, and translations in a number of little literary journals. An avid amateur pianist who loves both Chopin *and* George Sand, he currently resides in Gulfport, Florida.

A. F. WADDELL writes multigenre fiction, is a film lover, and lives in California. Works include the *Thelma and Louise* parody "Tina and Lucille" in *The Mammoth Book of on the Road;* "Cashmeres Must Die" in *Leather, Lace and Lust,* also to be published in 2005 in *The*

Mammoth Book of Best New Erotica; "The Road Killers" in *The Wildest Ones: Hot Biker Tales;* and "Whitewood" in *Foreign Affairs: Erotic Travel Tales*. For more, visit www.afwaddell.com.

FIONA ZEDDE is a transplanted Jamaican currently living and working in Atlanta. She spends half her days as a starving artist working in the city's fabulous feminist bookstore Charis Books and More, and the other half chained to her computer working on her second novel and an endless collection of bent and dirty stories that she hopes to get published someday. Her fiction has been published in *Best Lesbian Erotica 2004, Necrologue: Diva Book of the Dead and the Undead,* and *Va-Va-Voom: Red Hot Lesbian Erotica*. If you see her, please don't make jokes about her getting a life. She might bite. Her first novel, *Bliss,* will be published by Kensington Books in August 2005.

About the Editor

MITZI SZERETO is author of *Erotic Fairy Tales: A Romp Through the Classics* and *highway,* and editor of the anthologies *Foreign Affairs: Erotic Travel Tales, Erotic Travel Tales,* and *Erotic Travel Tales* 2. As M. S. Valentine, she's penned the erotic novels *Elysian Days and Nights, The Governess, The Captivity of Celia, The Possession of Celia* (all from Blue Moon and Venus Book Club); *The Martinet* (Chimera UK and Venus Book Club); and the special double volume *Celia Collection* (Blue Moon). Her fiction and nonfiction have appeared in *The Erotic Review, Moist, The Mammoth Book of Best New Erotica, Writing Magazine,* and *Writers' Forum*. She's the pioneer of the erotic writing workshop in the UK and Europe, conducting them from the Greek islands to the Cheltenham Festival of Literature. She appears frequently in the media, including the documentary series *3001: A Sex Oddity* (Bravo UK Television), *Nosolomúsica* (Telecinco TV 5, Madrid), and on BBC Radio. Mitzi's work as an anthology editor has earned her the American Society of Authors and Writers' Meritorious Achievement Award. She's currently work-ing on a pair of anthologies and writing a novel. She lives in Leicestershire, England.